PALM BEACH BEDLAM

A CHARLIE CRAWFORD MYSTERY (BOOK 8)

TOM TURNER

Copyright © 2019 Tom Turner. All rights reserved.

Published by Tribeca Press.

This book is a work of fiction. Similarities to actual events, places, persons or other entities are coincidental.

www.tomturnerbooks.com

Palm Beach Bedlam/Tom Turner – 1st ed.

JOIN TOM'S AUTHOR NEWSLETTER

Get the latest news on Tom's upcoming novels when you sign up for his free author newsletter at **tomturnerbooks.com/news**.

1

CHARLIE CRAWFORD WAS HAVING ONE OF HIS RECURRING dreams. He and Wayne Gretzky were walking through the kitchen of his parents' house in Connecticut. Gretzky had dropped by to pick him up so they could make the drive into New York City to play hockey at Madison Square Garden: the New York Rangers against the Los Angeles Kings. It didn't seem to matter Gretzky played for the Kings and Crawford the Rangers, because they were pals and liked to hang out together. It also didn't seem to matter they were almost thirty years apart in age. After grabbing a couple of ice cream sandwiches from the Crawford Frigidaire, Crawford and Gretzky walked into the garage to get Charlie's hockey stick, skates, and gloves.

There was a thick smell in the garage—like a car's exhaust—and Crawford saw his father slumped over the steering wheel of his Lincoln.

That's when Crawford usually woke up. Sweaty and in a paralyzed panic.

In real life, his father had committed suicide, but Wayne Gretzky had not been there. And instead of hockey sticks, Crawford had actually gone out to the garage to get a lacrosse stick so he could toss a ball with a neighborhood friend. He did, in fact, find his father slumped over the steering wheel of his Lincoln Continental. Needless to say, it was an image he'd never forget.

It always took him a long time to get back to sleep after dreams like that. Sometimes it would start to get light in his bedroom and he'd get up because by then a million things would be pinballing around in his head. A murder case badly in need of a clue or an overlooked revelation. Bills that he had been putting off paying. Dominica McCarthy or Rose Clarke? All kinds of stuff.

This time he had actually fallen back to sleep when his cell phone rang. He reached over to the bedside table and knocked over the alarm clock groping for his iPhone.

Finally, he located it. "Hello."

"Charlie," his partner, Mort Ott, said, "we got a dead female on the ocean side of The Colony."

That was a hotel located on Hammon Avenue in Palm Beach.

Crawford was immediately focused. "How'd it happen?"

"For one thing, looks like she got tossed off a high floor. For another, she's got multiple stab wounds."

Crawford slid out of bed and put his feet on the floor. "I'll be there in fifteen."

"I got the coffee."

CRAWFORD GOT THERE AT A LITTLE AFTER TWO A.M. The Colony Hotel was blocked to the west and the south by Palm Beach Police Department cars. Crawford hadn't seen so many blue and whites at any one place since the Knight Mulcahy murder up on the north end the year before. Not to mention what looked like a couple of football fields' worth of yellow tape strung up already.

He parked at the corner of Golfview and South County, spotted Ott a block away talking to a uniform, Art Ryan, and walked toward them. As he got closer, he saw the woman's body behind Ott and Ryan with two crime scene techs down in crouches.

Ryan saw Crawford approach and said something to Ott. Ott turned and handed him a coffee. "Hey," Ott said. "Vic's name is Grace Spooner, staying at the hotel."

"How do you know that?"

Ryan stepped forward. "Guy at the desk came out and ID'd her. Just before Mort got here. She was staying in one of the penthouses."

Crawford walked over to the woman's body. One of the techs looked up. Her name was Sheila Stallings. "Hi, Charlie."

"Hey, Sheila," he said, looking down at the body. "How many stab wounds, you figure?"

"Lots."

"That's not very scientific."

"I haven't counted yet, but I'd say at least twenty."

The other tech, Robin Gold, looked up. "But that's not the worst part."

Crawford got down in a crouch. "What do you mean?"

Gold, wearing vinyl gloves, pried open the victim's mouth with both hands.

Grace Spooner's tongue had been cut out.

2

Grace Spooner's mouth had a pool of blood in it, but the cut was clearly visible. Instead of the end of her tongue being rounded, it ended in a straight line.

"Jesus," Ott said, shaking his head. "Poor woman."

Crawford stood up. "No kiddin'. Let's go check out the penthouse."

Ott nodded. "Gotta be security cameras all over the hotel."

"Yeah, I'm sure," Crawford said, turning toward the entrance of The Colony.

Then he turned back to the techs. "We're going up to the room she was staying in. You coming up after here?"

"Yup," Stallings said. "See you up there."

Crawford turned, and he and Ott started walking toward the main entrance of The Colony.

Crawford flashed to his last case, in which the victim was buried alive up to his neck on the beach on the north end. Between a pack of hungry crabs and the incoming tide, it did not end well for the buried man. The killers turned out to be from a Mexican cartel. Cutting someone's tongue out reminded Crawford of how the cartels did things.

He and Ott walked into the opulent lobby of The Colony.

There were clusters of people there, sitting and standing. They all had one thing in common: frightened and troubled looks on their faces. At quarter after two in the morning, they weren't there to socialize. It reminded Crawford of the minutes after a fire alarm has sounded. He assumed between hearing police sirens and seeing flashing lights, sleep had become impossible for the guests. They had no doubt come down to the lobby because they were curious about all the commotion. Some of the people were fully dressed, others in bathrobes. One woman was holding a tufted quilt over her shoulders. A man was bare-footed and wore a white undershirt and pajama bottoms.

Crawford decided to take advantage of them being there and walked into the middle of the crowd and raised his voice. "Can I have your attention, please." He waited a few seconds. "My name is Detective Crawford, Palm Beach Police, and"—he extended an open hand toward Ott—"this is my partner, Detective Ott. It is important if any of you knows of, or saw, anything that might be relevant to our investigation of a woman's death here"—several gasps of shock and fright—"you come forward and tell us what you know."

The man in the pajama bottoms and undershirt stepped toward Crawford and Ott. "What exactly happened? Nobody's told us anything at all."

"As I mentioned, there's been a homicide ... Obviously, we want to do everything we possibly can to get to the bottom of it as quickly as possible."

Ott raised his voice to the crowd. "We'd be most appreciative if anyone here who saw anyone or anything that looked suspicious would please step forward."

Several people glanced around at each other and shook their heads, but no one made a move.

"How about, did any of you hear anything?" Crawford asked. He didn't want to be any more specific than that, like saying a scream or a shriek.

A woman in a fluffy white bathrobe shyly raised a hand. "I thought I heard a thump sound. I was reading because I couldn't sleep."

Crawford nodded. "A thump sound, thank you," he said, knowing exactly what it was. "Did you hear anything before that?"

The woman shook her head. "Sorry."

"Well, thank you again. Anyone else?"

"I just heard that party down in the restaurant," the man in the pajamas said. "It got pretty loud."

Several people nodded their assent.

"What party was that?" Crawford asked.

The man in the pajama bottoms shrugged. "I don't know exactly. I was told there was a private party in CPB."

That was the name of The Colony restaurant. Crawford guessed it stood for The Colony Palm Beach.

"A birthday party, I think it was," volunteered the woman with the quilt around her shoulders.

"Thank you," Crawford said. "Anything else any of you might think would be helpful to us?"

A few shook their heads, several others shrugged, and then a woman came up to them.

"I don't know whether it's helpful or not, but I saw a very drunk man wearing a bathrobe wandering around in my hallway."

"What floor, ma'am?" Ott asked.

"Third."

"Thank you," Ott said, making a note of it in his old leather notebook.

Crawford turned to Ott, flicked his head toward the reception desk, and lowered his voice. "Let's go talk to the guy over there. Get the key to the vic's room."

"Can you imagine," Ott said, lowering his voice, "reading a book in the middle of the night and suddenly you hear a thump sound."

"Yeah, I know," Crawford said grimly.

The two walked up to the man at the desk.

"We're Palm Beach Police detectives," Crawford said. "Are you the man who ID'd Ms. Spooner?"

The man nodded. "Yes, I'm Rick Hodding."

"Anything you can tell us about Ms. Spooner, Rick?"

Hodding shrugged. "Not much. She had a reservation for just tonight in Penthouse B. Checked in around five, seemed very nice. Friendly and all."

"Did you see her talking to any other guests? Or did she have any visitors that you're aware of?" Ott asked.

"No, sorry. I saw her go out at around seven. I assumed for dinner. But she was by herself when I saw her. She came back around eight, or eight fifteen maybe. Also alone."

Crawford nodded. "Can we get a key to her room, please?"

"Of course," Hodding said. He reached down for a nearby plastic card as though he'd been expecting them to ask for it. He handed it to Crawford.

"Thanks," Crawford said. "Will you be around for a while in case we have other questions?"

"I'm here until eight this morning."

"Graveyard shift, huh?" Ott said, then grimaced at his unintended double entendre.

They got into one of the elevators, and Crawford reached into his pocket for his vinyl gloves and put them on. Ott did the same. The elevator operated without a security card, which surprised Crawford.

"Doesn't look like someone *not* staying here would have a problem getting up to one of the rooms," Crawford said.

"Yeah, I noticed that too," Ott said as the elevator stopped and they got out. "But she'd still have to open her door to whoever it was."

"Yeah, unless he had a key."

Ott nodded as they walked down the hallway to Penthouse

B. They got to the door, and Crawford slipped the card into the slot and pushed open the door.

There was a breeze in the room, and they immediately saw a slider that went out to a balcony was wide open.

Next, they noticed a lamp tipped over on the floor and blood stains on the putting-green-colored carpet. Just beyond that, the round glass top of an overturned table was also spattered with blood and leaning against a sofa.

"She didn't give up without a fight," Ott said, carefully examining the glass top.

"No way he cut out her tongue when she was conscious," Crawford said.

"So, you think he killed her first, then did it?"

Crawford thought for a moment. "Maybe she wasn't dead, just unconscious."

"Why the hell would someone go to the trouble of cutting someone's tongue out in the first place?"

"I been thinking about that," Crawford said. "Only thing I can come up with is it was a message."

Ott nodded. "Okay, but to who?"

Crawford shrugged as he glanced out at the endless black expanse that was the ocean. "That's the question."

"Gotta be honest with you," Ott said with a grim look, "I'm not real keen on finding a tongue."

Crawford wasn't either, particularly because he couldn't see how finding it would help advance the case. "Remind me to ask the techs if there's anything under the vic's fingernails," Crawford said. "Good chance she may have scratched the guy. Got some DNA."

Ott nodded. "Maybe some of this blood is his."

"Yeah, maybe," Crawford said, crouching down and lifting the skirt of a sofa. He looked underneath for a knife even though he knew it was a long shot. Not much chance the killer would leave that behind.

Unlike his short, stout, balding partner, Charlie Crawford

looked nothing like a cop. More like a male model who'd just popped out of the pages of *GQ* (minus the snappy threads). Six-three with dirty-blond hair on the long side, he had burned out on high-profile homicides in New York City four years before and headed south. Ott preceded him by a year, having happily left high crimes and misdemeanors in Cleveland in the rearview mirror. The two, most agreed, had a quite functional marriage of opposites.

The trail of blood led out to the terrace.

Taking pains to step around it, Crawford and Ott went onto the terrace and up to a brick wall around its perimeter. They looked down. In addition to the two techs, they could see Medical Examiner Bob Hawes had arrived.

Ott picked up a nearby flowerpot. "I could drop this on Hawes's head."

Crawford chuckled. The man was not their favorite.

Crawford noticed something off to the side on the terrace floor. He crouched down, picked it up and showed it to Ott. It was a wide strip of duct tape, which Crawford guessed the killer might have used to cover Grace Spooner's mouth. "Maybe lift a print off this."

Ott nodded. "Unless the guy was wearing gloves. What do you think, maybe he tasered her at the door, then stuck that over her mouth?"

"Yeah, he'd have to do something pretty fast, or she'd start screaming."

"Unless she knew him."

Crawford nodded. "Let's go back in and look around some more."

They spent the next half hour looking under furniture and all around the large living room. Then they went into the bedroom, but it seemed apparent nothing had taken place in there.

"Not much to work with," Ott said as he followed Crawford out into the living room.

"Yeah, might as well take off," Crawford said, walking to the door and opening it. "Our best chance is if they lift a print off that duct tape."

"Yeah," Ott said, approaching the elevator, "'cause without that we ain't got squat."

3

CRAWFORD GOT BACK TO HIS CONDO IN WEST PALM Beach at 4:25 a.m. He was tired but couldn't get back to sleep right away. Too many thoughts about the murder racing around in his mind. But finally, he fell back to sleep.

He was in the middle of that dream everyone has: the one where you wake up in a sweaty panic about not having done your homework. It was terrifying. Talk about being riddled with guilt about not hitting the books as a kid.

Another recurring one hit Crawford before he woke. He was playing in a lacrosse game, Dartmouth against Cornell this time, and running down the field cradling the lacrosse ball when his legs suddenly downshifted from a full sprint to slow-motion ... and that was when his alarm went off. He was glad to see it still worked after knocking it over reaching for his iPhone earlier.

He flipped over to the other side of the bed and eyed the alarm clock with scorn. Eight thirty. An hour of tossing and turning, three hours of fitful sleeping and disturbing dreams, many of them familiar replays.

Two feet on the floor, followed by a long yawn.

Forty minutes later, after a quick stop at Dunkin' Donuts, he was at his desk.

First thing he did was Google Grace Spooner, figuring someone who could afford a five-hundred-dollar-a-night penthouse might show up in a web search.

He was right about her surfacing on Google, but not about her fitting the profile of someone who could afford a five-hundred-dollar-a-night suite. According to what he found, she was a twenty-five-year-old employee of a PR firm in Tampa called Advance Team that had twenty employees. That was all he could find. Nothing about where she lived or about her personal life or how she ended up in a penthouse in Palm Beach.

He walked down to where the crime scene techs were stationed. Neither Sheila Stallings nor Robin Gold was in yet. But Crawford's good friend Dominica McCarthy was.

She smiled up at him. "Caught a real nasty one last night, I heard," Dominica said, leaning back in the chair in her cubicle.

Crawford nodded. "Well, officially this morning."

Dominica grimaced. "Her tongue was ..."

Crawford nodded. "Yeah, you believe it?"

Dominica raised her arms. "Who would do something like that?"

"A real sicko, I'd say."

"Yeah, no kidding," Dominica said. "So, you got anything yet?"

"Not much."

She smiled. "You will. You always come up with something."

"Thanks for the vote of confidence. Maybe we can catch dinner when I slow down."

"Sure. I'd like that."

Crawford looked around. No eyewitnesses. He leaned down and kissed her.

"Very unprofessional, Charlie," she said with a smile.

"Yeah, I know. Tell Stallings or Goldie to call me, will ya?"

She nodded. "You got it."

Crawford walked back to his office with a little bounce to his step.

His landline was ringing as he reached his desk.

"Hello."

"Is this Detective Crawford?"

"Yes."

"Detective, my name is Quinn Casey from *The New Yorker* magazine. Can I ask you a few questions?"

The New Yorker? What could they possibly ... "About what?"

"The murder last night. Grace Spooner," Casey said. "I was supposed to meet her for breakfast this morning, but she never showed. Then I went to the hotel where she was staying and found out what happened."

"Why were you meeting with her?"

"I'd like to come talk with you."

Crawford pushed it. "And I'd like to know why you were meeting with her."

Casey resisted. "I'll tell you when we're face-to-face."

"Okay, when do you want to meet?"

A pause. "How about five minutes from now?"

"Okay. You know where I am."

"Sure. The police station on South County."

"See you in a few." Crawford clicked off.

The New Yorker? What the hell was that all about? He opened his MacBook Air to Google Quinn Casey as he heard familiar, lead-footed footsteps.

Ott walked in. "Hey, man."

"Hey. You're an informed guy. Ever heard the name Quinn Casey, a reporter for *The New Yorker?*"

"Sure. Wrote that exposé about the Russian mafia. Also, he's the guy who busted that movie guy who was hitting on all the actresses."

"'That movie guy hitting on all the actresses ...' I need a few more clues."

"You know, the famous director."

Crawford's landline rang again. It was the receptionist.

"Yeah, Dottie?"

"A Mr. Casey's here to see you."

"That was fast. Okay, send him back." Crawford clicked off, then turned to Ott, nodding. "I think I know who you mean. The director. Worked together with his sister, right?"

"Yeah, that's the guy. He—"

A man in khakis and a short-sleeved blue shirt walked in and put his hand out to Crawford. "I'm Quinn Casey. I'm guessing you're Charlie Crawford"—then he glanced at Ott—"and you must be Mort Ott, right?"

They shook hands, and Crawford and Ott said their nice-to-meet-yous.

"Have a seat," Crawford said, pointing to the chair next to Ott.

Casey did and pulled a micro recorder out of his pocket. "You mind if I—"

Crawford held up a hand. "Let's just talk a little first."

"Kinda like, get to know each other?"

"Kinda like."

Casey lay the recorder down on Crawford's desk. "Okay," he said. "Don't worry, it's off. Kind of a force of habit. So, I'm a man of few secrets; you first want to know why I—a reporter from New York—was meeting Grace Spooner for breakfast."

"Yup. That would be the first question," Crawford said.

"Do you know the name Asher Bard?" Casey asked.

It was vaguely familiar to Crawford, but he couldn't quite place it.

But Ott was nodding. "The guy with the young girls," he said. "Did some time, right?"

Casey turned to Ott. "Exactly. Like five minutes. Took

place ten years ago. Word was he had underage girls coming and going at his house on Ocean Lane."

"And on his yacht, as I remember," Ott said.

"Correct," Casey said.

Now Crawford remembered. "Didn't he also fly 'em down to some place in the Virgin Islands, too? Nassau or somewhere?"

"Close. The Caribbean. Same guy, though."

"The way I remember it was the parents of one of the girls, who was like fourteen or fifteen, went to the cops," Ott said. "Then like five more girls came out of the woodwork, implicating not just Bard, but a bunch of other men. Some of them famous. Wasn't there gonna be a big trial"—Ott paused—"but then it kind of went away?"

"Good memory," Casey said. "That all took place before I was at *The New Yorker*, but I read about it. It was obvious there was a big pay-off. Bard's lawyer pled it down to like ... jaywalking. So, he got a month in jail. A country-club jail, to be exact. I've been interviewing a lot of people over the last six months. Seems like the parents of the girls who were going to testify ended up with new Mercedes or went from trailer parks to million-dollar homes."

"So, we're talking *big* money," Crawford said.

"Yeah, *really* big money," Casey said. "Bard owns the second-largest media conglomerate in the country."

"Okay," Crawford said. "So how exactly does Grace Spooner fit into all of this? I'm guessing she was one of the underage girls?"

Casey nodded. "Ten years ago, Grace Spooner was a fifteen-year-old homeless girl living on the streets of Riviera Beach some days, other days in this facility for kids who ran away from home or had no home. How it worked was there were these guys—pimps, effectively—who would go out and round up young strays. Cute young strays, that is. And that's exactly what Grace Spooner was. Anyway, she heard

I was doing the story and contacted me—" Casey exhaled. "She was going to tell me everything she knew about the whole thing this morning. And then ... well, you know the rest."

"She was stabbed twenty times and got her tongue cut out," Ott said, turning to Crawford. "You were right about the tongue. Bet it definitely was a message."

Casey was shaking his head. "You're kidding. Her tongue was—"

"Uh-huh," Crawford said.

"Any guy who'd do that is one seriously sick fuck," Casey said.

Crawford nodded.

Ott cocked his head and stared at Casey. "So, sounds like your guess is Asher Bard is our guy?"

Casey leaned back in his chair so it was resting on the two rear legs. "He's the most obvious suspect, but there are a few others who wouldn't want to see my story in print."

"Give us a list," Crawford said.

"I'm not going to give you specific names, because I've been sued for libel more than once—"

"Come on," Ott said. "We're discreet."

Casey shook his head. "I can't, but what I will tell you is that one is a certain ex-senator. Another is a high-profile lawyer and author who likes to describe himself as a 'noted civil libertarian.' Another one is a Saudi Arabian prince. Another is an English lord—"

"Wait a minute, you're going too fast," Crawford said.

"Yeah," said Ott, "we're a couple of small-town detectives. Our brains don't move as fast as yours."

Casey laughed. "Don't give me that. I've heard all about you. Like the Mounties, you always get your man ... or in some cases, woman."

He was right. Palm Beach was not a place where men had an exclusive on murder.

"Okay, I think I figured out who the first two are," Crawford said.

"What you're saying," Ott jumped in, "is all these guys might have had sex with underage girls, right?"

Casey tapped the arm of his chair and nodded. "According to the rumor mill and some pretty reliable sources."

"Who are they?" Crawford asked.

"Can't tell you. Journalists don't reveal sources."

Crawford groaned. "We can subpoena you, you know."

"Charlie, Charlie, must you threaten me?" Casey said. "I've been subpoenaed before, and, funny, whenever it happened, I just got really forgetful."

Ott chuckled and glanced at Crawford. "I'm beginning to like this guy."

"Okay, who else?" Crawford said.

"Well, let's see, there's a certain man of foreign descent who owns a certain airline, a certain director who's won two Academy Awards—"

"That Weinstein dude?" Ott asked.

"No, that Weinstein dude's only won one. *Shakespeare in Love*."

"I saw it," Ott said. "It sucked."

Casey laughed. "Tell the Academy."

"Come on, who else?" Crawford asked.

"A certain ex-golf champion," Casey said. "The clue is he's left-handed."

Crawford shrugged. "No clue who that is."

"There are others, but that's a start."

"You just reeled off half of Palm Beach," Crawford said.

"Yeah," Casey said with a nod. "Those are the famous ones. There're a bunch of no-names, too."

"'No-names?'" Ott asked.

"You know, friends of Bard's who are not public figures. Men you've never heard of who want their names kept out of the paper. Guys who aren't real keen on going to trial for having sex with minors. That's not good for a marriage, know what I mean?"

"I get it," Crawford said.

No one said anything for a few moments.

"So, now I've opened up to you," Casey said, "and never once turned on my recorder. How about keeping me in the loop on your investigation?"

Ott shot a look at Crawford.

Casey smiled and cocked his head. "I can make you famous," he said. "'The two intrepid, tenacious detectives who tracked down the killer of Grace Spooner.'"

"We don't want to be famous," Crawford said.

"Speak for yourself," Ott said.

"And we're a long way from tracking down the killer of Grace Spooner," Crawford said. "What was she like, anyway?"

"I just met her once," Casey said with a shrug. "But I had a lot of conversations with her. She was a straight-talking, no-bullshit kind of a woman. She told me the whole thing with Bard screwed up her relationships with men. I think she finally had something going with a guy, but she told me she still had a lot of baggage."

"I can believe it," Crawford said. "Do you know the name of the boyfriend?"

"I asked her, but she wouldn't tell me." Casey smiled and raised his arms. "Hey, how come I'm the one laying out all the info? How about a little quid pro quo here, boys?"

"We already told you she got her tongue cut out," Crawford said. "That's about all we got at the moment."

"You think I could tag along with you when you interview suspects or something?"

"No," Crawford said.

Casey chuckled. "Well, that's definitive."

Crawford glanced at Ott. "We can talk to you from time to time, but we're not gonna let you just 'tag along.'"

"Let me ask you this, Quinn," Ott said. "Have you ever interviewed Asher Bard?"

Casey shook his head and smiled. "No, but I did get the opportunity to interview one of his ... employees, I guess he was. He was a very large African-American gentleman by the name of Tyrell. It was a very short interview. I rang the bell at Bard's house, Tyrell came to the door sporting a giant frown and massive biceps and asked me what I wanted. I told him I wanted to interview Asher Bard, and he told me to get the fuck outta there and never come back." Casey laughed. "I did as I was told."

4

CRAWFORD AND OTT MADE THE SHORT DRIVE BACK TO The Colony after Quinn Casey left.

"I liked that guy," Ott said about Casey. "Seemed like a straight-shooter."

"Gotta watch out for reporters," Crawford said. "They'll act like they're your best friend then stab you in the back with their typewriter."

Ott laughed. "Interesting image, Charlie. I think they're using computers these days."

"You know what I mean. Anything for a damn headline or blockbuster story."

The night before, after inspecting Grace Spooner's hotel room, they had checked camera footage from the lobby and at the reception desk but found nothing suspicious. Today they planned to spend a lot more time looking at footage from the hotel's many other cameras in hopes one caught Grace Spooner or the person who was her killer. Scanning hours of footage for someone who lurked, looked out of place, or in any way seemed suspicious was typically a long, slow, tedious process, but one that had paid off in the past. Crawford and Ott planned to have their hands full for the better part of the afternoon.

This time, they focused on footage from the hallway of the penthouse floor where Grace Spooner had been staying, the elevator bank on the ground floor, and the front entry of the hotel, through which most guests came and went.

One of the latter caught Grace Spooner opening the passenger side door of a car and getting in. They ID'd the vehicle as a blue Cadillac CTS, but the footage did not show the license plate and the driver was only a blur. They couldn't even tell if it was a man or a woman. The timestamp was 7:06, which coincided with the time the desk clerk saw Spooner leave the hotel, presumably for dinner. Ott suggested he take it to the crime lab on Gun Club Road in West Palm and try to blow up the image of the driver. Crawford agreed it was worth a shot, though he wasn't particularly hopeful.

The camera covering the bank of hotel elevators caught a lot of people coming and going, but since they didn't know who they were looking for it wasn't particularly productive. They hardly expected to spot a person with a sinister, foreboding presence and go, *Aha! There he is. That's our guy.*

Their biggest hope was the camera that scanned the penthouse hallway and the door to Grace Spooner's room. But it, too, was a bust. It showed Grace Spooner put her plastic card in the slot and enter her room but caught no other person in the area. They went even further back, thinking the killer might have gained access to Spooner's room ahead of time and lay in wait for her, but they found no one.

They had been doing this at The Colony for more than three hours when Crawford's cell phone rang. It was Rose Clarke, the top real estate agent in Palm Beach and Crawford's former *friend with benefits*. He had called her earlier and left a message. Rose was always one of his first calls when he caught a murder because she knew everybody in town and tended to hear about things five minutes after they happened.

"Hi, Rose."

"Hi, Charlie. I'm not sure I can help you on this one."

"As usual, you're way ahead of me. So, obviously, you heard what happened?"

"Yes, but I've never heard of the poor woman. The victim."

"She actually lived up in Tampa. What about a man named Asher Bard?"

She groaned. "The scum of the earth. I avoid him like the plague." Then, like she had an afterthought, "You know who used to be friends with him? Your buddy, David."

"Balfour?"

"Yes. I say 'used to' because I remember David telling me they had a falling-out."

"That's very helpful, Rose. I appreciate it."

"You're welcome. Someone really threw her out a window?"

"Off a terrace, actually."

"Oh, God. The poor woman," she said again.

"I know," Crawford said. "Well, I'm going to give David a call now."

"All right, Charlie. Go do what you do...Make the streets safe again."

Crawford turned to Ott as they walked out of The Colony toward their Crown Vic. "David Balfour apparently knows Asher Bard pretty well, Rose said."

Crawford punched in Balfour's number on speed dial.

Ott nodded as David Balfour answered.

"Hello." It was not Balfour's usual exuberant 'hello.' Crawford thought he sounded either hungover or possibly despondent about something.

"What's wrong, David?"

"Charlie?"

"Yeah, it's me."

"It's about Missy."

"What about her?"

"It's over."

Crawford didn't hesitate. "I'll come right over."

"Yeah, please, I really need a shoulder to lean on."

Crawford dropped off Ott at the station and headed toward Balfour's house. The good thing was he could kill two birds with one stone: commiserate with Balfour and pick his brain about Asher Bard.

Ten months before, Crawford had been an usher at Balfour's wedding to Missy Barnes. Balfour, despite being one of the most eligible bachelors in Palm Beach, had never been married and on the day of his wedding was one of the happiest bridegrooms Crawford had ever seen. He toasted his bride effusively, saying how it was the best day of his life, and then he danced with her until the wee small hours, paying the band extra not to stop at their scheduled time. He and Missy were the last to leave at one thirty in the morning. And now, only ten months later ...

Crawford had first met Balfour when he went to his house to question him about a woman—well, actually a high-class prostitute—who Balfour knew and who had died, horrifically, from snake bites suffered while skinny-dipping in a pool on Barton Avenue.

Even though Crawford had arrived in the role of a cop asking tough questions, the two hit it off almost immediately. Balfour was clearly a rich and pampered patrician. One quick glance was all you needed. The perfect part of his hair, the confident smile, the stylish Maus & Hoffman silk sport shirt, the Belgian suede shoes with cute little bows. Normally, those things would be a turnoff to Crawford. But he liked Balfour's easygoing, unpretentious, self-effacing manner and the fact that he didn't seem to take himself too seriously. Self-absorption was a condition Crawford had observed in many Palm Beach men, but not in Balfour.

Balfour seemed to like him, too. Crawford didn't know why, but he suspected Balfour felt they shared some personality traits, not to mention interests. They'd played golf a couple of times at Balfour's private club, the Poinciana—which was a far cry from Crawford's public course, the scruffy par-three down at the south end. They both were big fans of the New York Giants football team and had commiserated through the last few seasons of sub-par performance. In fact, Balfour still had Crawford over for the occasional Giants night game, during which they both favored the same beer: Sierra Nevada Torpedo.

A few days ago, Crawford had been given a warning about the shaky state of Balfour's marriage when Balfour told him on the phone that things were "pretty rocky" with Missy.

"It's over," his latest pronouncement, was a whole lot more conclusive, if not completely shocking. Balfour had already admitted to Crawford that his relatively short engagement with Missy might have been due to his rebound from a failed relationship with a woman named Brie Ackerman, who he had been madly in love with. Turned out, though, Brie was having an affair while ostensibly dating Balfour. But ... that was another story.

Crawford parked and pressed the buzzer of Balfour's two-story Georgian.

A few moments later, Balfour opened the door. "Thanking for coming," he said in an uncharacteristically dead monotone.

"You all right, man?"

Balfour rolled his eyes. "I've been better. Come on in."

Balfour turned and walked—shuffled was more like it—through his living room into his library. Balfour was way too young to be shuffling, Crawford thought, but kept that to himself. Balfour sat down in his big leather chair, Crawford opposite him.

"I don't get it," Balfour started out.

"What?"

"Why women have affairs behind my back," Balfour said. "I must suck as a lover."

Crawford smiled. "Missy was? Having an affair?"

"Yup. Apparently, she met some struggling artist ... and now wants to live in squalor in West Palm."

"That's the place to do it," Crawford said. He, too, lived in West Palm, not in squalor, but not exactly high on the hog either.

"This is not real good on my ego, Charlie," Balfour said, shaking his head dolefully. "What am I going to do?"

"Jesus, man. It seems like you two were just walking down the aisle five minutes ago."

Balfour patted the arm of his chair. "I know. I just keep wondering what I did wrong."

"I doubt you did anything wrong. It was just"—he started to say "one of those things" but felt he could do better—"not meant to be, maybe."

He wasn't sure that was much better.

He looked around the library. The same place they watched the Giants lose Sunday after Sunday. A space that had more athletic trophies than books.

"So, I just got served," Balfour said. "This lowlife process server. Looked like someone out of *The Walking Dead*."

Crawford chuckled, conjuring up a mental image. "So, you got a good lawyer?"

"Yeah, but she's got a better one. This ballbuster from New York."

"A woman?"

"No, a she-devil," Balfour said. "Can we *not* talk about it anymore?"

"Sure."

"What did you call me about anyway?"

Crawford leaned forward in his chair. "Oh, yeah. Rose told me you know Asher Bard. What can you tell me about him?"

No hesitation. "That's easy: he's a sleazy lowlife and one

of the richest guys in Palm Beach. Used to be a friend of mine, until he showed his true colors. Why?"

"There was a murder early this morning. A woman who was one of his underage victims ten years ago."

Balfour sat up straight. "No shit. What happened?"

"It was pretty grisly. She got stabbed a bunch of times then got tossed from the penthouse terrace at The Colony. Her tongue was cut out, too."

"Oh, my God, that's terrible."

"Can you see Bard doing something like that?"

Balfour sighed and thought for a moment. "Personally, no. But if she was going to, as you guys would say, rat him out, who knows?"

"She was."

"Really?"

Crawford nodded. "So I'm led to believe."

Balfour shook his head slowly. "Cut her tongue out ... Jesus, how sick is that?"

There was clearly unanimity on that.

"I was invited to his sixtieth birthday party last night," Balfour said. "No way in hell I'd ever go, though."

"Where was the party?" Crawford asked. "His house?"

A pause, like Balfour was trying to remember. "No, come to think of it, it was at The Colony."

5

AFTER LEAVING DAVID BALFOUR'S HOUSE, CRAWFORD went straight to Ott's cubicle.

Ott, typing something on his computer, looked up. "What's up?"

"Guess where Asher Bard was last night?"

"Girl Scout meeting?"

"How 'bout his sixtieth birthday party at The Colony?"

"You gotta be—"

"Nope. David Balfour told me, and I just called The Colony. They said Bard rented out the entire restaurant there. The CPB. Even though there were only about twenty people who came."

Ott put his feet up on his desk. "Why so few?"

"I'm guessing he's not the most popular guy in Palm Beach," Crawford said. "Did you try him again? The birthday boy."

"Yeah, I've got three calls into him. Nothing back."

"All right, let's wait an hour, and if we haven't heard from him, just show up on his doorstep."

"What about that guy at his house? The guy Quinn Casey told us about? Tyrell," Ott said.

"You can handle him."

Asher Bard did not call back in the next hour, so Ott tried him again.

No luck.

He walked down to Crawford's office. Crawford was on a call. He had been trying to locate Grace Spooner's next of kin. From what they could tell, there was no mother or father in the picture. Which made sense, given Casey's account of her teen homelessness.

Someone at her PR firm said she had a sister in Palm City whose last name was Henderson, and Crawford was trying to track her down. So far, unsuccessfully.

Crawford looked up when Ott walked in. "No call back from Bard?"

Ott shook his head. "Let's go break the guy's door down."

Asher Bard had a house at the end of Ocean Lane. It looked to be on at least two lots, maybe three, and was huge. Crawford was surprised they could drive right up to it, that it had no gate or, as was the case with some Palm Beach houses, a gatehouse manned by someone whose job it was to stop anyone who wasn't friends or family or driving a Rolls.

Ott, who was at the wheel as usual, drove right up to the oversized front door and parked in front of it.

Crawford pointed. "They *do* have a parking court, you know."

"Screw that. I like to save shoe leather."

They walked up the steps to a landing that had big marble columns on either side of the front door. Ott hit the buzzer.

Nothing. He leaned forward to press the buzzer again just as the door opened.

It was a large African-American man who had a flattop you could land a drone on and biceps that resembled the house's stone columns.

"Tyrell?" Ott asked.

"Yes. Who are you?"

Another large African-American man came up behind him. Not as tall but just as wide.

"We're detectives," Crawford said, flashing his ID. "Palm Beach Police." Then to the other man, "And you are?"

"His brother, Darnell," the man said with a smile.

Crawford nodded. "We need to talk to Mr. Bard."

"Sorry, man, not here," Tyrell said.

"Where is he?" Crawford asked.

"Halfway to Costa Rica. In his plane."

"What's he doing there?"

Tyrell shrugged. "I'd say 'whatever he feels like,' but you probably wouldn't think that was a satisfactory answer."

"You're right. What's he doing there?" Crawford asked again.

"Just a little golf vacation. He'll be back in three days."

"When did he leave?"

"Couple hours ago. Why, what you want him for?"

Ott stepped in front of Tyrell. "We're asking the questions here, Tyrell. Who went with him?"

Tyrell's wide smile revealed a large diamond stud in his tongue. "Well, tough guy, I don't know the answer to that. You'll have to ask his assistant, Jennifer."

"How do we contact her?"

"The office. 350 Royal Palm Way. Jennifer Atwood."

"Thank you, Tyrell," Ott said.

"You're very welcome, Detective. Got any more questions?"

Ott glanced over at Crawford, who shrugged.

"Just one," Ott said.

"Well, fire away."

"Y' ever get food stuck on that diamond?"

OTT WAS PULLING OUT OF ASHER BARD'S DRIVEWAY. "Costa Rica's a long way to go to play golf."

"Sure is."

"So, what was your first thought when he said Bard had gone there?"

Crawford was tapping his fingers on the console. "Probably same as you."

"What?"

"Sex."

Ott nodded. "Yup, exactly what I was thinking."

"What else is going through that brilliant analytical mind of yours, Mort?"

"I was just thinking of Ward Jaynes."

"Huh?"

"This reminds me of him."

Crawford flashed back to their first case together in Palm Beach. Ward Jaynes was a billionaire Wall Street tycoon who also had a thing for young girls. One in particular. Whose brother Jaynes ended up killing because he was trying to extort a million dollars from him. Jaynes was ruthless and diabolical, and it took them a long time to take him down, but eventually they did.

"I know what you mean," Crawford said. "So, if we play this right, maybe Bard ends up Jaynes's roommate in prison."

Ott smiled and nodded.

"Could be wishful thinking, though, since we got a long way to go," Crawford said. "I remember my brother telling me about Costa Rica."

"Your rich brother?"

"Yeah, he went there once. He liked it and was thinking about buying a house."

"What happened?"

"Told me he got turned off after seeing a bunch of old American guys with young Costa Rican girls."

"Your brother's got class."

Crawford nodded wistfully. "Yeah, if only he could knock off the booze."

Ott took a left instead of going straight to the station. He parked in front of 350 Royal Palm Way. They got out and took the elevator up to the second floor.

It turned out Jennifer Atwood was Asher Bard's only employee.

"His main office is up in New York," Jennifer explained as they faced her in the tidy office. "He uses this when he's down here on weekends and vacations."

"He flies down on weekends?" Crawford asked.

Her office had a distant view of the Society of the Four Arts building and its garden beyond. Jennifer was a short woman in her forties who had a nice smile and pretty brown eyes.

"Yes, comes down almost every weekend. Except in the summer."

"Probably has a place in the Hamptons for then, huh?" Ott said.

Crawford turned to his partner, surprised. How did a cop from Cleveland and the son of a locker room attendant even know about the Hamptons? He saw Ott was checking out her left hand. For a ring, was his guess.

"No, actually Nantucket," Jennifer said.

The other place captains of industry summered, Crawford knew.

"Must be nice," Ott said. "What kind of plane does he have?"

"A Cessna Citation X. Goes about seven hundred miles an hour."

"So"—Ott did the math—"takes him about an hour and a half to get down here?"

"Yes, well, not door to door. He's in the air that long, though."

"I imagine some people in New York have commutes that long," Ott said.

"I guess that's true. I've never lived up there," she said with a bright smile.

"Ms. Atwood," Crawford said. "We are looking into that murder that took place at The Colony Hotel. I'm sure you've heard about it by now—"

She nodded. "That was so horrible."

"Yes, and we know your boss had a birthday party there last night."

"Yes, but you don't think—"

"We don't think anything at this point. We're just talking to a lot of people and asking a lot of questions. Since Mr. Bard and his group were there where it happened, naturally we want to talk to him and the others. Do you have the guest list for the birthday party?"

"I sure do," Jennifer said, reaching into a desk drawer. "It was not a very large group."

She handed Crawford two pieces of paper. "The ones with checks next to their names came. Or accepted, at least. The others ... had other plans, I guess."

Or like David Balfour, didn't want anything to do with Asher Bard.

Crawford scanned the list. By his unofficial calculation, one in every three invited had accepted.

"So, it looks to be about twenty," Crawford said.

"Another question." It was Ott's turn. "How many went to Costa Rica with him?"

"Well, that I don't need a list for. There were three other men."

"And they were going there for ... what reason?"

"A golf trip. Apparently, there're some really good golf courses in Costa Rica."

"Is that right?" Ott said. "And who were they, the men who went with him?"

"Well, there was Joe Mitchell, Ainslie Sunderland, and Jerry Reposo."

Ott wrote the names down in his old leather notebook. Joseph Mitchell was the lawyer and author Quinn Casey had mentioned as a frequent interviewee on Fox News about legal matters. Ainslie Sunderland was an English lord who had become well known because his daughter had just married into the royal family. Jerry Reposo was an unfamiliar name.

"They're all good friends of Mr. Bard," Jennifer said.

"And I see all of them went to his birthday party, too," Crawford said, scanning the list. He noticed the ex-senator Quinn Casey had mentioned was not on the birthday list, either as an invitee or an attendee. He must have been told by his wife to clean up his act.

"Yes, that's true."

"So, did you make reservations for Mr. Bard and his friends at golf courses in Costa Rica?" Ott asked.

She glanced out the window then turned and shot Ott a smile. "Ah, no. Actually, I didn't. He did that."

"Is that the kind of thing he usually does?" Ott asked.

"No." She shifted in her chair. "Usually I do."

Ott smiled at her. "Just not this time, huh?"

She smiled back at him. "Exactly."

"And I assume Mr. Bard belongs to a golf club around here," Crawford asked. "The Poinciana, maybe?"

"No, Seminole up in Juno Beach."

Crawford nodded, then thought for a moment. "Well, I

don't have any more questions"—glancing at Ott—"how about you?"

"Just curious," Ott said, "have I maybe seen you at St. Edward Church, by any chance?"

That was about the last question Crawford expected to come out of his partner's mouth.

"Ah, no. I go to St. Ann's," Jennifer said.

Ott nodded and smiled.

Crawford got to his feet. "Well, thank you so much for meeting with us, Ms. Atwood."

"Yes, we really appreciate it," Ott said, shaking her hand with both hands. "Especially it being spur of the moment and all."

"It was my pleasure," Jennifer said. "So nice to meet you both." Crawford could have sworn she winked at Ott.

Crawford waited until they got to the elevator. "She winked at you, didn't she?"

Ott's face went crimson. "You're seeing things, my friend."

Crawford shook his head and laughed. "I don't think so," he said. "And what was that thing about the churches?"

"I just noticed the cross she was wearing."

"So, let me guess: You figured you'd let her know you were a good God-fearing, church-going man? That it, Mort?"

Ott shrugged. "Never hurts."

"You're hopeless," Crawford said. "I bet the last time you went to church was back in Cleveland."

"Not true. Remember when we went to church on the Palmer-sisters case?"

"Yeah, you were working ... not praying."

For once, Ott had no rejoinder.

Crawford pulled out his iPhone as the elevator door opened. He started dialing.

"Who ya calling?" Ott asked.

Crawford held up a hand. "Yes, can you give me the

number of the Seminole Golf Club in Juno Beach, please." He listened. "Thanks."

Then he dialed the number. "Yes, hello. Can you connect me to the pro shop, please?"

Pause.

"Yeah, hi. My name is Tyrell, and I work for Asher Bard, a member there. He's out of the country, and I just wanted to know whether his clubs are there or whether he took 'em up north with him?"

Pause.

"They *are* there," Crawford said into his phone. "Okay, great, that's all I need to know. Thanks, I appreciate it."

Crawford clicked off.

Ott patted Crawford on the shoulder. "Good thinkin', Charlie."

"Yeah, but all it does is confirm he wasn't going to Costa Rica for golf. Unless maybe he's got two golf bags. Doesn't get us any closer to finding our killer."

6

When Crawford and Ott arrived back at the station, Crawford's landline was ringing in his office.

"Hello?"

"Charlie"—it was the receptionist, Janine—"it's Harlan Brody on the phone. He's the—"

"Thanks, Janine, I know who he is."

Harlan Brody was the state attorney for Palm Beach County. A powerful man who led a team of 120 prosecutors and had a vast professional staff in five offices throughout Palm Beach County.

Crawford clicked on. "Hello."

"Charlie, Harlan Brody here. I'd like to come see you right away."

Sorry, I'm busy, didn't seem like it would be an acceptable answer. "Okay, I'm assuming this has to do with the Grace Spooner murder?"

"Yes, it does. I'll be there in fifteen minutes."

"Okay."

Brody clicked off.

Crawford loved it how men like Brody expected men like him to just drop everything. What if he had an interview lined up? What if he had an arrest to make? What if ... It didn't seem to matter to the Harlan Brodys of the world.

And, sure enough, fifteen minutes later—not sixteen or fourteen—Harlan Brody stormed into Crawford's office at a business-like clip. He was a man of medium height, short hair, and a marshmallow-white face, as if he'd never stretched out on a local beach. But he shook hands as if he were intent on breaking every knuckle in Crawford's right hand. Crawford's read: an over-compensator.

"Nice to meet you, Charlie," Brody said. "I've heard good things about you."

"Thank you," Crawford said, not knowing what to call Brody. "State Attorney" was a mouthful and "sir" ... well, he refused to call him "sir."

"Call me Harlan," Brody said, making it easier.

He sat down in a chair facing Crawford's desk. "So, let's talk about Grace Spooner."

"Hang on a sec. I want to get my partner in on this," Crawford said, hitting the intercom for Ott. "Hey, Mort, can you come in? I'm with the state attorney."

"Yeah, sure, be right there," Ott said.

A few seconds later, Ott walked in. Crawford introduced the two and Ott sat down. It was then Crawford saw the insignia on Brody's maroon tie. It was the unmistakable shield of one of Crawford's old college rivals, Harvard University.

"So, I was just about to ask Charlie," Brody said to Ott, "what you guys got on the Grace Spooner case?"

Ott nodded and glanced at Crawford.

"At this point we've got a few suspects," Crawford said, "but no one who we'd call a key suspect."

The instant frown on Brody's pasty white face indicated that was not the answer he was looking for. "You gotta be kidding. Why the hell isn't Asher Bard locked up right now? He was at the murder scene. He's got a clear-cut motive. What the hell else do you need?"

"For one thing, he's in Costa Rica."

"You're kidding. When did he go there?"

"This morning."

"Well, hell, I'll get him extradited."

"We have no reason to believe he was fleeing. Or that he's a flight risk. He went there with three other men on a planned trip."

"Yeah, I've heard all about his trips," Brody said. "So, when is he supposed to come back?"

"Day after tomorrow."

"So arrest him at the airport." Not a suggestion, an order.

"On what charge?"

"You got two days to dig up evidence to charge him with."

Crawford looked down and tapped his desk with a pen. "What makes you so sure it was Bard?"

Brody sighed and shook his head like he was in the presence of a couple of dopey high-school boys who needed to be spoon-fed. "Jesus, have you been listening to me? Because he was at the murder scene, and because he had a motive. My witness, Grace Spooner, was about to go to trial and put him away for twenty years."

Crawford nodded. "But, wait a minute, there already was a trial ten years ago. And a conviction. Wouldn't that be double jeopardy?"

Brody smiled. "Very good, Charlie"—it was a touch condescending—"I see you're a lawyer *and* a detective. The charge this time is different from the one the first time. But, in reality, pretty similar."

Crawford nodded. "I gotcha. So the other three from back then, they were also going to trial on the new charges?"

Brody nodded. "But forget the other three. Bard did it. Trust me."

"Well, Bard's definitely our leading suspect, but we haven't ruled out the others at his birthday party," Crawford said. "We don't have any physical evidence yet. We're hoping to get a print or DNA but don't have the results yet."

"Well, hell, man, you need me to speed things up?" Brody asked.

Crawford glanced at Ott, who nodded. "Wouldn't hurt."

"Right after this, I'll make the call."

Crawford nodded.

"But, goddamn it," Brody said and pounded Crawford's desk, "I'm telling you, Bard did it."

Crawford held up his hands. "Okay, as soon as he's back, we'll be all over him. In the meantime, we still have the others at his party to interview. Question: Was there a statute of limitations on the sexual battery charge against Bard and the others?"

Brody nodded slowly. "That's a good question, and the answer is, it was going to run out in six months."

Crawford nodded. "So that gave you enough time?"

"Yeah, and based on everything Grace Spooner told me, she was going to be a very convincing witness. With enough detail to put Bard away for, as I said, a long time."

Brody stood up. "All right," he said to Crawford. "We'll be talking on a regular basis. I need your cell phone number, too."

Crawford gave it to him. "We'll let you know when we have something."

As he walked toward the door, Brody turned back to Crawford. "No, that's not good enough. Get something in the next three days so you can greet Bard at the airport with your handcuffs out."

7

No sooner was State Attorney Harlan Brody out the door than Police Chief Norm Rutledge walked in the door. "What was that all about?" Rutledge asked Crawford.

Crawford and Ott were still standing, having just done another quick knuckle-breaker handshake with Brody before his hasty exit. "Seems the state attorney wants to see Asher Bard put in solitary for life up at Raiford," Crawford said.

"Yeah, with no parole," Ott added.

Raiford was the notorious state prison west of Jacksonville.

"Yeah, well, who can blame the guy after what Bard did to him," Rutledge said.

"What? What exactly happened?" Crawford asked.

"Guess it was before you guys got down here," Rutledge said. "I'd say it was maybe five or six years back. Anyway, Brody was the chief assistant in the state attorney's office. Young—like late twenties—and ambitious as shit. He was out to nail Asher Bard and add another scalp to his belt. He had, or so he thought anyway, an iron-clad case against Bard and the other three. Three teenage witnesses who were going to detail what went on at Bard's house and on his yacht." Rutledge had

Crawford's and Ott's complete, undivided attention. "So, he called the first girl to the stand, and she gets up there and says with a straight face how Bard and one of the other guys just helped her with her homework—math in particular—whenever she came over."

"You gotta be shitting me," Ott said, shaking his head incredulously. "That's what she said?"

"Yup," Rutledge said. "And when Brody started questioning her about giving the men massages or any kind of sex having occurred, she denied everything. Said very innocently that nothing at all like that happened. They were all perfect gentlemen."

"That's unbelievable," Crawford said. "So, what happened next?"

"When Brody saw where it was headed, he dismissed her quick and called the next girl. So, she gets up and says that Bard and the other men were all very generous with their time and gave her advice on how to set up and successfully run a lemonade stand—"

"Bullshit!" Crawford said in total disbelief. "*Really?*"

Rutledge nodded his head. "Half the people in the courthouse were stifling laughs at this point. Brody's up there red-faced, looking like a total idiot, and the judge decides it's time for a recess. Long story short, it's over. Brody wisely doesn't call the third girl, and all but one of the charges were dismissed. They got him for something minor, I forget what. Got, basically, a wrist slap."

"Wow," Crawford said, looking at Ott. "I guess we know why Brody wants Bard's ass so bad."

"Yeah, the whole thing was a big setback in his career," Rutledge said. "But, gotta hand it to him, the guy hung in there and a few years later got the job he was after. And, word is, he's now thinking about running for senator in 2022."

"And it sure wouldn't hurt to have a murder conviction for

a high-profile guy like Asher Bard on his résumé, would it?" Crawford asked rhetorically.

Rutledge nodded. "Sure wouldn't."

"So, this is way more than just politics."

"Sure is."

8

Asher Bard and his fellow passengers aboard his Citation X were indeed primary suspects, and if Harlan Brody had his way, Crawford and Ott would be on their way to Costa Rica to arrest them all. Even though Brody didn't seem to have much interest in considering Ainslie Sunderland, Joseph Mitchell, Jerry Reposo, and another man, Monte Bittar, whose name had surfaced, as suspects in the murder of Grace Spooner. A year ago, Crawford and Ott pursued a suspect all the way to Mexico. Back then, they had substantial evidence that their suspect, a Mexican national, was the killer. In the Spooner case, though, they had nothing to justify spending good money and wasting a lot of time going after Asher Bard and company in Costa Rica.

They were in Crawford's office figuring out a plan of attack. Typically, they used something resembling a spreadsheet, on which they designated and split up people they needed to interview, locations they wanted to revisit, and follow-up conversations they were eager to have, typically with the ME and crime scene techs.

There were twenty people on the list they had gotten from Jennifer Atwood. They had to interview all of them. It went without saying that one interview could be quite different from the next one. There was the interview in which a subject was ruled out almost immediately. An airtight alibi, usually. Or, as in a previous case, a physical handicap that made it impossible for a suspect to commit a crime.

Crawford decided the best way to proceed was to talk to David Balfour about the men on the list. Get his impressions. He called Balfour, who sounded even more dispirited about his deteriorating marital situation than before, but who readily agreed to help on the Spooner case in whatever way he could.

So Crawford and Ott drove over to Balfour's house. As usual, they met in Balfour's library.

Crawford had just handed Balfour the list.

"So, you're asking me who on this list could be a murderer?"

"That would be nice," Crawford said with a smile. "You tell us who did it, we go read him his rights and lock him up. But somehow I see it being a little more complicated than that."

Balfour was scanning the list. He stopped at one. "Wow, Khalid Al-Ansani was there?"

"Who's he?"

"You don't know?" Balfour asked.

"Name is vaguely familiar," Crawford said.

"He's what's called an international arms dealer by some, a legendary philanderer by others … Me, I just call him a rogue. A lovable rogue sometimes; other times, kind of a sinister rogue."

"What nationality is he?" Crawford asked.

"He's a Saudi. Makes deals all around the world. S'posedly speaks, like, seven languages and has five wives and ten mistresses."

"Is he the kind of rogue who kills people?" Crawford asked.

Balfour chuckled. "Not that I know of personally, but I've heard stories."

"Really? Like what?"

"He can play a little rough, supposedly."

Crawford made a mental note to follow up on him right away.

"Who else on this list jumps out at you?" Ott asked, shifting in his chair.

Balfour turned to Ott. "Well, you saw the golfer, Roddy Sproul, right?"

Ott nodded. "Yeah, what's he like?"

"I don't know him that well, even though he's a member at the Poinciana," Balfour said. "I hear he's got a temper, though. Throwing clubs, stuff like that."

Ott couldn't resist. "How 'bout throwing women?"

"Kinda doubt that," Balfour said.

They went through the rest of the names on the list. Three of them Balfour didn't know at all. The rest of them were men he knew to varying degrees. Crawford asked him again if he had to choose someone on the list to be a murderer, who it would be.

"Well, this is obvious, but Bard is your leading candidate at this point, right? I mean, talk about motive. That woman's testimony could put him in jail for a hell of a long time. Or else one of the other men from the trial ten years back, who she was going to implicate again."

"You mean Sunderland, Mitchell, and Bittar?"

"Yes, but I'm not telling you anything you don't know."

Crawford nodded, his mind veering in another direction.

"What are you thinking?" Ott asked.

"Just that in my experience, the most obvious suspect turns out to be the killer about sixty percent of the time."

"Someone else forty percent?" Ott said.

"Yeah, what would you say?"

Ott nodded. "Sounds about right."

"So, the sixty percenter is Bard, and the forty percenters are Monte Bittar, Joe Mitchell, and Ainslie Sunderland."

"Yeah, so far, but something tells me we're going to be adding to the list."

"I agree."

Crawford turned to Balfour. "Let me ask the question another way. Who on this list would you rule out?"

Balfour looked down the list and thought for a few moments. "This is hard, especially since a couple of these guys are friends of mine."

"I hear you," Crawford said. "See, one of our problems is that none of them have alibis, since they all were at The Colony. Unless they can prove they left early and went home. You know, where their wife can alibi them or something. We can usually rule out people pretty fast, assuming they have solid alibis."

"I understand," Balfour said, reaching into a coffee table drawer next to him and pulling out a pen. "Tell you what I'm going to do: I'm going to put checks next to ones I'd call 'least likely.' Does that help at all?"

Crawford nodded. "It definitely does. But then again, I've run across a murderer or two who everyone describes as the nicest guy they've ever met"—he turned to Ott—"know what I mean?"

"Oh, yeah, for sure," Ott said. "Boy Scouts, class presidents, Most Likely to Succeed ... Murderers don't all look like Charlie Manson."

Crawford nodded.

"In fact," said Ott, "Ted Bundy was an honor student in high school and went to law school for a while."

Balfour looked up. "Is that right?"

"I had one guy when I was up in Cleveland who was the choirmaster at the Unitarian Church. Taught Sunday school and turned out he got his jollies by hacking up people into tiny little pieces in his spare time."

"You're kidding," Balfour said, shaking his head.

"Nope. Sidney Machowski. I'll never forget ol' Sid."

"That reminds me of something," Balfour said. "Does the name Sid Sherman mean anything to you?"

Crawford and Ott both shook their heads.

"He's a Broadway producer whose wife, I heard, is having an affair with Bard."

"Does Sherman know about it?"

"I doubt it. But even if he does, I'm not sure he'd care much because—"

Crawford held up his hand. "Don't tell me. Because he's having a thing with someone else's wife."

Balfour nodded. "You catch on quick, Charlie. By the way, we never had this conversation. Bard's not my friend, but I sure as hell don't want him as an enemy." He turned to Crawford. "On another subject—Missy—I hired a private investigator my friend recommended. He's looking into her and her boyfriend. I get the sense the P.I. knows what he's doing."

"Sounds good," Crawford said. "Keep me up to speed on it. Let me know if there's anything I can help with."

"I will," Balfour said. "In the meantime, good luck on your case."

"At this point, we sure could use some."

CRAWFORD AND OTT WENT BACK TO THE STATION, SPLIT up the list, and started making calls right away. Two men were eliminated quickly. One had the flu the night of Bard's party and never left his house. Crawford confirmed that by phoning Jennifer Atwood, who said the man called the day of the party and said he didn't want to give the flu to the others at the party. Another man Ott called said he'd only gone to the party for one drink because his wife had had a fender-bender the afternoon of the party, banged up her knee a little, and he'd come home early to take care of her.

And then there were eighteen.

Crawford was able to reach Roddy Sproul, the PGA golf professional, who seemed accommodating. They made a date for an interview at five o'clock. He lived in Delray Beach, about a half hour from the station. Crawford also heard back from Khalid Al-Ansani, and they agreed to meet at Al-Ansani's house at six thirty. It was one of those phone calls that goes like this:

Crawford (answering the phone): Hello?

Voice: Detective Crawford?

Crawford: Yes, who's this?

Voice: Hold for Mr. Al-Ansani, please.

Which Crawford did for a full minute until Al-Ansani finally came on.

The upshot was that Al-Ansani was willing to meet, but he wanted to know what the purpose of the meeting was, though Crawford was convinced he knew already. When Crawford told him, Al-Ansani said, "Oh, I heard about that. Was that the same night we were there?" Again, Crawford was convinced he knew perfectly well that it was.

Having the two men lined up for interviews was unusual because normally the men and women of Palm Beach treated a visit from a detective as they would an IRS man climbing over the wall behind their house. After Al-Ansani, Crawford made calls to four other men, but got only voicemails.

Finally, he called the last man on his list, and he answered.

"Hello. Dan Wright."

"Yes, hi, Mr. Wright, my name is Detective Crawford, Palm Beach Police. I'm calling because you were at Asher Bard's birthday party the night before last at The Colony, where the murder of a woman took place. I'd like to come talk to you."

A pause. "Okay, but what is it you'd like to know?"

"Just some general questions," Crawford said. "What you may have observed or heard at Mr. Bard's party."

"I didn't observe a damn thing except a bunch of guys getting drunk."

"I'd still like to talk to you. How is tomorrow morning?"

Reluctantly, Dan Wright agreed. He said he had an errand to run on Royal Palm Way at nine, and they agreed he'd stop by the station at ten.

Something Wright had said triggered a thought, and Crawford walked down to Ott's cubicle. Ott was in the middle of an animated conversation with someone, gesturing excitedly with his left hand, his ninety-five percent bald head alternately nodding, then shaking side to side. "Okay, great, thank you, Mr. Greer. I'll stop by tomorrow morning at eleven. Look forward to meeting you."

Ott clicked off.

Crawford recognized Greer as one of the names on the Bard party list. "Got a live one there?"

"Got a real talker is what I had," Ott said. "Among other things, he said he didn't know Asher Bard very well."

Crawford shrugged. "But he was invited to his sixtieth birthday party?"

"I know. Turns out he thinks it was because of his sixteen-year-old daughter."

Crawford cocked his head. "Wait, I'm not with you."

"Greer was with his daughter at Publix and bumped into Bard there. Greer said, in retrospect, Bard was paying a little bit too much attention to his daughter. Then, at the birthday party, Greer says Bard started asking him all kinds of questions about her."

"Like what?"

"Well, like where she goes to school. What sports she plays. Shit like that. But then he asks him when her birthday was. And Greer thinks that's a little weird, so he goes, 'Why do you want to know that?' And Bard says, "Cause I thought I might get her a birthday present.'"

Crawford shook his head. "I'd say that's more than a little weird."

"I agree. So did Greer. He says to me he steered the conversation to some other subject after that."

"If it was me," Crawford said, shaking his head, "I'd steer it to accusing Bard of being a world-class perv and tell him to not go within a hundred miles of my daughter. Man, this guy gets worse by the second. I mean, he's major-league sick."

"Yeah, no shit. I get why Harlan Brody wants to take him down so bad," Ott said. "Why'd you come by?"

"I think I know something that might help us."

Ott leaned back in his chair. "What's that?"

"The guys at Bard's party had no reason to leave the restaurant."

"Keep going."

"Like any restaurant, there's a men's and ladies' room, so for what reason would they possibly go outside the restaurant?"

"That's a good point," Ott said. "Other than to have a smoke maybe, I can't think of any reason unless to pay a visit to Grace Spooner."

Crawford nodded. "And, as I remember, there was a camera at the entrance that connects the restaurant and the hotel."

Ott nodded. "So, we go see if anyone walked out of the restaurant into the hotel?"

"Exactly," Crawford said. "We both don't need to go. I thought I'd head over there now. I've got appointments with Sproul at five and the arms dealer at six thirty."

"Ever interviewed an international arms dealer before?"

Crawford shook his head. "Only arms dealer I ever met was a guy selling stolen Kalashnikovs out of the trunk of his car up in Riviera Beach."

After Crawford examined the surveillance footage from the door connecting the CPB restaurant with The Colony Hotel, he discovered that four men from Asher Bard's birthday party had left the restaurant. One of them, it turned out, was one of his upcoming interviews, Khalid Al-Ansani. Al-Ansani was easy to recognize: he was wearing a thobe and a turban. Crawford had no idea who the other three men were. One was tall, had a shaved head, and was wearing a blue blazer and pink pants. Another was skinny, had Gordon Gekko slicked-back hair, and was wearing a tan suit.

The third was a mushy-looking man with drooping eyebrows and curly reddish hair who had a wide grin. Crawford snapped a shot of all three men with his iPhone. He intended to have Roddy Sproul identify them, then show the photos to Ott.

He took a look at his watch. It was 4:35. He walked out to The Colony parking lot, slid into his Crown Vic, and headed south to Delray Beach. He pulled into the peach-colored ranch house at the address he had for the professional golfer.

Sproul, who answered the door, was an older version of the man Crawford had seen walk off the eighteenth green of Augusta National to thunderous applause fifteen years before. The Masters champ was a little grayer and paunchier but still had the hawkish look and penetrating blue eyes. He was wearing a straw hat with a Poinciana club logo on it, beige shorts, and a green collared shirt.

"Welcome, Detective. Can I get you something to drink?" Sproul asked in a South African accent.

Crawford had forgotten he was from there.

"Just a water would be great," Crawford said, shaking Sproul's hand.

"Oh, come on, Detective. It's five o'clock. How about a beer or something?"

"No, thanks. I appreciate it, though."

"Well, come on back." Sproul gestured with his hand. "I'm going to have a beer."

Crawford followed Sproul into his large, antiseptically white kitchen and up to the refrigerator.

Sproul reached in and pulled out a green bottle. Crawford didn't recognize the name on the label. "Windhoek?" he said. "Thought I knew my beers, but I don't know that one."

"It's from South Africa. Sure I can't—"

Crawford shrugged. "Why not?"

Sproul smiled and reached in for another bottle. Then he got an opener from a drawer and opened them both. They walked out to a sunroom in the back of the house and sat down facing each other.

"Terrible thing, that murder at The Colony," Sproul said.

"Sure was," Crawford said. "When you were there for Bard's birthday party, did you see anything ... out of the ordinary?"

Sproul chuckled. "I saw quite a few things out of the ordinary, but not what you mean."

Crawford squinted. "I'm not with you."

"Well, I think what you're asking is did I see anything out of the ordinary that might have had to do with a murder, and the answer is no. But at the birthday party, there sure as hell were a few things out of the ordinary."

"Like what?"

Sproul cocked his head. "Have you spoken to any other guys who were there yet?"

"No, you're the first."

Sproul paused as if he wasn't sure he wanted to tell tales out of school. Finally: "Okay, well, fasten your seat belt."

"It's fastened."

Sproul leaned forward. "And I'm assuming this is confidential. You won't ever quote me."

"You have my word. Nothing you say will go outside this room."

Sproul took a long sip of his Windhoek. "Okay, well, the first thing that struck me was it seemed more like a bachelor party than a birthday party."

"How so?"

Sproul paused again. "'Cause there were dancing girls in attendance."

"Dancing girls?" Then it clicked. "Wait, you don't mean strippers, do you?"

Sproul chuckled. "I never used that word."

"But that's what they were, right?"

Sproul nodded. "Second of all, when I left, Asher told me we had gone through two cases of Pommery Cuvee."

"I'm guessing that's something you drink?"

Sproul nodded. "A very expensive brand of champagne," he said, shaking his head. "And that's with two guys who are teetotalers."

Crawford did some quick math: Twenty minus the man who didn't show, minus the one who just had one drink, minus the two teetotalers. That meant the sixteen remaining men had averaged a bottle and a half each. "That's a lot of champagne."

"No kidding," Sproul said with a laugh. "Judging by how I felt the next morning, I might have single-handedly knocked off a couple of those bottles."

"I noticed on a surveillance camera that several of the men walked out of the restaurant with women. I'm assuming they were—"

Sproul leaned even closer. "Between you and me, dancing girls who doubled as working girls. I heard Asher had booked a couple of rooms in the hotel for, let's just say, amorous activities."

"And a few of the guys ended up in these rooms?"

Sproul put his hands up. "Not me, mind you. I'm a happily married man."

"So, what I saw on the surveillance tape was several women walk out with some of the men."

"Yeah," Sproul said, shaking his head. "One of the girls started to leave the restaurant very skimpily clad, but Asher didn't think that was a good idea. He headed her off at the pass."

"Speaking of Bard, did you see him leave with one of the girls?"

"I'm not going to comment on that," Sproul said. "I've given you a lot already."

"Yes, you have, and I appreciate it, but I didn't see Bard leave with any of them. Or go into the hotel at all."

Sproul dropped his voice, like he thought Asher Bard might have a spy planted behind one of his curtains. "Maybe if there was a camera in the kitchen ..."

Crawford nodded. "Are you saying Bard went into the kitchen with one of the girls? Then ... what? Through the kitchen into the hotel ... maybe?"

Sproul shrugged. "Could be."

Crawford chewed on that, then reached into the breast pocket of his jacket. He pulled out three photos. "Who are these three men?"

Sproul took the photos out of Crawford's hand. "That's Jerry Reposo," he said, pointing at the man with the shaved head. "And that's Tom Schiller, a heavy hitter on Wall Street. And that"—he was eyeing the photo of the man with reddish hair and drooping eyebrows—"that's Ainslie Sunderland."

"And the women? Do you remember their names?"

"Well, they didn't exactly flash their driver's licenses around, but the one with Tom is Betty and the one with Jerry, I think, called herself Ronnie, as I recall."

"And the one with Sunderland?"

"Sorry, no clue."

Crawford made a mental note to talk to Jennifer Atwood, Asher Bard's secretary. See if she knew anything about Betty and Ronnie.

Crawford couldn't think of anything else to ask Sproul. "Okay, Mr. Sproul—"

"Call me Roddy."

"Roddy, I really appreciate all your help."

Sproul nodded. "My brother's a cop back in Cape Town. I've always been partial to law enforcement. Plus, just in case one of your guys pinches me for going ten miles over the speed limit, it's good to have a friend in high places."

Crawford smiled. "Not sure I can help you there, but thanks again. Say," he said, "are you playing on the senior circuit these days?"

"Yeah, a little bit. Got a second last month. Won the Chubb Classic last year."

"Good for you. Well, I'll be looking for you on TV." Crawford pulled out his wallet and got a card. "You think of anything else that might be helpful, please give me a call."

"You got it," Sproul said, and he walked Crawford to the door. "Remember, you didn't hear a thing from me, right?"

"Not a word."

9

Khalid Al-Ansani was wearing stylish white linen pants and a blue and white striped sport shirt that Crawford thought he had seen in the window of Maus & Hoffman on Worth Avenue. He remembered thinking, when he walked past the store, that the shirt probably cost half his paycheck. A third, at the very least. It was a far cry from the thobe and turban surveillance cameras had showed him wearing at Asher Bard's party.

He greeted Crawford at the front door of the huge, olive-colored Mediterranean, and, as Roddy Sproul had, he asked if Crawford would like something to drink. This time Crawford thanked him but declined. Al-Ansani led him outside, and they sat on a patio overlooking a pool and the ocean beyond. It was a familiar view for Crawford, as Al-Ansani's house was only two doors down from Rose Clarke's home, where he had spent many a night.

"Thanks for seeing me, Mr. Al-Ansani. I'd like to ask you a few questions, if that's all right."

"Of course, Detective, that's what you came for," Al-Ansani said, raising his martini to Crawford.

Crawford reached into his breast pocket for the photo of Grace Spooner. "Have you ever seen this woman before?"

Al-Ansani took the photo and looked at it. "No, I never have. So, she's the woman who was killed."

Crawford nodded. "You never saw her in The Colony Hotel the night of Asher Bard's party?"

Al-Ansani shook his head. "No, I did not."

Crawford studied his eyes. He didn't blink or look away.

"Did you either hear or see anything at Mr. Bard's party or in the hotel that looked in any way suspicious? Anything that made you think a crime might be in the works?"

Al-Ansani tapped the arm of his chair a few times. "No, nothing at all. We were just a group of men eating and drinking and toasting our host on his birthday."

"A group of men, you say. Were there any other people there?"

Al-Ansani thought for a moment. "Well, yes, waiters and bartenders."

"But nobody else?"

Al-Ansani shrugged. "No."

"You're sure?"

Had the man contracted a convenient case of amnesia or was he just a willful liar? The latter, Crawford decided.

"Yes, unless someone came after I left."

"And when did you leave, Mr. Al-Ansani?"

"I think it was around eleven fifteen or eleven thirty." He took a quick, nervous sip of his martini.

Crawford reached into his pocket again and pulled out another photo. He held it up for Al-Ansani. "Do you mean when you left with this woman to go into the hotel or when you left to go home?"

Some men would have been embarrassed; some men would have looked guilty. Khalid Al-Ansani just looked colossally pissed off. "Is this what the Palm Beach Police Department does? Goes around and spies on private parties? This is outrageous. Why don't you go after the murderer of that poor woman instead of focusing on a bunch of men celebrating another man's birthday?"

There was a lot to be said for the maxim, the best defense is a strong offense.

"Mr. Al-Ansani, I can assure you neither I nor any other members of the Palm Beach Police Department have any interest in investigating a man's birthday party. But this particular birthday party took place *when* and *where* a murder took place. So, I repeat, when you left with the woman in the photo, did you see Grace Spooner, or possibly a man who might have looked suspicious?"

Al-Ansani polished off the last of his martini. He seemed to be trying to rein in his anger, but he was still fuming. "I don't think we have anything further to discuss, Detective."

Crawford smiled and made no move to get up. "Well, I do, Mr. Al-Ansani, because I know you have, in fact, seen the murder victim before."

Al-Ansani could no longer hold back. "What the hell are you talking about?" A little spittle flew with the question.

"You met Grace Spooner back when she was a teenager. When she was fifteen years old. And my understanding is she was now on the verge of testifying about what happened back then at an upcoming trial." Crawford sighed. "But, of course, she can't do that anymore."

"That's an absolutely outrageous charge." More spit flew. "I have never laid eyes on that woman in my life."

Crawford reached into his breast pocket again. This time he pulled out a photo Harlan Brody had sent to him. It was of Al-Ansani, Asher Bard, and Ainslie Sunderland on the upper deck of a yacht with three young women by their sides. It had been taken by an investigator from the state attorney's office, and, clearly, the three men had absolutely no idea it was being taken.

Crawford held it up to Al-Ansani. "That is Grace Spooner ten years ago ... standing right next to you."

He had Al-Ansani dead to rights. "Okay, Detective, I met with you as you requested, but now I'm done. And the next time, if there is one, my lawyer will be present."

"The more the merrier," Crawford said. "My last question: do you have any plans to leave the country?"

"I might. Why?"

"Because, Mr. Al-Ansani, I'm instructing you to cancel them."

MONTE BITTAR LIVED IN A BRUTALIST HOUSE ON EDEN Road. It was built in 1961, when Brutalist architecture had a toehold in various, mostly urban, parts of the country. The home featured reinforced concrete on three sides and rough-hewn stone on the fourth side. *Aesthetically pleasing* was not a phrase that jumped to mind to describe it—more like *muscularly unappealing*.

Ott and Bittar were seated in a living room dominated by sparse, modern furniture. Ott was doing a quick warm-up to the hard-core Q&A, which would be coming along shortly. Bittar was a movie director who did big-budget action movies. The kind Bruce Willis and, more recently, actors like The Rock and Jason Statham starred in. Generally speaking, the movies were not candidates for Academy Awards nor were they showcased at either Sundance or the Cannes Film Festival.

"I was a huge fan of *Full Throttle*," Ott said, referring to a movie about rival race-car drivers that came out in 2017. "Must have been fun to shoot that. I read a lot of those scenes were shot at actual races."

"It was a complete pain in the ass," Bittar said. "It rained for a solid week in Monaco. We had to sit around and wait for the weather to clear. Got to know the gin mills pretty well, though."

"I'll bet," Ott said, flashing on the ingénue who played the love interest of both race-car drivers. "Just out of curiosity, did Eva Strange hang out with you in those gin mills?"

Bittar chuckled. "Eva Strange was barely old enough to drink legally. She's also one of those 'my-body-is-my-temple' women. Strictly green tea and Perrier."

"That's no fun." It was officially time to get to work, Ott thought. "Mr. Bittar, as I mentioned on the phone, me and my partner are the detectives on the murder that took place at The Colony yesterday, and, since you were there, I have some questions for you."

"Sure, fire away," Bittar said, "But I doubt I'll be much help."

Ott reached into his jacket pocket and pulled out a photo of Grace Spooner. "Did you see this woman at The Colony night before last?"

Bittar shook his head. "The only place I've ever seen her is on the front page of the *Glossy*." He was referring to the local weekly newspaper, the Palm Beach *Daily Reporter*. "I can't believe that happened while we were there."

"When did you get there, and when did you leave?"

"Too early and too late," Bittar said, rolling his eyes. "Got there at about seven, left around eleven thirty."

Ott straightened up in his chair. "What do you mean, 'too early and too late?'"

"I mean, two of those hours were bullshit toasts about how Asher Bard was, basically, the second coming of Christ. All about his charitable giving, his various philanthropies, his being an incredible father and blah, blah, blah, blah, blah." Bittar leaned in close to Ott. "I mean, what's wrong with tellin' it like it is? Asher's a helluva businessman, very generous with his friends, but he sure as hell ain't no saint."

"And what about the other two hours, Mr. Bittar?"

"The other two hours were a damn good dinner, lots of top-shelf bubbly, and—if you don't know now, you're gonna find out sooner or later—women who are paid to make middle-aged men happy."

Ott nodded. "Matter of fact, I did know that."

"I figured," Bittar said. "You and your partner, I hear, have a pretty good rep for catching bad guys."

Yeah, eight for eight, to be exact, Ott thought. "Thank you," he said. "You never went outside the CPB restaurant, did you?"

Bittar shook his head. "Nope, just sat there and listened to all that hot air," he said. "Watched the girls pop out of a cake or wherever the hell they came from. Can't really remember that well."

"So, is it safe to say you never saw or heard anything related to the murder?"

Bittar nodded. "It is very safe to say that."

"Going back to something you said ... Mr. Bard's charities. Can you tell me a little about them? If you know the specifics."

"Well, what I know is that he's the financial backer of a whole slew of non-profit rehab centers up and down the east coast," Bittar said. "What I heard was his nephew had a pretty serious drug problem when he was a kid, died of it eventually, and that's what got Asher involved in the first place."

"So they're drug and alcohol rehab centers?"

"Yes, drug, alcohol, troubled kids, the whole nine yards, is what I've heard. He got some humanitarian-of-the-year award for his efforts."

Ott was taking notes in his well-worn leather notebook, which he'd had since his days back in Cleveland. He looked up and locked eyes with Bittar. "Gee, I wonder if any of those troubled kids ever ended up on his yacht."

10

DAVID BALFOUR CALLED AT JUST PAST SEVEN THE NEXT morning and asked Crawford if he would come over. He apologized for the early hour but said he really needed to meet with him. He went on to say he hadn't been able to sleep a wink the night before. The whole thing was odd because Balfour usually slept until nine, followed by twenty laps in his pool and breakfast at nine thirty. Crawford knew this because Balfour had once given him a blow-by-blow of his typical daily schedule, and Crawford had been more than a little envious. Especially when Balfour described his typical nine-thirty breakfast, which was meticulously prepared by Bonnie Lynn, his cook: fresh-squeezed orange juice, Sumatra coffee—Crawford had no clue where Sumatra even was—eggs Benedict, bacon he'd had shipped down from Peter Luger Steak House in New York, and Peter Reinhart's multigrain toast (whoever Peter Reinhart might be.)

Balfour'd had Crawford drooling after reeling off that "typical" breakfast menu. Rich guys might have problems like everyone else, Crawford concluded, but they didn't have breakfasts like everyone else.

Crawford had planned to have his own breakfast afterward at Green's Pharmacy, which was his main go-to, along with Dunkin' Donuts. He pulled up to Balfour's house at seven thirty, figuring he'd spend a half hour there, then head over to Green's.

Balfour opened the front door seconds after Crawford hit the buzzer, then led him back to Balfour's trophy room. Balfour had a Bloody Mary in hand, "a little bracer in my time of need," as he referred to it, and soon Crawford was savoring a cup of the aforementioned Sumatra coffee.

"I don't normally drink at this hour, Charlie, but Missy's going to turn me into a raging alcoholic."

"Why, what's the latest?"

"She's going after half of everything," Balfour said as a look of shock popped up on Crawford's face.

"What? You had a prenup, right?"

"Yeah, but my lawyer said it's not a very good one. 'Not very tight,' were his exact words."

"But wasn't he the one who drew it up?"

Balfour shook his head and put down his Bloody Mary. "No, actually, I got it from one of those online sites."

"Jesus. Really?" Crawford said, not wanting to make Balfour feel any worse than he already did. But that was truly a bone-headed move. Spending ninety-nine dollars, or whatever, for a form prenuptial agreement.

"Yeah, this friend of mine told me about it. This site called Rocket Lawyer."

Crawford felt bad for his friend, but how could such a wealthy man cheap out on a document that important?

"Well, the good news is no judge is going to award anyone half of someone's estate who they were married to for five minutes," Crawford said.

"That's what I'm hoping. I mean, I think her affair started about six months into the marriage."

"How do you know that?"

"Remember I told you I hired a private eye."

"Oh, yeah, who is he?"

"He's not from around here," Balfour said. "A Miami guy."

"I hope he's good and you're paying him a lot of money."

"Trust me, I really checked him out. And he ain't cheap. Plus, he had lots of references. I spoke to three of them."

"Well, good. So, he thinks the affair started six months in?"

Balfour nodded and took another sip of his drink.

"What else did he find out?"

Balfour stood and motioned to Crawford. "Follow me. I need to do a show and tell."

Crawford followed Balfour into his living room. It was a beautiful, elegant space that Balfour had once told Crawford was decorated by a famous decorator. Mario somebody, he seemed to remember. There was a lot of cheery-looking chintz that to Crawford made it look more like the living room of an older woman or elderly couple. It clearly didn't bother Balfour, though.

As they reached the center of the living room, Balfour pointed at a painting. "That's my Franz Kline," Balfour said of the artist. "Paid just under a million bucks for it twenty-two years ago. About three years ago one sold for forty million. Mine's a pretty good example of his work, so it might be worth *more* than forty in today's market."

Crawford's mind was reeling. He loved art and had ever since taking a gut at Dartmouth called *Art: The Last Fifty Years*. He'd become totally consumed by it at the time. He still went to galleries and to the Norton Museum in West Palm when he had time or wanted to take his mind off murder. But Franz Kline was an artist he'd never gotten excited about. To him, Kline's paintings were a lot of thick black lines that occasionally crisscrossed and looked dark and foreboding. Which, come to think of it, was how Kline the man looked: dark and foreboding, and to whom a smile seemed like a foreign element.

Balfour turned to him and smiled. "Only problem is it's a Roy Jenkins, not a Franz Kline."

Crawford searched his brain. Roy Jenkins was not an artist he was familiar with. So he asked the obvious question. "Who's Roy Jenkins?"

Balfour turned to Crawford and smiled. "Missy's boyfriend."

It took Crawford a few moments to put together the pieces. "You gotta be kidding."

Balfour shook his head, still smiling.

"That's incredible. Missy's boyfriend knocked off Franz Kline? So ... where's the actual Franz Kline?"

"Glad you asked. My P.I., being an enterprising man, found out where Jenkins' studio was and just happened to gain access to it in the middle of the night—"

"You mean, broke in?"

"Charlie, Charlie, that would have been illegal," he said, chuckling. "Yeah, so he ... found an open window or something, and guess what he found?"

"The real Franz Kline that used to hang where the Roy Jenkins does now," Crawford said, pointing.

"Not only the Kline, but see that one," Balfour said, pointing to another painting of a woman in a swimming pool that Crawford had always been keen on.

"David Hockney, too?"

Balfour nodded. "Yup. As a painter of his own stuff, Roy Jenkins pretty much sucks. My P.I. showed me a few photos he took of his stuff. But as a knock-off artist, he's not too shabby."

Crawford pondered the whole thing and shook his head. "Jesus, that's unbelievable. So the plan was for Missy to end up with your forty-million-dollar Kline and ... What's the Hockney worth?"

"I don't know exactly. Twelve million, maybe."

"So, to own a forty-million Kline and a twelve-million Hockney and stick you with two worthless Roy Jenkinses?"

Balfour nodded. "Yeah. Pretty much."

Crawford brightened. "Something tells me Missy's going to end up with a whole lot less than half when she finds out what you got on her."

"How much you think I should give her?"

"When she knows you've got her on art forgery and art theft ... oh, I don't know. How about a buck ninety-eight?"

"No, seriously."

"I *am* serious," Crawford said. "Far be it from me to be a vindictive man, but that woman was out to screw you *bigtime*."

"So, what do you think? Give her a couple hundred thousand?"

Crawford chuckled. "That sounds very generous to me. But then, I don't have any perspective."

"What do you mean?"

"Well, a couple hundred thousand to me is like a vast fortune. To you, it's like a tip, so I can't really advise you on this."

"Maybe a hundred thousand."

"Sure, if you're good with that," Crawford said. "In my opinion, though, you don't have to give her anything. Just threaten to call the cops about the whole scam. Tell 'em how she was going to screw you."

Balfour chuckled again and shook his head. "Yeah, and not in the way I wanted her to."

11

CRAWFORD PULLED UP TO GREEN'S PHARMACY AT 8:10, having left David Balfour to do his pool laps, followed by an extravagant breakfast prepared by his chef extraordinaire, Bonnie Lynn.

He walked in, nodded at Ruthie, the Green's waitress, and went over and sat down at "his" table. It was actually his and Ott's table, but Ott had an early morning car repair appointment and wouldn't be joining him.

Today, Crawford felt like having one of his favorites: a couple of big, greasy sausages and a triple-egg Swiss cheese omelet.

"Hey, Charlie," he heard a voice say.

He looked to his right and saw the reporter Quinn Casey parked behind an open *New York Times*.

"Hey, Quinn. Didn't take you long to find the best breakfast in town."

"Hey, man, I'm a reporter." He opened his hand. "Join me?"

"Sure," Crawford said, getting up, walking over, pulling out a chair, and sitting down. "Not the 'detectives table,' but I suppose it'll do."

"I imagine you were very particular about what table was going to be the 'detectives table.'"

"What do you mean?"

"Well, you wanted to be where you could see everyone coming and going. And where nobody could sneak up on you."

Crawford nodded. "You know your stuff. Wouldn't want to end up like Wild Bill Hickok, right?"

Ruthie, the gawky waitress, came up to the table. "Top of the morning to ya, Charlie. The usual?"

"Hey, Ruthie. Yeah, but I'm gonna have tea instead of coffee."

Ruthie nodded and walked away.

"Tea?" Quinn said, shaking his head. "That doesn't jibe with my profile. I got you pegged as a black-coffee guy."

"Profile. What profile?"

"The detective who takes down Grace Spooner's killer. *Strong, lantern jaw, ramrod-straight posture, long, athletic stride*—"

Crawford held up his hands. "Whoa, whoa, first of all, you're way ahead of the story. Got a way to go before we 'take down' Grace Spooner's killer. Second of all"—Crawford laughed—"my posture ain't all that great."

Quinn rubbed his brow. "How long were you on the job up in New York?"

"How'd you ... Oh, yeah, you're a reporter."

Quinn smiled. "First of all, you hardly struck me as a guy born and bred in Florida, so I looked into your background. You had some pretty high-profile cases up there. How long were you there?"

"Thirteen fun-filled years."

"I bet. And how'd you end up here, of all places?"

"Burned out up there. Wanted a beach and palm trees instead of black snow and honking horns."

"You miss it at all?"

"Sometimes in the summer."

"The heat down here?"

"And humidity."

Quinn nodded as Ruthie showed up. She set a plate down in front of Quinn. On it was a bowl of oatmeal with a banana on the side.

"Jesus, Quinn," Crawford said. "You didn't research this one too well."

"What do you mean?"

"Well, if you had, you'd know that when in Green's you gotta go with either bacon and eggs or big, greasy sausages and eggs. Or a stack. Pancakes are pretty damn good, 'cept you gotta use about five of those." Crawford pointed at a bowl containing syrup packets. "What do you think this place is, a health-food joint?"

Quinn laughed. "I got a little cholesterol problem." He pointed at his oatmeal. "You think I like this stuff?"

"I would hope not. Might start to wonder about you."

Quinn chuckled. "Hey, and you, the hard-boiled detective who drinks ... tea?"

Crawford smiled. "Not on a regular basis," he said. "See, I read this article about all the antioxidants in tea. Plus, it's got less caffeine than coffee and supposedly lowers your risk of a heart attack."

"Hell, man, you sound like a commercial," Quinn said. "Plus, you don't seem like a candidate for cardiac arrest."

Ruthie showed up with Crawford's plate: the cheese omelet, two sausages, and wheat toast slathered with butter covered virtually every square inch of his plate.

Quinn's eyes got big as he took it all in. "But then again," he laughed and pointed, "if you were to look up 'heart attack' in the dictionary, that would be the perfect illustration for what causes it."

They were finishing up their respective breakfasts.

"So"—Quinn did some calculating—"it's been two days since Grace Spooner's murder. Whatcha got so far?"

"Not enough," Crawford said, wondering just how much he actually wanted to tell Quinn Casey. "Did you know Asher Bard was having a birthday party at The Colony the night it happened?"

Quinn put his spoon down. "Get out of here. Well, isn't that a coincidence? So I guess that gives you a few new suspects."

"Eighteen, to be exact."

"You know everyone who was there?"

"Yeah, we got a list."

"So, you go talk to all of them?"

Crawford nodded. "Already knocked off a few." He took a bite of his squishy sausage.

"Who?"

"Sorry, can't tell you."

"Come on," Casey said, smiling broadly, "I'm not gonna tell anyone."

"You mean, except for the millions of *New Yorker* readers?"

"Only one-point-two million, but who's counting?"

Crawford leaned in closer to Casey. "Let me ask you something: You said that first time we met, in my office, you thought Asher Bard was the most obvious suspect in Grace Spooner's murder. Did she ever say she was scared of him?"

Casey shook his head. "No, it never came up. I was going to probe that in the interview that never happened."

"When did you first get together with her?"

"A month ago was our initial contact. It was a quick meeting. I didn't really get into the nitty-gritty with her at that point. Kind of had to build a little trust, if you know what I mean."

Crawford nodded. "Got it. So, the morning she was killed—"

"Was going to be the big interview. Figured I'd spend a couple hours with her, anyway."

Crawford thought for a moment, then shrugged. "I just don't get why she was there. At The Colony, I mean. A woman making ... I don't know, fifty, sixty grand a year in a five-hundred-dollar-a-night suite."

Quinn shrugged back at him. "Can't help you there."

"By the way, where are you staying?" Crawford asked.

"The Brazilian Court."

"That's pretty nice," Crawford said. "But I guess for their star reporter, *The New Yorker* can splurge a little."

Casey smiled. "I guess," he said. "By the way, have you talked to Bard himself yet?"

"No. He's a long way from here at the moment."

"Let me guess," Quinn said, peeling his banana, "Thailand?"

"Nope. Costa Rica."

"Figures," Quinn said. "I've heard his jet can pretty much go on autopilot to Bangkok or Costa Rica."

"Costa Rica's not as bad as Thailand, is it?"

"You mean, as far as young girls go?"

Crawford nodded.

"You can bet any country where prostitution is legal is gonna be on Bard's radar screen," Casey said, taking a bite of his banana.

"Gotta tell ya," Crawford began, "whenever I think of prostitution, I think of venereal disease, beds with slimy bugs crawling around, and pimps with switchblades."

"Yeah, well, something tells me Asher Bard and his pals take the high road."

"Yeah, I guess. Whatever that may be."

"Thousand-count Egyptian sheets, disease-free, well-scrubbed young girls, and pimps who majored in economics."

Crawford cocked his head. "Sounds like a subject you know something about."

"High-class hookers?" Quinn gave a disapproving shake of his head. "Nah, I'm a happily married man. But in my line of work you learn a little bit about everything."

12

Dan Wright, the man Crawford had made an interview appointment with the day before, turned out to be no help. He struck Crawford as a supercilious jerk who was happy to spend their half hour together making derisive comments about Asher Bard and all the "drunks" at his party, as if he were a saintly fellow who'd somehow fallen out of the sky and landed in Gomorrah against his will. He had nothing to contribute, and Crawford was happy to see him go.

An hour later, Crawford and Ott met in Crawford's office to discuss their interviews from the day before and map out their plans for the day.

"Rehab centers?" Crawford said after Ott told him about his interview with Monte Bittar.

"Yeah, it got me thinking, too," Ott, slouched down in his chair, said. "I haven't had a chance to look into them yet."

"Might be just a worthwhile humanitarian philanthropy, but then again, it might be something else altogether," Crawford said. "Speaking of worthwhile, I got a job for you I know you're gonna like."

"What's that?"

"I think you should go have a little talk with that woman

you were winking at." He was referring to Asher Bard's secretary, Jennifer Atwood.

Ott shook his head. "I didn't wink at her."

"Oh, then maybe you just got something stuck in your eye. But one thing's sure, you shook her hand like you never wanted to let go," Crawford said. "We need to find out who the dancing girls were at Bard's party. Find out what they know."

"You think she hired them?"

"I don't know. Maybe. Maybe not. But I'm pretty damn sure Bard won't tell us who they are when we talk to him."

Ott nodded.

"Just give her your ol' charm-school act," Crawford said. "She'll tell you everything you want to know."

"Okay. In the meantime, you're going up to Tampa, right?"

Crawford nodded. He had mentioned he thought it was worth the drive to go talk to people at Advance Team, the company where Grace Spooner had worked. "How long's it take? Never been to Tampa before."

"Little over three hours," Ott said. "I went up there to see my Cleveland Browns destroy the Tampa Bay Bucs."

"Did they?"

"Hell, no. They got crushed."

"Sorry to hear that."

"Well, at least the Giants aren't my team."

Crawford sighed. "Never miss an opportunity to dis my boys, do you."

"Get a new quarterback and you'll be all right."

"Leave our old man alone," Crawford said, standing. "All right, I'm going to head up there now. I'll put in a call to Hawes on the road to see whether he was able to lift a print or get any DNA."

"Yeah, also ask him if he can blow up that frame of Grace Spooner getting into the car in front of The Colony."

"Will do." Crawford gave his partner a theatrical wink. "Meanwhile, time to give your new girlfriend a call."

"Ms. Atwood?" Ott said.

"Yes?"

"Hi, it's Detective Ott," he said in his most cultured intonation. "We met at—"

"Of course, Mort, how are you?"

"I'm fine, thanks. I wonder if I could stop by and see you. I have a question or two regarding Mr. Bard's birthday party at The Colony Hotel."

"Sure. When do you want to come over?"

"How's right now? I'm not far away."

"I know. I drive by the police station every day. Come on over."

"Thanks. See you in a few minutes."

Ott was in Jennifer Atwood's office ten minutes later. Eager? Maybe. Jennifer greeted him with a kiss on Ott's fleshy left cheek, a gesture he was not entirely comfortable with. When was such a greeting appropriate? After the first meeting? The second? The third? Never?

But in this case ... he rather liked it and hoped she'd do it again when they were done talking and it was time for him to go.

For the moment, though, the question was how to start the conversation on the potentially touchy subject of the strippers.

"So," he said with a sigh, "this is a little bit tricky."

She smiled innocently. "What is?"

"The subject I want to ask you about."

"I'm a big girl."

"I know, it's just ... All right, here goes: There were three women at Mr. Bard's birthday party who were there for, ah, entertainment purposes—"

"Oh, you mean the strippers?"

Ott decided that description would suffice, even though their duties went well beyond just stripping. "Yes, exactly. Was that one of your, ah, tasks ... to, to hire them?"

Jennifer shook her head. "Oh, no, Lord Sunderland was in charge of that. I think he'd had them entertain at one of his parties in the past."

"I'm just curious, do these kinds of parties take place on a regular basis?"

"What kinds, Mort?"

Well, you know, where nubile young women strip and hook while drinking top-shelf bubbly, he wanted to say, but cleaned it up. "The kind where a bunch of men eat and drink and ... watch women disrobe," he said instead.

Jennifer laughed. "I hear that Lord Sunderland is a randy old codger. And my boss, well, you've heard the stories, I'm sure."

Glad she went there. "Yes, I certainly have. And as far as what you've observed about your boss, what is true and what is —well, let's just say—exaggerated?"

Jennifer Atwood sighed and thought for a few moments. "Well, Asher definitely likes women. Young women, not-so-young women, short women, tall women, blondes, brunettes, redheads, you name it. But I think a lot of what you hear *is* exaggerated. And that whole trial thing ten years back, I think that was all about a man who had an agenda to advance his political career and make an example out of a high-profile target like Asher."

"Harlan Brody you're talking about?"

"That's him. And the way I've heard it, he'd throw his own mother in jail to get a headline."

Ott nodded. "He's obviously an ambitious man."

"There's a big difference between ambitious and ruthless," Jennifer said, cocking her head. "Are you single, Mort?"

Ott smiled and held out his hand. "Yup. No ring. No commitment."

"A lot of men don't wear rings. Or take them off at convenient moments," she said. "Maybe we could have a drink one night?"

"I would like that very much," Ott said, amping up his 1000-watt smile. "But if I could go back to the three women who were at Bard's party ... You have no idea what their real names are?"

"No, neither Asher nor I had anything to do with them being there. They were, I guess you could say, Ainslie Sunderland's birthday present to Asher."

Ott nodded. "Different strokes for different folks, I guess."

"What do you mean?"

"I mean, I usually just give a friend a tie or something."

13

Crawford saw the sign for Kissimmee and wondered where the name had come from. Native American, he guessed. A little farther along, he saw a similar sign on which some enterprising graffiti artist had painted Xs over the letters I-M-E in Kissimmee. As if everyone seeing the name hadn't thought of that the first time they saw the word.

His cell phone rang, and he looked down and saw caller ID: Bob Hawes. The ME. Calling him back.

"Hey, Bob, whatcha got?" Crawford asked expectantly.

"Nothing you're going to be very excited about," Hawes said. "You're welcome to come take a look. The person driving the car the dead woman got into the night of was definitely a man. But it's impossible to make out any features, just that he was wearing a dark baseball-style cap."

"What about any prints off of—"

"*Nada.* Must have been wearing gloves. Not even a partial. Sorry, can't help you there."

"All right," Crawford said with a sigh. "And nothing on the woman's body. No DNA or blood from the perp?"

"Still looking into that. I'll let you know if we get something. All we've established is that she was likely dead before she got tossed. And, I hope for her sake, before the guy cut her tongue out."

"Yeah, me, too," Crawford said. "Thanks."

Hawes chuckled. "For nothing, you mean."

"Keep me posted." Crawford clicked off and checked his GPS. He was about ten miles from Tampa.

Before Hawes called, he had been thinking about what Ott told him about Asher Bard's rehab centers. He was eager to look into them and see if anything hinky came to light.

Up ahead, the skyline of Tampa came into view. It was pretty impressive. And new. Clearly a lot of it had been built in the last ten or twenty years. He had no idea it was such a big city.

Fifteen minutes later, he had parked and was walking into the reception area of Advance Team on the thirtieth floor of the Bank of America Plaza building. He had an appointment with the owner, a man named Kevin Malchoff.

"Hi, I'm Detective Crawford," he said to the receptionist. "I have an appointment to see Mr. Malchoff." It was just past two.

She gave him a smile and a nod. "I'll tell him you're here."

A few minutes later a tall man who looked to be in his fifties walked into the reception area and up to Crawford.

"Hello, Detective. How was your drive up from Palm Beach?"

Crawford shook his outstretched hand. "Pretty easy, thanks. Never been to Tampa before."

"Well, welcome," Malchoff said, motioning with his hand. "Come on back."

Crawford followed him back to his office, which looked out over a big stadium in the foreground and what he guessed was the Gulf of Mexico off in the distance. "Pretty amazing view you have here."

"Yeah, that's the Ray Jay," Malchoff said, pointing. "The Raymond James Stadium, where the Buccaneers play. Then

Clearwater beyond and the Gulf off on the horizon. Have a seat."

"I look out over a couple of dumpsters," Crawford said, sitting down.

Malchoff laughed, but his expression changed as he sat behind his desk. "So, you got anything yet on Grace?"

"Wish I could tell you I did, but it's still early," Crawford said. "What can you tell me about her?"

"She was the hardest worker I had here. She worked on the Aquarium, the Bucs, the Convention Center, and one of our local banks. She was a dream to work with, and I miss her a lot."

Crawford glanced out the big picture window, then back at Malchoff. "Do you know anything at all about her history, by any chance? Specifically, her past relationship with a man named Asher Bard?"

There was a knock on Malchoff's closed door. "Perfect timing," he said, getting up, walking over, and opening the door.

"Come on in," Malchoff said to a young woman with blonde hair and horn-rimmed glasses.

"Detective, this is Kathleen Esposito. I asked her to join us because she and Grace were very good friends."

"Nice to meet you, Kathleen," Crawford said, shaking her hand. "Thanks for joining us."

"You're welcome. Anything I can do to help find that murderer—" The words seemed to strike an emotional chord and her voice quavered. "I'm sorry, I still can't even believe it."

"I understand," Crawford said. "Please have a seat."

She sat down.

"Get you a water or something, Kath?" Malchoff asked.

"No, I'm fine. Thanks." She was clearly trying hard to hold it together.

"So, maybe if you could just start anywhere you want and

tell me about Grace. Her past, her parents, relationships with men, anything you feel might be helpful to my investigation."

"Sure, I'll do my best," she said.

Crawford pulled his Sony digital recorder out of his jacket pocket. "You mind if I record this?"

"No, not at all," Kathleen said. "So, as far as her childhood went, it was pretty awful. Her mother took off when she was, like, two. Grace didn't even remember her. I think her father abused her mother pretty bad. Then he got killed."

"Her father?"

Kathleen nodded. "He was a member of a biker gang. The Outlaws, was what Grace told me. He got killed in a barroom brawl in Daytona, I think it was."

"How old was she when that happened?"

"As I remember, about nine or so. Then she went to a bunch of foster homes and had problems at all of them. She got into drugs, told me she got arrested for shoplifting when she was twelve. Ended up at a place for, quote, emotionally troubled teens, when she was thirteen. Place was called Cedar Knolls, in Jupiter, I think." She glanced at Kevin Malchoff. "If you don't mind, I'll take you up on that water offer."

"Oh, sure," Malchoff said and stepped out of the office.

"She told me she liked Cedar Knolls at first, but then something happened, and I'm not sure exactly what it was. I think it had to do with some guy she met."

"From Cedar Knolls?"

Esposito shook her head. "No, definitely not. He was on the outside, and she told me he later got arrested for sex trafficking."

Malchoff returned and handed Kathleen a bottle of water.

"Thanks. See, what was happening," Kathleen continued, "is a lot of the girls were disappearing from Cedar Knolls. And nobody seemed to know, or care much, where they were going. Turned out this guy and his brother were targeting girls with, ah, behavioral and emotional problems. You know, the really vulnerable ones."

Crawford nodded. "I think I read about something similar to that up in New York."

"I hope they got those guys," Kevin Malchoff said.

"Yeah, I think eventually they did," Kathleen said.

"What's amazing to me," Malchoff said, "is how she turned out so normal. Or at least on the surface, anyway."

Kathleen smiled. "Under the surface, too. It's a testament to her character that somehow—God knows how—she turned her life around."

"That's amazing," Crawford said, then to Malchoff. "When did she start work here?"

"Three years ago. She was an intern while she was at University of Tampa. When she graduated, I hired her."

Crawford turned back to Kathleen. "Tell me about relationships with men that she may have had."

"Well, that was difficult for Grace. You know, the trust aspect."

"I can imagine," Crawford said.

"I mean, 'cause she was attractive, she had a lot of guys interested, but in college and up to about a year ago—maybe a year and a half—she didn't really go out with anybody for long. Then she met a guy it clicked with. He was just back from Afghanistan, kind of a loner, had a tough childhood, too."

"What's his name?"

"Jack. Jack Marin. She was head over heels about him … but then, like, a few months ago she met this other guy and suddenly broke it off with Jack."

"And what was the other man's name?"

"I don't know."

Crawford frowned. "She didn't tell you?"

Kathleen shook her head. "Nope. I asked her, and she just said he was handsome, smart, funny, and—"

"Let me guess, married?"

Kathleen pointed a finger at Crawford. "Yes, unfortunately. I also know he wasn't from around here. I got a feeling he was from up north."

Crawford shrugged. "So, maybe here on business?"

"Maybe. I just don't know."

"So, back to Jack Marin? She just broke it off and that was the end of it."

Her eyes narrowed. "Well, she broke it off, but that *definitely* wasn't the end of it."

"Why, what happened?"

"She told me he followed her around. Like one time she looked out the window of her apartment and saw him parked in his car. Another time he followed her to her gym. Stalker-type stuff."

Suddenly, Jack Marin was taking on special interest to Crawford. So was the married man.

"So, Marin lives here?"

Kathleen nodded. "Yeah, up in Zephyrhills."

"Where's that?"

"North of here," Malchoff said.

Crawford nodded. "This is all very helpful, Kathleen. I really appreciate it. Anything else you can think of?"

"No, that's about all ... except, boy do I miss her. Sorry, I can't help you with the other man's name."

"That's okay," Crawford said. "Is there anybody else, another friend of Grace's maybe, who might know the name of the second man?"

"I'm not sure," Kathleen said. "You could try Natalie Weir. Grace may have told her. They've been friends for a really long time."

"Natalie ... how do you spell the last name?"

"W-e-i-r. She works at Anderson Insurance here in town."

"Thanks, and what about Jack Marin. Do you know where he works?"

Kathleen put her hand on her chin, then smiled. "Pretty sure he does what you do."

Crawford's eyes widened. "A detective, you mean?"

"Yes, except not for the police. A private investigator, I'm pretty sure. I know he works a lot at night because Grace told me once they had a hard time getting together sometimes."

Crawford had a silent chuckle: there were getting to be enough investigators for a convention. "Thank you. Again, that's very helpful. You don't happen to know the name of the agency where he works?"

"No, sorry."

"Well, I really appreciate everything," Crawford said.

Kathleen got to her feet. "You're very welcome."

Crawford reached for his wallet, took out a card, and handed it to her. "If you think of anything else, please give me a call."

"I sure will."

"Thanks, Kath," Malchoff said as she walked past him.

"Anytime."

"I'm really glad I spoke to her," Crawford said. "I'm thinking while I'm here, I'll pay a visit to Jack Marin."

"You want to use a computer? Look up where he lives?" Malchoff asked.

"Thanks," Crawford said, holding up his iPhone. "Got an app here that oughta tell me."

CRAWFORD HAD JUST CALLED OTT AND CAUGHT HIM UP on his meeting with Kevin Malchoff and Kathleen Esposito.

"Sounds like it was worth the drive," Ott said. "Unlike mine with Jennifer Atwood. 'Course, that was only a three-minute drive."

"Why, what did she have to say?"

"Had no clue who the strippers were. Said they were a

birthday present from Lord Sunderland. And she seemed to think Harlan Brody is out to get Asher Bard for political reasons."

"So that was all you got?"

"No."

"What else?"

"I got a date."

"All right! Nice work."

"In a couple of days. I told her I was pretty busy at the moment."

"Attaboy. Playing hard to get."

Ott chuckled. "You headed back now?"

"No. I figured I'd go have a talk with Grace Spooner's ex-boyfriend."

"Where's he?"

"Some place called Zephyrhills. You've got two more interviews this afternoon, right? Guys at Bard's party."

"Affirmative."

"Ah, Mort ... love it when you talk cop-talk."

14

CRAWFORD HIT THE CLICKER AND SLID INTO HIS CROWN Vic, which was parked in the underground garage at the Bank of America Plaza building. Then he took his iPhone out of his pocket while reaching for his wallet. Quinn Casey had given him a card when they first met in Crawford's office. He pulled it out, saw the number, and dialed it.

"Don't tell me, you got the killer behind bars?"

Quinn Casey seemed typical of many New Yorkers, who answered their phones with a question or a statement because they were too busy for "hello" and "goodbye."

"No such luck," Crawford said. "I have a question for you. Actually two."

"Shoot."

"The first one is, in your conversations with Grace Spooner, did she ever tell you about when she was a teenager living in a place for quote-unquote emotionally troubled teens, called Cedar Knolls?"

"Sure did. Sounded like a place that if you had problems, it would only make 'em worse."

"And did she mention two brothers who lured some of the girls out of the place to have sex with johns?"

Casey fell uncharacteristically silent.

"You there?" Crawford asked.

"Is this totally confidential?"

"Totally. Having loose lips in my business is a big negative."

"Okay, those two brothers were going to be key players in my article. Their names are Frank and Johnnie Begay. Grace Spooner was going to tell me all about them at breakfast the other day. But, obviously, that never happened."

"But she'd mentioned them before?"

"In broad terms. Just that they were basically pimps who preyed on girls at places like Cedar Knolls in Jupiter. She mentioned she heard they got arrested and charged once, but they got off."

"For what?"

"She wasn't sure, so I looked it up. Lewd and lascivious battery, but like I said, they got off."

"And a lot of these girls were really young, right?"

"Yeah, thirteen, fourteen, fifteen."

"You have any idea where these brothers are now?"

"Sure do. Johnnie and Frank are the proprietors of a quaint little spot called Puss in Boots."

"What the hell is that?"

"Come on, Detective, you playing dumb? A strip club over in West Palm."

"Never heard of it."

"Then you haven't lived," Quinn said. "I think that place may be a side hustle to make 'em look quasi-legit while they still run women. Or teenagers, as the case may be."

"Okay, so now my second question: I interviewed a guy, friend of Asher Bard, who told me Bard is the money behind a chain of non-profit rehab centers on the east coast. For troubled kids, supposedly. I'm just wondering if—"

"Holy shit, Charlie, you're a better investigative reporter than me," Casey said. "So, you're thinking Cedar Knolls is one of them and that was the Grace Spooner-Asher Bard connection."

"That's what I was thinking," Crawford said. "I haven't had a chance to look into it yet."

"Tell you what, I'll do the legwork on that one. After all, you served up this scenario on a silver platter. It's the least I can do."

"All right, let me know," Crawford said. "You'll appreciate this ... Bard apparently got some humanitarian-of-the-year award for his support and charity toward emotionally troubled teens."

Quinn laughed. "What a scumbag."

"Yeah ... couldn't've said it better myself."

15

On the drive up to Zephyrhills, Crawford got the number of Anderson Insurance, workplace of Natalie Weir, the friend of Grace Spooner that Kathleen Esposito had mentioned. He got her voicemail and left her a message asking her to call.

It was three thirty when Crawford got to Jack Marin's house at 6565 Paden Wheel Street in Zephyrhills. The town with the funny name apparently had funny-sounding street names, too.

Parked in the driveway of the Paden Wheel Street address was a tricked-out black Chevy Silverado with big wheels. Its cab was way off the ground, and it looked to Crawford like you'd need a ladder to get up to it. He pulled in behind it and got out.

It was a nice neighborhood, the kind where all the houses look the same except for different paint colors. Like most of the buildings in Tampa, the house looked fairly new.

He walked up and pushed the doorbell.

He could hear a TV inside. A few moments later a man opened the door. He looked to be around thirty, had a Fu Manchu with flecks of gray, and was wearing sunglasses.

"Yes," he said.

"Are you Jack Marin?"

"Who wants to know?"

Crawford hated that response. It was so passive-aggressive.

"My name is Crawford. I'm a detective from Palm Beach."

"Okay, and what do you want?"

"I'm investigating a murder and have reason to believe you knew the victim"—Marin's eyes started blinking—"Grace Spooner."

Marin lowered his voice and looked down. "Yeah, I definitely knew Grace."

"You mind if I come in? Ask you a few questions?"

"Yeah, all right." Marin turned and walked into a living room.

The house was light on furniture but had the biggest flat screen Crawford had ever seen. On it was a women's tennis match. There was something incongruous about this big guy with a Fu Manchu, a former soldier from Afghanistan, now a P.I. with a macho truck, watching a women's tennis tournament.

Marin went over to a table, picked up the clicker, and clicked off the TV. "Have a seat," he said, pointing to a couch facing a beige recliner.

Crawford sat down as Marin took a seat in the recliner.

"I was told you went out with Grace for a while."

Marin nodded. "Yeah, I did. About a year."

"So, you know what happened to her?"

Marin nodded.

"How'd you find out?"

"I got a brother in Port St. Lucie. He saw it on the news—" Marin let out a long sigh and slumped in his recliner. "Guess I expected someone to come around sooner or later. This was just a little sooner than I expected."

"So, being a P.I., you know what the first question I'm going to ask you is, right?"

"Yup. Where was I the night she got killed?"

"You got it. So, where were you?"

"Hey, man, I loved that woman. The last thing I'd ever do—"

"Where were you, Jack?"

Marin sighed. "I was actually down in your neck of the woods."

"What were you doing?"

He broke eye contact and glanced at the blank flat screen. "I wanted to know who she was seeing."

"Why? You two had broken up."

"Yeah, but I wanted to get back together with her."

Crawford rubbed his forehead. "Did you think the way to do that was to dog her all over the state of Florida?"

"Who said—"

"I heard from someone you had been following her around, and you just admitted it." Crawford leaned closer. "Where were you between ten and twelve that night, Jack?"

"I was on the road back here. Got in a little before one."

Crawford tapped his fingers on the arm of the couch. "Okay, let's back up. So, you followed Grace down from her place in Tampa to The Colony Hotel?"

"No, this other hotel. The Chesterfield."

"What do you mean, 'the Chesterfield?' She was staying at The Colony."

"I'm telling you, she went to that place, the Chesterfield, first. Checked in at around two in the afternoon, but then checked out around five and went to The Colony."

"Why would she do that?"

"Beats the hell out of me, but she did."

"So, she ends up paying for both places?"

Marin shrugged. "Yeah, I guess."

"I don't get it," Crawford said. "So, you were tailing her all this time?"

Marin nodded.

Crawford shook his head. "I don't get that hotel change at all," he said again.

Marin shrugged again. "Neither did I."

"We were told that at around seven o'clock, she got picked up by someone"—Crawford suddenly wondered if it might have been Marin himself—"probably a man, in front of The Colony, and they went somewhere. Dinner, I assume. So, where'd she go, Jack? You were there. And I need you to describe the guy at the wheel."

Marin's red face got redder. "Can't help you with that."

"What do you mean? You were there," Crawford said again.

He shook his head. "No, I wasn't. I was starved. Went to Burger King at around six forty-five."

"Great timing," Crawford muttered. "You didn't see her when she came back?"

"I nodded off for a while in the car."

Crawford shook his head. "Jesus, Jack, how's this P.I. job working out for you, anyway?"

Marin looked offended. "Just fine. Gotta eat, gotta sleep, you know."

"Yeah, but your timing really sucks," Crawford said. "So, you came back to The Colony and nodded off. Then what?"

"At around ten o'clock I headed back here. Nothing more I could do."

Crawford nodded. "Got any proof of that? Buy gas along the way or anything?"

Marin sighed. "You're really looking at me as a suspect?"

"You and everyone else in the state of Florida."

"That's fucked up."

"Prove to me you took off from Palm Beach at ten."

"Listen, man—" Marin's gaze fell to the floor. Crawford heard bottled-up emotion in the two words. Marin cleared his throat. "I *loved* that woman. All I wanted to do was get her back. I just didn't know how to do it."

If he was acting, he was good. His voice brimmed with pain, regret, and sincerity.

Crawford got to his feet and reached for his wallet. "All right, you have any ideas you think might be helpful, call me." He handed Marin a card. "Meantime, I'll let you know when we get something."

Marin was on his feet. "I appreciate it." He walked over to Crawford and shook his hand.

Crawford gave him a pat on the shoulder. "Well, I guess you can go back to your tennis match now."

16

CRAWFORD GOT INTO THE CROWN VIC AND RIGHT AWAY his iPhone rang. It said Quinn Casey on caller ID.

"Hi, Quinn, what's up?"

"Man, you called it," Casey said. "Asher Bard's dirty hands are all over those rehab centers. There're thirty-one of them from New York down to Miami. And they may be non-profits, but Bard sure as hell gets something out of them."

"Meaning girls."

"Your words, not mine," Casey said.

"So, I'm adding the Begay brothers to my suspect list, along with Bard—"

"— and a couple dozen others you're not telling me about."

"Hey, a guy's gotta have some secrets."

CRAWFORD DROVE FROM ZEPHYRHILLS TO THE PUSS IN Boots strip club in West Palm in a little under three hours. He tried Grace Spooner's friend Natalie Weir again but, as before, only got her voicemail. He arrived at the Puss in Boots at seven forty-five. Its address was 31245 Zip Code Place and the location was, at best, sketchy. But what would you expect with that address? It wasn't exactly Worth Avenue. What it was, was a combination of industrial buildings and low-end housing. He got out of the Vic and walked to the front.

A big guy dressed all in black with weightlifter muscles and a shaved head stood just inside the door.

"Welcome to the Puss," he said in a lifeless monotone. "Ten bucks."

Crawford wondered how he'd explain this on his expense sheet.

He handed the guy a ten-dollar bill. "Receipt, please."

The guy looked at him funny. "You fuckin' kiddin' me?"

"No, boss makes me account for every penny."

The guy shook his head and brushed him along. "Whatever."

It was dark inside. Straight ahead was a large four-sided bar being worked by two female bartenders. In the middle of the bar was a stage with a woman, naked except for a leather g-string and motorcycle boots, dancing robotically to a rap song. She was a bleached-blonde and clearly had some mileage on her. Along with a hundred tattoos. The old expression "ridden hard and put up wet" occurred to Crawford.

Crawford walked over to an empty bar stool and sat down, trying to act like he was a regular.

One of the bartenders meandered over. "Hey, honey, what can I getcha?"

He smiled at her. She reminded him of Miss Polly, his old Sunday school teacher, except with nicotine-stained teeth and a stud in her nose. "A 7-Up, please."

"Sorry, we don't carry that," she said. "I'm kidding ... That's really what you want?"

Seemed she was challenging his manhood. "A seven and seven is what I meant."

"That's more like it, tiger," she said, turning to make the drink.

He felt a touch on his shoulder and turned around. "You're cute," said a tall, skinny brunette, her arms sleeved in tats. She was topless and had a bikini bottom and fake brown alligator boots. "Wanna go to the back room?"

Crawford had no idea how to respond to that. "Ah, what goes on back there?"

"Anything you want, cowboy."

Crawford cocked his head. "Cowboy, I like that."

He wondered if everyone there was going to give him a nickname.

She flashed a lopsided grin. "I aim to please."

"I just got here, so I think I'll wait a while," Crawford said with a nervous smile.

She leaned close to him and whispered. "Okay. You just let me know when you're ready."

"I sure will."

She started to walk away, then turned. "My name's Daffy, as in Daffodil. What's yours?"

"Ah ... Mort. As in Mortimer."

"That's a pretty name."

"Thanks."

Daffy walked away.

The girl up on the bar was now upside down on a silver pole. He had heard about poles in joints like this before. It dawned on him, *duh, hence the name pole dancers.* Her boobs were dangling low, almost touching the floor. It was not a sight likely to get anyone aroused.

Suddenly, the pole dancer caught his eye and winked at him. He gave her a quick nod and flagged down the other bartender. She came over. "Get ya 'nother?"

He had only taken two sips of his seven and seven. "No, thanks, just wondered if Johnnie or Frank were here."

She up-and-downed him. "Who wants to know?"

Christ, not again.

"Name's Mort."

"Okay, Mort, and what do you want with Johnnie and Frank?"

"Just wanted to say hi."

She rolled her eyes like she had expected him to do better than that. "Okay, then, I'll tell 'em Mort says hi when I see 'em. How's that?"

Crawford smiled gamely. "I'd like to say it in person."

"Well, here's the thing, Mort, they're really busy."

It was time to give up. For the moment, anyway. This was not going anywhere. "Okay, no problem."

Like Daffy, she started to walk away, then turned back. "But if you're looking for someone to say 'hi' to, I can send over Jasmine or Daisy."

So that was it: the girls' aliases were flowers. "How 'bout Petunia?" Crawford asked.

The bartender frowned. "Petunia? We don't have anyone by that name here."

Crawford put up a hand. "I'm good," he said, raising his seven and seven.

Turned out, though, Daisy came over anyway. She also was a bottle blonde, but unlike the other women, appeared tattoo-less. Like Daffy, she invited him to go to the back room.

"What exactly goes on back there?" he asked.

"Private dances," Daisy said, doing her best to turn her voice into a purr. "Just you and me, Mort."

Crawford shook his head slowly. "Sorry, but I'm on a pretty tight budget."

Without another word, she turned and walked away. Men on tight budgets were apparently as welcome as men who drank 7-Up.

Crawford realized he wasn't getting anywhere, so he turned to the man next to him. "'Scuse me."

"Yeah?"

"Have you been here before?"

The man, wearing a hipster fedora, nodded. "Yeah, more than I should. Why?"

"Just wondered if you know who the owners are?"

"Yeah, there's one," the man said, flicking his head at the other side of the bar. "Dude in the baseball cap. Johnnie's his name."

Johnnie was talking to the bartender. The one who'd said the brothers were busy.

"Thanks," Crawford said, getting up from his stool and walking over to Johnnie. He plopped onto an empty stool next to him.

Johnnie, a scarecrow of a man with acne scars, turned to him. "Can I help you with something? My bartender said you wanted to ... say hi?"

"Yeah," Crawford said. "My name's Detective Crawford, Palm Beach Police. I'm investigating the death of a woman named Grace Spooner that happened three nights ago. Name ring a bell at all?"

"No, can't say it does. But I read about the murder."

"How about a place called Cedar Knolls? A place for emotionally troubled teenagers?"

"Doesn't ring a bell either."

"'Cause someone who I think is pretty reliable told me that back in your pimping days, that's where you got a lot of girls from. One being Grace Spooner."

Johnnie shook his head and glared at Crawford. "You come into my place and insult me with some bullshit allegation?"

The pole dancer, no more than ten feet away, was perpendicular to the pole now, her boobs twisted unnaturally.

"Tell you what, Johnnie, I want you and your brother to come over to the Palm Beach police station tomorrow. Have a little conversation with my partner and me."

"I got a very busy day tomorrow."

"We're all busy, Johnnie. Be there by five or we'll come

after you with handcuffs. That can be a little embarrassing. Though ... maybe not for you."

Johnnie took a pull on his drink. "I'll see what my brother says."

"Is he the boss?"

"Hey, look, bro. We're done here."

He got up and walked toward a door in the back, opened it, and disappeared.

The bartender with the nicotine-stained teeth and nose stud was giving Crawford the evil eye.

Crawford gave her a wave, then looked at his watch. It was 8:40. He pulled out his cell phone and dialed Ott's.

"Hey, Charlie."

"Hey, where are you?"

"At the station. Had a late interview with one of Asher Bard's buddies, then came back here to catch up on a few things."

"I'll be there in ten. Got a lot to catch you up on."

"I'll be here," Ott said. "Hey, what's that music in the background?"

"It ain't music, it's hip-hop," Crawford said. "I'm at a place called Puss in Boots. Ever heard of it?"

"I'd be lying if I said no."

Crawford laughed. "All right, see ya shortly."

Crawford knocked back the last of his drink, which seemed to be nine-tenths 7-Up and one-tenth Seagram's, dropped a fiver on the bar, and headed for the door.

The muscle-bound man in black nodded as Crawford walked past him.

Crawford was halfway across the parking lot when he heard a footfall behind him then felt a heavy blow to the back of his head ... then ... lights out.

He came to and saw two young guys in black looming over him. He put a hand up to defend himself.

"Hey, we're just trying to help," one said. "You all right, man?"

"Want a hand?" said the other one, bending over and grabbing Crawford's right arm.

"I'm okay," Crawford said, as one grabbed his left hand and together they pulled him up to his feet.

"What happened?" one asked.

"Damned if I know," Crawford said, glancing at his watch. It said 9:10. He figured he must have been unconscious for a good fifteen minutes.

He was damned lucky he didn't get run over in the parking lot.

The other guy was still holding his arm. Crawford felt shaky at best.

"Did you pass out or something?"

Crawford laughed, which caused a pounding pain in his head. "No, someone whacked me over the head."

"Take your wallet?"

Crawford knew it wasn't a smash 'n' grab and didn't even need to check to see if his wallet was there. "Nah, they weren't after my money."

All of a sudden, a car came wheeling into the parking lot. Crawford recognized it as a PBPD Crown Vic and realized who was at the wheel.

The Vic screeched to a stop ten feet away from Crawford and the two young men. Ott came flying out of the driver's side. "What's goin' on?"

"Someone clocked me on the head coming out of this place."

Ott yanked his Glock out of his shoulder holster and stink-eyed the two young guys. "Who the hell are you?"

Crawford quickly added, "No, not them."

Ott moved closer. "Someone really hit you?"

"Yeah ... feels like a building fell on me."

"We just found your friend on the ground," one of the young men said.

"Let's go inside," Ott said to Crawford. "Get the fucker who did it."

Crawford held up a hand. "It's a waste of time. We're never gonna find him."

Ott pointed up at a CCTV surveillance camera. "Yeah, but maybe we got him on that."

Crawford nodded. "All right." He eyed Ott's Glock. "Bad idea to walk in with our pieces out, though." He gave the two young men a nod. "Hey, guys, thanks for your help. Appreciate it."

They nodded back.

Ott was already taking long strides toward the front door of Puss in Boots.

Crawford followed.

Ott got to the bouncer at the door first.

"Ten bucks," the muscle-bound man in black said.

"We're cops," Ott said, flashing ID, "here on business. You see someone take a two-by-four to my friend here?" He cocked his head, already guessing the answer. "No, 'course you didn't."

The bouncer shrugged. "Didn't see nothin'," he said to Ott's back.

Crawford caught up to Ott. "One of the guys I talked to went through that door." He pointed, walked toward it, and rapped on it. "Open up!"

A few moments later, a man opened the door. "Who are you?"

"Crawford and Ott. Detectives, Palm Beach Police. Who are you?"

"Frank. You the dude my brother talked to?"

Crawford gave the door a push. "Yeah, and we're gonna have another conversation."

"Sure, Detective," Frank said, opening the door to reveal a room with a huge flat screen tuned to a baseball game.

Johnnie was tilted back in a BarcaLounger, a sparsely clad woman in his lap, a Bud in the chair's cup holder. "Hey, Detective," he said. Then seeing Ott, "Who's your buddy?"

"Ott's my name." He pointed at the flat screen. "Shut that thing off. We need to talk."

Johnnie picked up the remote and clicked off the ball game.

"We're gonna need a little privacy here," Crawford said to the girl in Johnnie's lap.

Another woman walked into the room. It was Daffy.

"Oh, hey, Mort," she said to Crawford.

Ott scrunched up his eyes and looked confused. Daffy glanced at him. "And who are you?"

"His partner, Mort Ott. You gotta leave."

"Wait, you're both named Mort?"

"You heard the man, Daff," Johnnie said. "Get out of here."

"Okay, okay," Daffy said, holding up her hands and heading toward the door.

"So, what do you boys want?" Johnnie asked, tilting forward in the BarcaLounger.

"I got hit over the head with a bat or something in your parking lot."

"Ouch," said Johnnie, grimacing. "Sorry to hear that. Not the safest neighborhood around."

"So, you don't know anything about it?" Ott asked.

"No, 'course we don't," Frank said, like his feelings were hurt. "You think we make a habit of taking bats to our customers?"

"So you were just in here minding your own business?" Crawford asked.

"Yeah, watchin' the ball game," Frank said. "Having a drink with the girls."

"You got a security cam that looks out at the parking lot," Ott said. "We want to take a look at it."

Frank laughed. "Sorry, man, sucker's been busted for over a year."

Ott eyed him.

"Hey, go check it out if you don't believe me," Frank said.

Ott glanced over at Crawford. "And what about lunkhead at the door?"

Johnnie laughed. "Wouldn't call him that to his face."

"Guy could have followed my partner—"

"Hey, Clem's harmless. Just looks kinda nasty," Frank said.

"So, you saying someone from the neighborhood walked into your parking lot and, just for the hell of it, whacked my partner over the head?"

Frank started to say something but Crawford cut him off. "'Cause they weren't after my wallet, so what would be the point?"

Frank shrugged. "I don't know, some people are just ... angry individuals."

"You a philosopher, Frank?" Ott said.

"All right," Crawford said. "Forget about the parking lot. We're gonna talk about Grace Spooner now."

Johnnie shrugged. "Told you, first time I ever saw the name was in the article in the paper."

"What paper?"

"*Palm Beach Post.*"

"When?"

"Day after it happened, I guess."

"That's interesting," Crawford said, "because her name hasn't been disclosed yet."

Johnnie shrugged. "Well, I heard it somewhere."

"Your story's starting to leak, Johnnie," Ott said.

"What the hell's that s'posed to mean?"

"It's got holes in it," Ott said.

Crawford took a step toward Johnnie. "What do the words

'lewd and lascivious battery' mean to you, Johnnie?" Then he shot a glance at Frank. "Either one of you can answer."

"Lascivious?" Johnnie said. "Don't even know what that means. Don't sound good, though."

"It's what you got charged with ten years back," Crawford said. "But I guess you had a good lawyer and got off."

"Hardly remember yesterday. Do you?" Johnnie asked his brother.

"Nope. Ain't got no recollection what you're talkin' about."

"You got any recollection of ever meeting, or doing business with, Asher Bard?"

Frank looked at Johnnie and shrugged. "Nope," said Johnnie. "Can't help ya there neither. Sorry."

"So, Tuesday night from ten to twelve, where were you?" Crawford asked.

"Right here," Johnnie said with a smile. "In my favorite seat with my favorite gal"—then dropping his voice—"one of 'em, anyway."

Ott shook his head. "You're a real prince."

Crawford took a step back from Johnnie. "All right," he said. "I can guarantee you boys, you haven't seen the last of us." Then to Ott, "Let's go."

"Hope your head feels better," Johnnie said, in a tone drenched with sarcasm.

"On your way out," Frank said, "you mind telling our lady friends to come back in?"

"Yeah," Johnnie said. "So we can pick up where we left off."

"TOLD YOU IT'D BE A WASTE OF TIME," CRAWFORD SAID, sliding into the passenger side of the Vic.

He was feeling woozy and his eyesight was a little hazy so

he had decided to leave his car there and pick it up the next day.

"But we couldn't just drive away like nothing happened," Ott said, turning the car key. "Those are two guys who never met a crime they didn't like."

"Yeah," Crawford said. "I'm gonna check 'em out tomorrow, see if they got a sheet."

"How you feeling, anyway?"

"Damn head's killing me," Crawford said, feeling the back of it gingerly. "Got a big old goose egg, too."

"Sorry, man. You want to drive around the neighborhood, see if we can find someone who might know something?" Ott asked, approaching a dilapidated gas station.

"Nah, whoever did it was carrying out an order from Johnnie and Frank."

"I agree," Ott said, pulling into the gas station.

"What are we doin' here?" Crawford asked.

Ott pointed at a sign that said "Ice."

"Get you a bag ... to put on your head."

17

In Crawford's haste to get up to Tampa to interview Grace Spooner's Advance Team boss and friend, he hadn't gotten around to meeting with the three other men who had left the CPB restaurant with the strippers and gone into The Colony.

He had spoken to two of them and was scheduled to meet with them the morning after he got cracked on the head in the Puss in Boots parking lot. At nine he met with Jerry Reposo, who sheepishly came into the station. He had wanted no part of Crawford coming to his house, and Crawford assumed that was because he was married and didn't want to have a conversation conducted in whispers about what he had seen while in the company of a woman named Ronnie. Or was it Betty?

Crawford quickly ruled him out. He was very convincing in his denial of not knowing who Grace Spooner was, having just moved to Palm Beach three years before. He struck Crawford as a man who probably was an okay husband and father but had the occasional one-night dalliance when it was easy and he'd had too much to drink. In any case, he seemed consumed with guilt. Or was it just that he had gotten caught?

It didn't much matter because Jerry Reposo was no cold-blooded killer.

At eleven that morning, Crawford drove up to Wells Road to the house of the third man from The Colony surveillance footage. His name was Tom Schiller. Crawford walked up the six steps to his porch and rang the bell.

A woman in her fifties with flaming red hair opened the door and smiled ear to ear.

"Hello, hello," the woman said. "You must be Horst?"

He had been called a lot of things, but never Horst ...

"No, I'm Detective Crawford, here to see Mr. Schiller. Your husband, I presume."

"Yes, he is," the woman said without much enthusiasm. Then the smile came storming back. "I'm just sorry you're not Horst."

Crawford shrugged. "Don't know who that is."

"My new masseur. My friend Janie recommended him."

"I see. Well, is Mr. Schiller here? We have an appointment."

"He's out by the pool." She didn't move.

He smiled. "If you would, please, let your husband know I'm here."

"Oh, all right, I'll go get him."

"Thanks," Crawford said, still on the stoop.

While waiting, he heard footsteps on the walk behind him and turned. A short man with a Yosemite Sam drooping mustache and a receding hairline walked up the steps, one arm around a folded masseuse table.

"A wild guess. Horst?" Crawford said.

"That's me," Horst said, stepping up to the stoop. "Who are you?"

"Crawford, Palm Beach Police."

"Somebody do something wrong?"

"Not that I know of."

Mrs. Schiller pushed open the half-opened door. The disappointment on her face was evident. "So, you're Horst?"

Horst nodded. "Yes, ma'am. You ready to go?"

She forced a smile. "Yes. Come on in." Then she glanced at Crawford. "Nice to meet you, Detective."

"Nice to meet you, too."

As she and Horst went inside, Tom Schiller appeared.

Crawford introduced himself. The two had a short conversation on the porch. Schiller hemmed and hawed for a while, but after Crawford told him he had him on camera, Schiller lowered his voice and admitted to walking out of The Colony with a woman whose name he didn't remember. Crawford was ninety-five percent sure Schiller was not his man. Just a man who didn't get enough attention on the home front. He asked him a few more questions until he was a hundred percent sure, then he left.

Next on Crawford's agenda was lunch with Rose Clarke at her palatial British Colonial on the ocean. It was really a fact-finding mission, but that's the last thing he'd tell her it was. He had phoned her earlier in the morning and asked her out for lunch. She told him she was working at home and he should come over for a salad and a couple glasses of rosé. "Even though manly men like you probably don't drink rosé," she'd said.

He assured her that he did drink rosé on occasion, just not on the job. She then reminded him that he had come over once, it was a Wednesday, and had a chicken avocado wrap and several glasses of chardonnay, followed by what she daintily referred to as a "roll in the hay ... no, actually several." He remembered it fondly, but clarified, "That was back when there was a long stretch when nobody was getting killed in Palm Beach, which is not the case at the moment."

And besides, he reminded her, that had been before the "moratorium." The moratorium, also referred to as "the deal," was something Rose and her good friend Dominica McCarthy had cooked up. Rose and Dominica—both former *friends with benefits* of Crawford's, but still friends—had implemented a sex ban after bringing it to his attention that he'd had it too good for too long—having sex with both of them alternately on a somewhat regular basis. He had objected strenuously, but they were resolute. The moratorium had been in effect for eight months now, and Crawford was feeling a little desperate to change the status quo.

They were sitting at a glass-topped table out by Rose's infinity-edge pool, which gave the impression from Crawford's angle that the ocean beyond was a continuation of the pool. They were eating Cobb salads and, turned out, Rose was a hell of a good amateur chef.

"This is so good," Crawford said, having taken his first bite. "Is there anything you don't do well?"

Rose smiled. "I suck at tennis."

"Which is *not* true. I've seen you play and you're not bad. You just have such incredibly high expectations for yourself."

"Yeah, that's true. Perfectionist, I guess," Rose said, putting down her wine glass. "So, Charlie, I know you have no time for me when you have a murder except to pick my brain, so what is it you want to know?"

"Am I that transparent?"

"Yup."

Crawford laughed. "All right, so tell me about a few people. First of all, Lord Ainslie Sunderland."

Rose smiled and shook her head. "Well, first of all, he's not."

"What do you mean? Not what?"

"A lord," Rose said. "He was born Ainslie Lord Sulcher. Lord being his middle name. Son of a hod carrier. Know what a hod carrier is?"

"Yeah, isn't that a laborer who hauls bricks around? An English thing."

"Very good. That Ivy League education comes through again."

Crawford shook his head. "Nah, I remember it from a crossword puzzle."

"You do crossword puzzles?"

"Did. I was too impatient. Gave up on 'em."

"Another thing I suck at."

"Yeah, 'cause of your perfectionism, I bet. If you didn't get every word in fifteen minutes, you gave up. Right?"

"Yeah, maybe. Back to Sunderland. As I said, he started out life as Ainslie Sulcher, working in the dry-cleaning business. Flash forward twenty years, and he owns, like, ten of 'em and is pretty rich. Along the way, he knights himself Lord Sunderland and buys a broken-down castle—"

"Wait, I thought only the Queen could knight you?"

"Yes, that's correct, but it didn't stop him from doing it in some underhanded, back-channel kind of way. Bribed someone, I'm sure."

Crawford leaned back in his chair; the woman could sure spin a yarn.

"And before you know it, in the great tradition of British aristocracy and rich American women, Ainslie marries a Pratt."

"What's a Pratt?"

"Descendant of a guy who was John D. Rockefeller's partner in the oil business. Owned a chunk of Standard Oil, I think it was."

"So, like a robber baron?"

"Exactly. And five years later, when he's around thirty-five, he divorces the robber baron's daughter but somehow ends up with half her money."

"So, now he's not just a lord but rich as hell?"

Rose nodded. "Ends up in Palm Beach ... Word is, trolling for another rich daughter or widow, even though he doesn't need the money anymore."

"I have a question."

"Just one?"

"Has every single person in Palm Beach reinvented themselves?"

"Only about half," Rose said.

"It's incredible," Crawford said. "I gotta get with the program."

"What do you mean?"

"I'm just the same ol' schlub I've always been."

"Yeah, but such a handsome, smart, and funny schlub."

Crawford reached across the table and patted her hand. "Thank you, Rose, that's very kind. So, Lord Sunderland ... aside from the thing with Bard and the girls ten years ago, any other scandal or skeletons in his closet?"

"Not that I can think of. He had a kid with the Pratt heiress who married into *the* royal family. But I'm told the Queen basically cold-shouldered him because she knew the guy was such a colossal phony."

"Wow, the man's come a long way from the son of a humble hod carrier."

"You're not kidding," Rose said, finishing off her glass of wine. "You know, Charlie, back in the old days I would have seduced you by now."

She was referring to the pre-moratorium days.

"Yeah," Crawford said, wistfully. "Gotta say, I really miss those days."

Rose's eyelashes flicked a few times and she tapped the glass-topped table. "I want to tell you about my new friend, Charlie."

It could only be one thing, Crawford knew. "I'm all ears."

"We-lll." She stretched the word out so it seemed like it was six syllables. "I'm seeing a man."

Crawford gestured for more. "Come on, girl, *details*. Gimme details."

"Okay, he's a really nice guy. Not as handsome or as funny as you, but he'll do."

"You forgot smart."

"Oh, yeah, he is that. Not to mention attentive and sweet."

"Sweet is good. What's he do for a living?"

"He's a doctor. A shrink, to be exact."

"Oh," said Crawford.

"What's that supposed to mean?"

"I just said, 'oh.'"

"Yeah, but it's how you said it."

"You're hearing things, Rose. What's his name?"

"John."

"John who? Don't make me pull teeth here."

"Muldoon." She frowned.

"What?"

She shrugged. "I just don't love that name."

"What difference does it make? You're not marrying him … or are you?" Crawford looked out on the ocean and saw an ocean liner way out on the horizon.

"No, of course not. We just met two weeks ago."

"Where? On his couch?"

Rose faux-laughed. "Funny. Do you think I need a shrink?"

"I think we all need a shrink from time to time."

"Maybe you got something there," Rose said. "You don't seem all that broken up about my news."

"I'm just faking it really well," Crawford said, taking a bite of tomato, bacon, and avocado.

"No, seriously, it's like you don't care that we won't be having our little nooners anymore."

Crawford laughed. "There's one thing I've learned in life."

"What's that?"

"Never say never."

"I didn't. I said anymore."

"Same thing," Crawford said. "Can I ask you about someone else?"

"You don't want to talk about my burgeoning love life?" Rose asked as she poured another glass of rosé.

Crawford shook his head. "Can I just run one more name by you?"

"Sure," Rose said with a sigh. "You're already bored with my love life, I see. Who do you want to ask me about?"

"It's not that I'm bored with it, I'm just," he sighed melodramatically, "not a part of it, so—"

"So it doesn't interest you, I get it. Who do you want to—"

"Khalid Al-Ansani."

Rose smiled and rubbed her hands together. "Oh, now there's a guy who's like a character out of a James Bond novel. Matter of fact, come to think of it, he had a yacht that actually was in a Bond movie. I forget which one, but the one where the bad guy was named Blofeld, I think it was."

"Oh, *From Russia with Love*, among others."

"Are you a James Bond expert?"

"Kind of."

"Anyway, Khalid's led a pretty colorful life," Rose said. "He was a billionaire back when there were only a handful of them around. But he's had some big-time reversals."

"So now he's slipped back to mere millionaire status?"

"Exactly," Rose said, taking a sip of her rosé. "Somebody once told me he had, like, eighteen or twenty houses all over the world at one time, though maybe he's down to only five or six. I think he spends most of his time here ... At least I see him around a lot."

"What about ... What's his history with women?" Crawford asked.

"Prodigious," Rose said. "I don't know if he's got as many wives and mistresses as houses, but it's probably pretty close."

"So, any good scandals on his résumé?"

Rose thought for a second. "With the exception of those girls ten years ago with Asher Bard, I can't think of any."

Crawford nodded.

"Oh, hey, you'll appreciate this," Rose said. "Khalid went to the company that makes the game Monopoly—like maybe fifteen years ago or so, when he was still flush—and had them make up a game board with all his houses on it. So instead of Park Place, it was some address in London. Mayfair, I think. And instead of Broadway, it was some address in Monte Carlo."

Crawford just shook his head. "Somehow I'm finding this a little hard to relate to."

Rose chuckled. "Then I heard he gave the custom games to family members and friends."

Crawford thought for a moment. "But the question is, did he ever have a condo in West Palm Beach with a spectacular view of the Publix parking lot?"

Rose laughed, started to say something but stopped.

"What?" Crawford said. "You were about to say something. About Al-Ansani?"

Rose held up her hands. "That's enough for now."

Crawford slowly shook his head. "Rose, you're holding out on me."

She heaved a long sigh. "Oh, all right," she said, hesitating. "So, this is about three years ago. Khalid called me up and said he was thinking about selling his house, and would I come over and give him some idea how much he should ask for it."

Crawford was nodding now. "I already know where this is going."

"What do you mean?"

"So, you go to Chateau Khalid and nobody's in the house except him and there's soft music playing and he offers you a drink. Champagne, probably."

Rose laughed. "You're not a detective, by any chance?"

"Then, he takes you around, gives you the grand tour of

the place—with several more champagne pit stops—and finally he squires you into the master bedroom. This big monster four-poster bed, like something out of Catherine the Great, am I right? And boom, he starts to slap those sly Saudi Arabian moves on you."

Rose shook her head in disbelief. "Jesus, were you *there* or something? Hiding behind a curtain, maybe?"

Crawford laughed. "No, I just know how men think. And it's always with their ... well, you know."

18

After lunch at Rose's house, Crawford drove to the Chesterfield Hotel at 363 Cocoanut Row. The Chesterfield was a boutique hotel a few blocks from Worth Avenue that, on its website, boasted of its "old-world charm, sophisticated interiors, and beautifully designed rooms and suites."

Crawford parked a half block away and walked into the lobby. A tall, skinny man was at the reception desk. "Yes, sir, welcome to the Chesterfield," the man said with a British accent.

"Thanks," Crawford said. "I'm Detective Crawford, Palm Beach Police. Is the manager here? I'd like to speak to him."

"Oh, yes, sir. Mr. Borland, his name is. I'll get him for you," the man said, walking to a closed door behind him. He knocked, then went in. A few moments later he walked back out followed by a bald man in a blue blazer.

"Hi, I'm John Borland. May I help you?"

Crawford shook Borland's hand. "Yes, I have a few questions about a guest who stayed here earlier this week."

Borland nodded. "I think I know who you mean."

"Grace Spooner was her name."

Borland nodded more emphatically. "The woman who was killed at The Colony."

"Yes."

"I was in my office just about to leave for the day when she checked out on Tuesday. It was a very odd time for a guest to check out. Right around five o'clock. Plus, she had already paid for the night and so was on the hook for it. I remember wondering why she'd check out at that time."

"She didn't offer any explanation?"

"No, not according to Justine, who was at the desk at the time. Just said she needed to go. Then when I read in the *Post* about her terrible death at The Colony, I wondered again why she would pay to stay *there* when she had already paid to stay *here*. Didn't make any sense to me."

"I agree, it doesn't make sense," Crawford said. "Do you know when she made the reservation?"

"I sure do, because I was the one who took the call. It was last Thursday, and the person who made the reservation was not Ms. Spooner, but a man."

"Really? Did he give his name?"

"No."

"But to make the reservation, he'd need to give you a credit card. Right? And give you his name?"

"Normally. But he said he was going to have a messenger come right over with cash. And, sure enough, an hour later a messenger showed up with five hundred twenty dollars in cash."

"I never heard of anybody doing that."

"I think it was a first for me, too."

Crawford thought for a moment. "Do you have any record of where the messenger came from? What service?"

"No, sorry, just a young guy in khakis and a blue shirt."

The whole thing was looking like a dead end, which was a huge letdown since it might have been a critical link in cracking the case.

"Did anyone visit Ms. Spooner when she was here? Or have a drink with her maybe? In the Leopard Lounge possibly?"

Borland glanced over at the tall, skinny man, who shook his head. "Not that I ever noticed," he said.

"Sorry," Borland said.

"Okay," Crawford said. "Well, thanks for your help."

"I'm afraid it wasn't much," Borland said.

He was right.

CRAWFORD TRIED AINSLIE SUNDERLAND ONE MORE TIME, but again only got his message machine.

Next stop was Cedar Knolls up in Riviera Beach. Crawford felt it was important to go there and confirm a few things. Maybe get some new facts, too. He drove to the station to pick up Ott for the short ride north up Route 1. Crawford was waiting for Ott outside the station when a man wearing cargo shorts and a red Coke T-shirt came into view in Crawford's rearview mirror. He was walking down the sidewalk at the same time Ott came out of the station. Crawford saw his partner's eyes light up when he saw the man on the sidewalk. The man, apparently recognizing Ott, rushed up to him and threw his arms around him in a full-on bear hug.

The two had a short conversation, then Ott pointed at Crawford's Crown Vic, and the two shook hands and said good-bye.

Ott opened the passenger side door of the Vic. "Sorry about that," he said. "That was an old buddy from Cleveland. Renting a place in Boca for a few months."

"Not a fan of Cleveland winters, huh?"

"Yeah, you know how it is: the older you get, the lower your tolerance."

"I hear you."

"Speaking of fans, I'm not a big fan of man hugs," Ott said.

"Why not?" Crawford knew Ott to be outspoken on just about every subject known to man.

"I don't know exactly. Half the time it just feels ... awkward. I mean, shit, what's wrong with a good old-fashioned handshake."

"Nothing," Crawford said. "It's my greeting of choice."

"Yeah, the one time I saw you hug a guy," Ott chuckled, "it was like you were hugging a cactus. Not into the experience *at all*."

"Well, you see these guys do it, and they barely touch."

"Or where it's like one of 'em's thinking, 'I just met you once, why the hell are we hugging?'"

"I'm with ya."

"So I guess we're both in the old-fashioned handshake camp."

Crawford nodded. "I guess."

Cedar Knolls was a large three-story colonial style house that looked inviting at first. It reminded Crawford of his grandmother's house in Massachusetts that always smelled of gingerbread. Then he drove closer and saw the bars on the windows. It was beautifully landscaped in front with a massive live oak surrounded by palm trees. He had gone on Google and read some disturbing articles about the place from ten years ago and wondered whether the live oak was the same tree one of the troubled teens had hanged himself from. There was a parking lot off to the side that was large enough to park twelve to fifteen cars, Crawford drove in and parked. "We don't have an appointment or anything, right?" Ott asked, getting out of the Vic.

"Nah, unannounced visits can be the best kind."

"Sure can," Ott said as they walked up the steps to the front door.

Crawford pushed the buzzer. They waited a full minute and no one came to the door.

"Why don't I go around back?" Ott said.

"Sure. Give it a try."

Just as he stepped down, the door opened and a plump woman who looked to be in her forties peered out. "Can I help you?"

"Yes," Crawford said as Ott walked back up the steps, "are you the person in charge here?"

"One of them. And you are?"

"Detective Crawford and my partner, Detective Ott. Could we talk? We have a few questions."

"Ah, sure, come on in. I'm Janice, by the way."

"Hi, Janice," Crawford said, following her in.

She led them into a small room that had a bookcase on one wall, a few old paintings—for the most part, dreary-looking landscapes—and furniture that looked like it had been moldering there for a long time. "Have a seat," she said, motioning to two wooden chairs.

She sat facing them. "So, tell me what you'd like to know."

Crawford leaned toward her. "How long have you been here at Cedar Knolls?"

"I'm almost a lifer," Janice said. "Sixteen long years."

"Then I'm sure you remember back about ten years ago, when quite a few girls in their teens were disappearing. And it turned out, some of them anyway, had been lured into prostitution."

Janice's expression had slowly changed and was now unmistakably grim. "I certainly do. I call it 'the bad ol' days.' I was pretty young then, but I definitely remember it. The only good that came out of that was the people who ran Cedar Knolls back then all got fired. They ran a pretty loosey-goosey operation. Mr. Jauron, the head now, has a military background and runs a very tight ship."

"Is he here now?" Ott asked.

"No, he's gone for the day. He'll be here tomorrow morning."

"Do you remember names from back then?" Crawford asked.

"Some."

"Grace Spooner?"

"Yes. I remember Grace. Beautiful girl and nice, but she had her issues."

"Like what?"

"Just had a really terrible family life. She was very ... what's the word? Impressionable. I got the sense she had never been loved and was desperate for someone to love her. Enter a guy named Frank."

Crawford glanced at Ott, then back to Janice. "Frank, huh?"

"Mm-hm. He was bad news. Convinced some of the girls to run away, told 'em they'd get lots of money and dope. That's when they got involved with that prostitution thing."

"Did Frank have a brother, do you know?" Ott asked.

"Yeah, he was the ringleader. The brother. But he wasn't here. He was on the outside."

"Do you remember their last name?" Crawford asked.

"I forget, but I'd remember it if you told me."

"Begay?"

"Yes, that was it. As I remember, they got arrested, but nothing ever happened to them."

"That's right." Crawford's face took on a solemn look. It was clear Janice hadn't heard the news. "I'm sorry to have to tell you this, but Grace Spooner was killed earlier this week."

Janice's hand went up to her mouth. "Oh, no. What happened?"

"She was murdered," Crawford said. "We're the investigators on it."

"Oh my God, that's just terrible," Janice said through her hand. "I hope you catch whoever did it."

"We will," Crawford said.

Janice was slowly shaking her head.

"Janice, do you happen to know who owns Cedar Knolls?" Ott asked.

She shook her head. "No. Just that it's some company up in New York. Like I said, it's really well-run now. Kids who are here really want to get straightened out. Want to get clean. You know, forge a new life. Back then, it was a different story. To make a place like this work, you've got to have committed people. Mr. Jauron is; so are the rest of us."

"That's good to hear," Crawford said, as he heard footsteps that seemed to be coming toward them.

Two girls appeared, one in blue jeans, one in a skirt. "Janice, is it okay if we go down to the library?" one asked.

"Yeah, sure, just be sure you're back for dinner."

"Don't worry," the girl said. Then to Crawford, "Sorry to interrupt."

"No problem," Crawford said with a smile.

The girls walked away.

"Where's the library?" Ott asked.

"A few blocks from here," Janice said. "Back in the bad ol' days I was talking about, girls would ask if they could go to the library and then never come back. They'd meet up with that guy Begay and get into big trouble. Not anymore."

Crawford and Ott thanked Janice, got back in their car, and headed south to Palm Beach.

"You buy all that?" Ott asked, turning to Crawford.

"What do you mean?"

"Well, the way she described it, the place used to be hell. Now it's heaven."

"Yeah, I know what you mean. It did seem a little too perfect," Crawford said.

Ott shrugged. "But now that I think about it, it could just be the difference between having those Begays around, and not."

19

CRAWFORD DROPPED OTT OFF IN FRONT OF THE STATION at four that afternoon. "Hey, do me a favor," Crawford said, rolling down his window. "Call Signature and find out when Asher Bard and his buddies get back, will ya?"

Signature was the company that serviced private planes at the Palm Beach airport.

"Will do. What are you up to?" Ott asked.

"I got a hunch about something."

"Is your hunch gonna land someone in jail?"

Crawford smiled. "I sure as hell hope so."

CRAWFORD DROVE OUT TO THE MOTOR VEHICLE Department in Royal Palm Beach. He could have called them, but last time he tried, he'd been put on hold for fifteen minutes and made to endure some extremely schmaltzy Lawrence Welk-type music. Then, when a woman finally picked up, she said all the people who could help him were celebrating an employee's fiftieth birthday and were unavailable. She took his number and said someone would call him back, but, of course, nobody ever did. The next time he ID'd himself as a cop and, exaggerating a little, said it was a matter of life and death. He immediately got disconnected.

So this time, screw it, he was going to go there in person. He stood in line at the counter, and when someone asked if they could help him, he said he was a police officer and told her he needed to know what kind of car a certain individual drove. She told him normally that was not something she could divulge. He got the sense, though, that if he sweet-talked her a little, he could wheedle the information out of her. He leaned closer to her and dropped his voice. "It's critical information to solve a brutal murder, ma'am."

Her eyes widened. "Well, in that case …"

Three minutes later, he knew Frank Begay drove a 2017 black Ford F-150 and his brother Johnnie a Cadillac CTS—the same make of car that had picked up Grace Spooner the night she was murdered.

CRAWFORD GOT A PANICKED CALL FROM DAVID BALFOUR. "I think I blew it. I know you're right in the middle of that big case, but I really need your help, man."

It all came at Crawford like machine gun fire. "Slow down, David. What happened?"

"So I had a come-to-Jesus conversation with Missy. Said I was going to give her a hundred grand and that I knew all about the paintings switch."

"Okay, so then what happened?"

"Then I went to the Poinciana for my Wednesday golf game."

"And then?"

"Came back five hours later and the real Kline and Hockney paintings were back on my walls."

Crawford scowled. "So, let me guess. Missy denied they

had ever been taken and acted like she didn't know what the hell you were talking about. And probably still wants half your money."

"Yeah, exactly, but it gets worse. The P.I. from Miami disappeared."

Crawford sighed as the reality hit him. "Oh, I get it, so Missy or probably Jenkins got to him and paid him off. So now you don't have him to testify about the paintings switch."

"That's what it looks like," Balfour said, his voice thin, his exhale loud.

"Well," Crawford said, "the good news is I took a few close-ups of the painting with my cell phone."

"Oh, thank God," Balfour said. "I was kicking myself for not doing that."

Crawford shook his head. "Problem is, that doesn't really prove anything," he said, then thought for a moment. "How are you at bluffing, David?"

"What do you mean? I'm a pretty good poker player."

"You're going to tell Missy that I broke into Jenkins' studio and got photos of the Kline and the Hockney."

Balfour sighed again. But this time it was a sigh of relief.

CRAWFORD WAS BACK AT THE STATION AT SIX THIRTY, reading whatever he could on the internet about Asher Bard, Lord Sunderland (nee Ainslie Sulcher), Joe Mitchell, and Khalid Al-Ansani.

At a little before seven, Crawford heard footsteps approaching his door.

"Hel-lo, Charlie."

Dominica McCarthy was wearing a short beige skirt and flashing a little cleavage but far from flaunting it. Personifying the old expression *she'd look good in a potato sack,* Dominica had thick brown hair, cat-like green eyes, full lips, and a slinky walk that was always a sight to behold. Sometimes Crawford slowed down to let her get ahead of him so he could take in her majesty hip-swaying.

"What? Are you out roaming the hallways again," Crawford said, "looking for someone to bother?"

"I take offense at that. Have I ever bothered you, Charlie?"

"Um. Never."

She raised her arms. "Are you going to ask me to join you or just stare at me?"

"I like staring at you but would be honored if you'd join me," Crawford said, pointing to a chair opposite him.

"Isn't that the one molded to Ott's ass?" she asked.

"No, it's that one." He pointed to the other chair as she sat down.

"So, how you doin' on Spooner?"

He tapped the top of his desk. "Got a few things. Not enough yet."

"I keep hearing the name Asher Bard."

"Yeah, he's high on the list. What do you know about him?"

"I just hear the same things you do. Rich sleazeball who's bad news with women."

"I think you're being generous."

"And I hear he's got some friends who are no day at the beach."

Crawford nodded. "The morning after the murder, Bard and some of those friends flew down to Costa Rica on a golf outing. Only problem is, they forgot their golf clubs."

"Isn't Costa Rica a place where old guys go to meet young girls?"

"Yup. Bard's flying back tonight. I'll be camped out on his doorstep tomorrow morning."

Dominica nodded, then yawned. "Well, I'm bored. What do you say I buy you a drink?"

Crawford tapped his desk. "I got a better idea. How 'bout I buy you a drink ... at a strip club?"

"Now there's an offer I've never had before."

"So, what do you say?"

"I say ... sure, what the hell," she said with a shrug.

"That's what I've always liked about you, McCarthy, your adventurous spirit."

"And what I've always liked about you, Crawford, you recognizing it."

"I think it's that Irish-Spanish-Hungarian blood in you."

"Irish-Spanish-Czechoslovakian."

"Even better."

"What's the name of this dive you're taking me to?"

"Puss in Boots."

"Cute," Dominica said, cocking her head to one side. "Who came up with that name?"

"Couple of dipshits named Johnnie and Frank. But the dancers actually do wear boots."

"And that's about all, right?"

"Yup."

CLEM THE MUSCLE-BOUND LUNKHEAD WAS AT THE DOOR of the Puss.

He gave Dominica a long, approving stare after he asked her for ID.

"Thank you, sir," Dominica said as she dug her ID out of the wallet in her purse. "You make me feel young and vital." She had turned thirty-one a few months back.

He grunted something and gave her a stubby thumbs-up.

They walked into the hallway. "Charming gentleman," Dominica said.

"Clem? Oh yeah, salt of the earth," Crawford said. "It gets better. Wait 'til you meet the rest of the gang."

They walked in and there were two mostly unclad women dancing on the stage in the middle of the bar. Boobs were bobbing and bodies grinding.

"Oh, my," said Dominica, eyes wide.

Crawford pointed to two bar stools. They sat.

The bartender with the nicotine-stained teeth and stud in her nose who reminded Crawford of his old Sunday school teacher sidled up to them. "Welcome back. Mort, right?"

Crawford nodded and turned to Dominica. "What are you gonna have?"

"Ah, got any pinot grigio?" she asked the bartender.

"Sure do."

Dominica smiled at Crawford. "How 'bout you ... Mort?"

Crawford studied the beers on tap. "I'll have a Hoppy Ending IPA."

Dominica's eyes shot to Crawford's. "A *what*?"

"It's a beer. Heavy on the hops, lame on the name," Crawford said, looking up at the women on stage. One of them blew him a kiss. She was the one from last time, her arms sleeved in blue ink.

Dominica noticed and chuckled. "You a regular here?"

"Nah, just the one time." Crawford flicked his head. "That's Daisy ... or is it Daff?"

"Daff?"

"Yeah, all the girls are named after flowers."

"Oh, really," Dominica said. "And why'd the bartender call you Mort?"

"'Cause that's my alias."

"Your partner know that?"

"Gotta keep *some* secrets from him," Crawford said. "All right. Enough small talk. We got a job to do."

"Talk to the brothers, you mean?" Dominica asked.

Crawford nodded. He had told her about Johnnie Begay owning a Cadillac CTS, the same car that had picked up Grace Spooner the night she died.

Crawford flagged down the bartender.

"What's up, Mort?" She eyed his three-quarter filled Hoppy Ending beer.

"Johnnie and Frank back in their office?"

She sighed and rolled her eyes. "You gonna hassle them again?"

"Yup."

She glanced at Dominica, then back to Crawford. "Gonna take your little friend along?"

Dominica got a steely look in her eyes. "I'm his boss. Name's Rutledge. We need to see Johnnie."

Crawford suppressed a laugh as the bartender held up her hand. "All right. All right." Then to Crawford, "You know where to go."

Crawford took another slug of his beer, then got up, leaving the Hoppy Ending half full. "You ready ... boss?"

Dominica took a dainty sip of her pinot grigio, then got up. "Let's do this."

Crawford walked back to the door to the brothers' office, noticing the bartender had just made a call on her cell.

They got to the door and Crawford banged on it. A few moments later, Frank Begay opened up. "Well, well, back like a bad penny."

"Hello, Frank. This is Dominica. We work together."

"Wow," Frank said. "Look at you." He went from her toes up to her long and lustrous hair. "Whatever the Palm Beach Police Department's paying you, we'll double it."

"Thank you, Frank, but I'm very happy where I am. Need to ask you and your brother some questions."

Johnnie was across the room in his recliner, watching a basketball game this time. A woman Crawford hadn't seen before was in his lap. "Johnnie, look who it is," Frank said. "Our old friend Detective Crawford, and a lady-friend."

Johnnie glanced over and did a double-take when he saw

Dominica. "Well, hel-lo, sweetness," he said with a leer. "You here for a job interview?"

"Screw off and get over here," Dominica said. "We got questions."

Johnnie clicked off the basketball game and stood. "Seems like all we ever do is answer questions."

Crawford reached into the breast pocket of his jacket as Johnnie walked up to them. "You got a blue Cadillac CTS, right, Johnnie?"

"Yeah, so?"

Crawford held up a photo. "Is this your car? 'Cause it's also a blue Cadillac CTS."

Johnnie took a quick look at the photo. "No."

"How do you know?"

"'Cause I know you're trying to place that woman who got killed in my car, but she was never anywhere near it."

"'That woman.' You know who 'that woman' is?"

"No idea."

Crawford held up the photo of Grace Spooner getting in the car again. "Take another look."

Frank and Johnnie both shrugged.

Crawford shook his head and raised his voice. "I'm getting sick of you assholes lying all the time." He looked at Frank. "You lived in the same house with 'that woman' ten years ago." Then to Johnnie, "And you, you lowlife pimp, you had her in your teenage girl stable."

"I have no idea what you're talking about," Johnnie said.

"Yeah," Frank said. "And how you expect me to remember some chick from ten years ago?"

It was Dominica's turn. "How 'bout 'cause you just saw her a few nights ago?"

Frank shook his head. "How 'bout ... never happened."

"That ain't my car," Johnnie said. "Gotta be hundreds of blue Cadillac CTS's in the state of Florida."

"Eighty-three, to be exact," Crawford said. "But only seven registered in Palm Beach County."

Johnnie looked impressed. "How you know that?"

Crawford ignored the question and looked over at Dominica. "Got anything else?"

"In case my associate didn't ask you before," she said to Crawford, then to the brothers, "where were you Tuesday night?"

"Right here, girlfriend," Johnnie said. "Sitting in my easy chair over there, girl in my lap, nursing an adult beverage." Then, as an afterthought, "Maybe you could join me one night, when you're not out hassling innocent men."

"Thanks a lot, but you're really not my type," she said. "Pleasure chatting with you, though." Then to Crawford, "Let's get out of this armpit."

"Yeah, let's go," Crawford said, then he smiled at Johnnie. "You're not my type either."

THEY WERE OUT IN THE PARKING LOT. "CAN I SEE THAT shot of Grace Spooner getting into the car again?" Dominica asked.

"Sure," Crawford said, reaching into his breast pocket, sliding it out, and handing it to her.

She took it. "Thought I noticed something before." She pulled the photo closer. "Yeah, see that."

She was pointing at something on the passenger side door.

"Oh, yeah," Crawford said. "A scratch."

"So, assuming the Caddy's somewhere in the lot here, let's see if it's got a scratch."

Crawford nodded and patted Dominica on the shoulder. "It takes a tech to spot something that subtle. Good catch."

"Thanks," Dominica said, then pointed at a blue car. "Over there, is that it?"

"No, that's a Lincoln."

They spent the next few minutes walking around the parking lot but didn't spot a blue Cadillac anywhere.

"Let's check around back," Crawford said.

Dominica nodded.

They walked around to the other side, and there, parked next to a black Ford F-150 pickup, was a blue Cadillac CTS.

"Bingo," Dominica said.

They went around to the passenger side and looked down at the door.

There was no scratch.

"Could have had it painted in the last couple of days," Dominica said, looking up at Crawford.

"Could have, but I doubt it. I mean, he'd have to think that, one, the car would be caught on a camera, and two, the camera could pick up the scratch—"

"Yeah, you're right, and three, that we'd ever track him down," Dominica said, getting down in a crouch and examining where the scratch was in the photo. Then, holding the photo, she touched where the scratch would have been, leaned forward, and sniffed it. "No fresh paint."

"Bummer," Crawford said, shaking his head. "Guy was looking like such a good suspect."

"Too bad. What do we do now?"

Crawford shrugged. "Get a drink. But not here. I'm sick of looking at tattooed women with bad boob jobs."

20

They decided on a place called E.R. Bradley's, a saloon at the end of Clematis and overlooking the Intracoastal in West Palm. Crawford had a vague recollection of reading that E.R. Bradley was a gambler and racetrack owner who donated land he owned in Palm Beach that later became the site of Rosarian Academy.

Dominica was halfway through her first pinot grigio, and Crawford had just ordered his second Stoudts Smooth Hoperator IPA.

"What's with all those stupid names?" Dominica asked, pointing to Crawford's beer bottle.

"I can't tell you. Tastes pretty good, though."

"That's all that counts, right?"

Crawford nodded. "So, I assume you heard the Rose newsflash?"

"Oh, you mean about John?"

"Yeah. John the shrink. You met him?"

"Just briefly. I stopped by her house and had a quick drink with them."

"Jesus. She's having cocktail parties, and I'm not on the guest list."

"Don't be so sensitive, it wasn't a cocktail party. She just asked me over, and he showed up as I was leaving."

"So, what did you think?"

"Nice guy. Kind of reserved. Struck me as one of those strong, silent types."

"So, it seems pretty serious?"

"Too early to tell."

Crawford glanced away and saw a big yacht heading up the Intracoastal. "Would you ever have figured she'd end up with a shrink?"

"Charlie, first of all, she hasn't ended up with anybody. They just started going out. And second, what's wrong with shrinks? Just 'cause you're so normal you never had to go to one."

"I went to one once."

"Once? That doesn't count. Why'd you go?"

"My ex-wife suggested it."

"You mean, the ex-wife you never talk about."

"What's to talk about?"

"I don't even know her name."

"Would you like to?"

"Yes?"

"Jill."

"That's a nice name."

"I thought so, too."

"This is a pretty lame conversation."

Crawford laughed. "Ask me whatever you want. Let's just say, it was a good marriage for a while but kind of ran out of gas."

"That doesn't tell me anything."

"Well, what do you want to know?"

Dominica sighed. "I just know you're going to give me Charlie answers."

"What the hell are 'Charlie answers?'"

"That's what Rose calls them. Short. Succinct. Pithy. But not volunteering a damn thing."

"Let's talk about Rose and John the shrink?"

"We just did. What's to talk about? I met him for five minutes, and you've never laid eyes on the man."

"It's still more interesting than Jill and Charlie."

"Because you don't like talking about yourself."

"True," Crawford said. "You want to get something to eat?"

"No."

"You don't?" Crawford said with a shrug, "Well, what do you want to do then?"

Dominica leaned in close and lowered her voice. "How 'bout ... go back to your place and mess around."

Crawford smiled. "Seriously?"

"Don't act so surprised."

"Well, it's just—"

"The moratorium Rose and I came up with?"

"Yeah, the thing that's been in effect for seven months, two days, five hours, twenty-three minutes and"—looking at his watch—"fourteen seconds."

Dominica laughed. "Well," she said, twisting a strand of hair around her ear, "now I'm proclaiming it's over."

Crawford raised his fist. "Hallelujah."

"So, finish your drink and let's go celebrate its official end."

They were at Crawford's condo after Dominica elicited a promise from him that he'd prepare his trademark breakfast the next morning: a cheese omelet, Nueske's smoked bacon, and toast slathered with marmalade.

He would have promised her anything.

"Back when you smoked," Dominica asked, out of breath

from their just-concluded lovemaking, "did you smoke a cigarette after...you know?"

She was lying on her back, the sheet pulled up just above her breasts, her tanned, lean arms out to her sides. She had a few beads of sweat on her forehead.

Crawford nodded. He was facing her, his right hand propping up his head. "I think I did because James Bond did. Anything 007 did was in my playbook."

"Which one?" Dominica asked, then she turned and kissed him.

"Which James Bond?"

She nodded.

"Sean Connery, of course. Roger Moore, a distant second. Daniel Craig, not even in the running."

"Pierce Brosnan?"

"Too pretty."

"And Sean Connery and Roger Moore weren't?"

Crawford slipped his left hand up to her breasts and traced gentle circles around them. "They were, but they were more ... rugged."

"'Rugged?'"

"You know, manly, virile. I never really felt Pierce Brosnan was up to the task of taking on Sean Bean in *Goldeneye*."

"Who's Sean Bean?"

"The actor who played Alec Trevelyan. Also known as Agent 006. He faked his death and took over the Janus crime syndicate. One seriously bad dude."

"Jesus, Charlie, sounds like you got 'em all memorized."

Crawford kept stroking around Dominica's nipples. "Did you know the first Bond movie was filmed in 1962?" He did the math. "Fifty-seven years ago."

"*Dr. No*, right?" she said. Then with a soft smile and a sigh, "Oh, yes, that feels sooo good."

Crawford didn't hear her. "Yeah ... man, did I ever lust after Ursula Andress."

"She was Pussy Galore, right?"

Crawford laughed. "You should be ashamed of yourself. Honor Blackman was Pussy Galore. Ursula Andress was Honey Ryder. Had posters on my bedroom walls of both of 'em."

"They didn't exactly go on to become major starlets."

"True. Pretty much one-hit wonders, but wow, were they hot."

"Don't stop," Dominica said, as Crawford seemed to be losing focus.

"And, oh my God, Daniela Bianchi and Claudine Auger—"

"Who in God's name are they?" Dominica asked, grabbing his inert hand and guiding it back to her breasts.

"Daniela Bianchi played Tatiana Romanova in *From Russia with Love* and Claudine Auger was ... Oh, God, what's her name in *Thunderball*—"

"No clue."

Crawford snapped his fingers. "Domino, that's it, Domino Derval."

Dominica turned to her side and put her arms around Crawford. "Charlie, do you realize you have a real live woman right next to you, who some might describe as—"

"—the hottest woman in south Florida and quite possibly the world? Yeah, I picked up on that. Just having a little flashback there."

He put his arms around her and kissed her with all he had. Then he moved his hands down to her perfect, rounded ass and pulled her into him. Three minutes later they were making love like James Bond only dreamed of.

21

It was seven fifteen and Crawford was serving Dominica breakfast in bed.

Dominica wore a pair of his blue boxers and nothing else, sitting at the end of the bed watching CNN. They were loose on her.

She had just finished off a piece of crisp Nueske's smoked bacon. "So, I have a question for you."

Crawford walked out with his tray of food. "Shoot."

"Were you thinking about any of those Bond girls when we made love?"

"Umm, maybe a little, the fourth time."

Dominica cocked her head. "Did we do it four times?"

"Five, actually," Crawford said.

"We had a lot of time to make up for."

"Seven months, two days, six hours, twenty-three minutes and—"

"—but who's counting?" Dominica shook her head and laughed. "What are you doing today on Spooner?"

"Asher Bard flew back last night. I'm about to go camp out on his doorstep."

"What about the guys that went with him? Are any of them on your shortlist?"

"Absolutely. Lord Sunderland and Joe Mitchell."

"Who's Joe Mitchell?"

"You've probably seen him on TV. A big-time lawyer from Boston. He's, like, the resident legal expert on Fox News and has a very impressive vocabulary. Whenever there's a legal question, ol' Joe always gets up there and gives some long-winded answer. I think he used to be a criminal attorney."

Dominica put her fork down after having finished her cheese omelet. "That was so good, Charlie. You could be a chef."

He shook his head. "That's the only thing I know how to do."

"Okay, you could whip up breakfast for the gang at Green's then," she said. "So, have you ruled out those sleazeball brothers from last night?"

"No, just 'cause the car didn't match doesn't mean they couldn't have done it. They still have motive."

"Which is?"

"Grace Spooner was going to talk to that reporter, Quinn Casey. The brothers sure as hell didn't want more press about what happened ten years ago."

"I hear you."

Crawford glanced away from the TV and down at Dominica. "You look good in boxers ... but then, you look good in anything. Even better in nothing, though."

She laughed. "Thank you, Charlie."

"You're welcome, Dominica," he said, looking at his watch. "It's a little early to show up on Bard's doorstep, so what do you say we—"

"Go for number six?"

Crawford nodded and smiled. "Can't hurt."

22

CRAWFORD HIT THE BUZZER AT THE BIG CONTEMPORARY oceanfront house at 6 Ocean Lane at a little after nine o'clock. When nobody came to the door, he hit it again.

Finally, it opened. It was the big redwood tree of a man, Tyrell, who went from a neutral expression to a frown. "You again. Whaddaya want, Detective?"

"Asher Bard."

"Well, you can't have him."

"You want me to get a warrant, Tyrell? Because that's easy enough. I'll just be back in a half hour." Which was bullshit, because sometimes it could take quite a while.

"Yeah, why don't you do that," Tyrell said as a face in white pajamas with blue piping appeared next to him. It was Asher Bard. He was a blocky man, no more than five-nine or five-ten with big cauliflower ears and a small nose. He had gray hair that stuck up in front and flattened out on the sides and back.

"Who's this?" Bard asked.

"A Palm Beach detective, I forget his name."

"You don't need to translate," said Crawford. "I can speak

directly to Mr. Bard. My name's Detective Crawford. I've been waiting three days to talk to you."

"Oh, yeah, what about?"

"I bet you have a pretty good idea. Grace Spooner. The woman who died at The Colony when you were having your birthday party there."

"I read about that."

"What? It made the *Costa Rica News and World Report*?"

Bard scowled. "Funny man. I read about it online. The *Glossy*."

"I'd like to come in. Ask you some questions."

"No. Right here is fine," he said, then glanced at Tyrell. "You can go, Ty. I got this." Then back to Crawford, "So, ask away."

Crawford first wanted to see if he could catch Bard in a lie. "Did you go into the hotel at all the night of your party?"

Bard thought for a second. "You've had three days to check all the cameras, so you know the answer. Yes, I did. As you know, I booked a couple of rooms there."

"Did you ever go up to one of the penthouses?"

"No."

"What floor was your room on?"

"The third."

"And who did you go there with?"

"Her name was Midge." He was eyeing Crawford's shoes. "Are those Skechers?"

Crawford looked down at them. "Yeah, why?"

Bard shrugged. "I don't know, I've just never met anyone who wore Skechers before."

It was clearly a put-down.

"They're very comfortable. You should get a pair."

"Maybe I will. Cost about fifteen, twenty bucks, right?"

Another put-down.

"A little more."

"And that tie. Is it rayon?"

Crawford looked down at it. "You know, I'm not really sure. Why the interest in my wardrobe?"

"It's just, I never talked to a detective before. So I'm kind of curious to know how a detective dresses."

"Well, now you know. Did you know Grace Spooner was staying at The Colony?"

"No idea."

"But you knew Grace Spooner?"

"Look, you've done your homework, you know what happened ten years back. And that nothing ever came of it."

"And you never saw her last Tuesday night?"

"No, as a matter of fact, I didn't."

"Did any of your guests see her? Like maybe Khalid Al-Ansani or Lord Sulcher."

Bard shook his head. "It's Lord *Sunderland*, and how the hell would I know? I wasn't keeping tabs on all my guests."

"Something else," Crawford said. "You own Cedar Knolls in Riviera Beach, right?"

"What's that?"

"A place for at-risk teenage boys and girls."

"Hey, look, I own a big company that's in the business of providing homes and care for kids like that. Maybe that place is one of them."

"Yeah, matter of fact, it is. And guess who did a stint there ten years back?"

"I have no idea."

"Yeah, you do ... Grace Spooner."

"Okay, so what?"

"You know damn well. She and some friends of hers spent time with you right here in this house. On your yacht. On your island. God knows where else."

Bard shook his head and jeered. "Are you here to arrest me for something, Detective? Because if not, my breakfast is getting cold, and you're really starting to get on my nerves."

"Sorry to hear that, and no, I'm not here to arrest you." Bard stepped back and pushed the door to close it. Crawford pushed it back at him. "Not this time, anyway."

23

Lord Ainslie Sunderland was a little more cordial than Asher Bard and not once tried to ridicule Crawford's wardrobe. They were in the living room of his house on Middle Road, in the heart of the estate section.

"So, you just walked to The Colony for Asher Bard's party?"

Sunderland was sitting in a lime-green club chair with a cup of coffee and a saucer balanced in his lap. "Yes, it's only a five-minute walk. Though, I must say,"—he guffawed noisily—"it took me a little longer to get home."

Crawford smiled. "All that champagne you were telling me about?"

"Oh, my God, yes. I got a little lost, I must confess."

They had become fast friends in five minutes. Crawford could tell Sunderland was one of those impish men who liked to tell war stories that invariably revolved around an excess of drink.

"Then I had to take a leak and almost walked into a Spanish bayonet tree."

"That would have been painful."

"Oh, my God. Can you imagine?"

"So, Lord Sunderland." It was time to get down to it. "As you well know, there was a brutal murder that night."

Sunderland moved the coffee cup and saucer to a side table. "I know. I heard about the poor woman. Simply awful."

"Yes, it was," Crawford said. "So, I'm just going to cut to the chase: I know there were strippers there who performed double duty. And I know Asher Bard had booked rooms in the hotel. And I also know you and one of the women spent some time together in one of the rooms."

Sunderland's face turned fire-engine red. Crawford paused, waiting to see if he would volunteer anything, but Sunderland just glanced off in the distance.

"So, my question is—no, actually, I have several questions. First one is, did you ever see the victim, Ms. Spooner?"

"No, definitely not."

"And you never went to the penthouse floor?"

"Ah, no, I had my hands full where I was."

"Did anyone, in your presence, ever mention the name Grace Spooner?"

Sunderland shook his head.

"Of course, I'm well aware of the incidents ten years ago involving Ms. Spooner."

The red face was back. "I'm not certain I would have recognized her had I seen her at the hotel."

"I understand. It's been a long time."

"It certainly has."

Crawford leaned closer to Sunderland. "I was told you were the one who hired the strippers as kind of a birthday present to Asher Bard. So, my question is, what are their names? Their *real* names. Or even if you just have, say, one name and a phone number?"

Sunderland shook his head. "Why do you need to know that?"

"It's very material."

Sunderland sighed. "I spoke to a bartender friend. He had one of them call me."

"What bartender? Where?"

Sunderland hesitated a few moments.

"Come on, I need to know."

"Dorian at Pistache."

Crawford wrote it down. "So, who called you?"

"Her name was Betty."

Crawford looked up. "Her number would be in your phone."

Sunderland shook his head. "I deleted the number after we made the ... arrangements."

"Why?"

"Ah, let's just say, I have a suspicious girlfriend."

Crawford nodded. "Okay, thank you, I think that will do it."

He looked at his watch. It was only eleven thirty. A little too early to go plunk himself down on a bar stool at Pistache.

MEANWHILE, ON THE NORTH END OF PALM BEACH, OTT was about to interview Joe Mitchell. Ott had found an address for Mitchell at 305 Indian Road, driven up there, and was now parked in front of the house. It was a two-story Tuscan villa, and as Ott walked up to the front door, he turned to his left and caught a glimpse of Peanut Island, the six-acre island where a bunker had been built for President Kennedy in case of a nuclear attack. After Kennedy's assassination, when it was no longer in use, Ott heard it had become a go-to site for beer-party blow-outs and romantic trysts.

Ott was met at the door by an Asian housekeeper who said Mitchell was taking a walk on the beach. Ott decided to try to track him down and asked her if there were any photos of Mitchell he could take a look at since he didn't know what

Mitchell looked like. She went and retrieved one of Mitchell and a youthful Bill Clinton in a silver frame. "He doesn't have quite so much hair these days," the housekeeper remarked.

"I'm going to walk over to the beach and try and find him," Ott said, taking his wallet out of his back pocket. "But if I miss him, could you ask him to call me at this number?" He handed her a card.

"I certainly will, sir." She dropped her voice. "Is there any problem?"

"No, I just have a few routine questions about a case I'm working on."

He thanked her and walked over to the beach. He took off his tie and jacket and rolled up his sleeves, but his shoes were problematic: he was wearing his Ecco Helsinki Bike Toe lace-ups. They were the most comfortable shoes he had ever worn but not for a stroll on the beach. He considered driving back to the station, where his gym bag was in his trunk along with his Nikes, but that was a half-hour round trip.

What's a little sand in your shoes? he thought.

Five minutes later he was slogging his way south on the wide, sandy beach.

He walked past two female sunbathers and nodded a hello. There were three surfers in the ocean; he watched one catch a wave and get a good, long ride. Then he glanced to his right and saw a familiar house: it was once owned by the famous talk-show host, Knight Mulcahy, who had been brutally murdered after having an illicit tryst in his pool house. There had been a multitude of suspects, as it seemed Mulcahy had antagonized half of Palm Beach, but Ott and Crawford had eventually tracked down the killer. Mulcahy's widow had put the house on the market soon after, but Ott heard that it took over a year to sell. The explanation, he remembered hearing from Rose Clarke, was that buyers tended to shy away from houses where murders or suicides took place.

Then as he looked back down the beach, he saw a single

man coming toward him wearing shorts and a polo shirt. He was pretty sure it was Joe Mitchell. As the man got closer, he saw what the housekeeper meant: Mitchell had a Friar Tuck fringe around his otherwise bald head and a well-developed double chin.

Ott felt sand shift in his Eccos as he approached Joe Mitchell. "Mr. Mitchell?"

Mitchell stopped. "Yes?"

"My name is Detective Ott. Your housekeeper said you were out here, and I have some questions related to the death of Grace Spooner at The Colony Hotel earlier this week."

Surprisingly, Mitchell didn't seem taken aback. "Okay, where do you want to do this?"

"Why don't we just keep walking. Back toward your house. By the time we get there, I'll probably be out of questions."

"Fine with me," Mitchell said. "Aren't you a little hot?" He was studying Ott's khakis and button-down dress shirt.

"Yes, well, I wouldn't want to walk a long distance dressed like this," Ott said. "So, my first question is, did you see or hear anything at Asher Bard's party or in The Colony Hotel that struck you as out of the ordinary?"

"Not even remotely," Mitchell said without hesitation. "It was just another party that just happened to be close to where a murder occurred. Asher could have had it at the Breakers, in which case you wouldn't be talking to any of us."

Which was not altogether true, Ott thought, because of the past relationship between Bard, Sunderland, Mitchell, and the victim, Grace Spooner.

"Besides, we were just in the restaurant, not the hotel," Mitchell added.

Was he going to play dumb about the rooms Asher Bard had rented in the hotel?

"Mr. Mitchell, are you not aware of the fact that Mr. Bard had rented four rooms in the hotel for the night?"

Mitchell changed his tone quickly. "Oh, yes, I certainly was aware of that. Some of the guys at the party lived off-island; the last thing they'd need would be to get a DUI on the ride home."

Should have expected a lawyer spin, Ott thought. "That was very considerate of Mr. Bard."

Mitchell shrugged. "Hey, who wants to have to go bail a friend out of jail?"

Ott had to hand it to him, it was a good cover story. "Mr. Mitchell, there were four young women at the party. You're aware of that, right?"

"Yes, of course I am. Some of the guys wanted to dance, and since no wives were invited ..."

Ott got the impression this was something Joe Mitchell had done all his life for clients: create alternative realities in order to get them off.

"Oh, I see," Ott said, looking deep into Mitchell's lying eyes, "so that's what the girls were invited for, to *dance* with some of the men."

"Exactly."

"Are you also aware that these women took their clothes off in the restaurant—some refer to it as stripping—then later went to those rooms Bard had rented and had sex with several of Bard's guests?"

Mitchell stopped walking and turned to Ott. "That's bullshit. How do you know that?" he demanded. "Do you even have a shred of evidence that anybody had sex with anybody?"

They were ten yards away from the two sunbathing women. Ott lowered his voice. "Admittedly, I am making a certain assumption: That is, when an older man who's had a lot to drink takes a young, attractive woman to a room in a hotel that it's not to watch *The Big Bang Theory* with her."

Mitchell shook his head and sighed. "You're being totally hypothetical. Were you at the birthday party watching what each of us consumed? How do you know who had a lot to drink? How much is a lot? How do you know what happened in those rooms?"

Christ, Ott had forgotten how much he hated lawyers.

Ott patted Mitchell on the shoulder, half-derisively, half *okay-I-give-up* gesture. "You are absolutely right, Mr. Mitchell. I was not there counting the men's drinks, nor was I a fly on the wall in one of those hotel rooms, but you know and I know that some of the men at the party should be looked at as serious suspects for what happened at The Colony."

They had walked off of the beach and onto a path that led to North Ocean Boulevard. Mitchell stopped walking and eyed Ott. "The same can be said for anyone—male or female—within a fifty-mile radius of Palm Beach."

This was never going to go anywhere.

"One final question," Ott said. "These women—from the Fred Astaire Dance Studio or whatever—do you happen to know their names? And I mean their real names."

Mitchell scrunched up his eyes as if he was thinking hard. It looked like it might have been part of his courtroom schtick. "Actually, I do remember two names. Ronnie and Midge."

Midge, thought Ott, now there was a name you didn't hear much anymore.

"All right, then," Ott said, walking over to his car. "Pleasure meeting you, sir."

"Thank you," Mitchell said. "Glad I had the opportunity to straighten you out on some of the facts."

Ott glanced at him to see if Mitchell was putting him on, but the lawyer's face couldn't have looked more serious.

IT WAS REHASH-TIME BACK AT CRAWFORD'S OFFICE.

"You know, Charlie, I always thought of you as a candidate for the *Best-Dressed List*. A little too preppy for my liking, but the chicks seem to dig it. That khaki and blue blazer look of yours, I'm talking about."

Crawford shook his head. "Yeah, but ol' Asher came down pretty hard on me. Gave me shit about my favorite rayon tie."

"And those stylish Skechers," Ott said. "Like he should talk. Standing there in his PJs."

"Yeah, no kidding."

Ott scratched the side of his head. "So, basically, we got nothin' out of the three interviews."

"Basically," Crawford said. "One of the things we still need to find out is the identity of the three strippers. That barkeep should know."

"Did you get the names, even if they were aliases? Mitchell told me two were Ronnie and Midge."

"And Sunderland told me the other one was Betty."

Ott cocked his head. "No shit. Betty, Midge, and Ronnie. Wonder if Ronnie is short for Veronica ..."

Crawford smiled and bumped Ott's fist. "Nice goin', man. Betty, Veronica, and Midge. The girls in the *Archie* comics."

Ott nodded. "My uncle had stacks of 'em. And who could ever forget Jughead, Reggie, Moose, and, of course, that carrot-top dweeb, Archie."

Crawford started scrolling on his iPad. "Wasn't there a TV show, too?"

"Millions," Ott said. "Every couple years a new one comes out."

Crawford first tried Craigslist, then when it came up, tried *girls*, then *hook-ups*. Nothing there.

"What are you looking for?" Ott asked.

"You gave me an idea," Crawford said, clicking *Escort Services*. And, *voilà*, there it was, the third one down, *Archie's Girls*. "Here we go. Under Escort Services. *Archie's Girls*. Gotta be it."

Ott leaned across Crawford's desk and raised his fist. They

bumped again. "Guess you don't need Dorian the barkeep anymore."

Crawford picked up his desk phone and dialed the phone number for *Archie's Girls*.

"Archie's Girls," the voice said, trying hard to sound sexy, but mostly just sounding weary.

"Veronica?" Crawford asked to make sure he had the right place.

"Nope. She's not here. Would you like to make a date with her?"

"No, thank you. Is this Betty?"

"Who's calling, please?"

"My name is Detective Crawford, and don't hang up or you'll be in a world of hurt."

Pause, but she was still on the line. Then, "What do you want?"

"A conversation with Veronica, Betty, and Midge," Crawford said. "I have no interest in hassling you, busting your business, or anything like that. I just have a few simple questions."

"O-kay." Tentative.

"So, tell all three of 'em I want to see them at the Palm Beach Police Station on County Road this afternoon at two. Okay?"

"I'll tell 'em."

"Tell them to ask for Detective Crawford or Ott."

"Promise you're not lookin' to shut us down?"

Charlie gave Ott a nod. "Scout's honor."

24

THE THREE WOMEN CAME IN LOOKING AS THOUGH THEY were attending high service at the Bethesda-by-the-Sea Episcopal church. Two wore skirts below the knees and the third a pants suit that might have come out of Hillary Clinton's walk-in closet.

Crawford led them back to his office as Ott dragged in two extra chairs from a nearby office. The trio sat directly opposite Crawford, with Ott off to one side.

"So, ladies, thank you for coming in on short notice. My partner and I appreciate it and hope you can help us with the case we're working on."

"You ladies are lookin' fly, by the way," Ott added.

Crawford shot him a look a parent gives a naughty child, but Ott just smiled.

Veronica, who told them her real name was Lila Broughton, leaned forward. "The murder of that woman, right? At The Colony."

"Yes," Crawford said. "That's why I asked you to come here. Since you were at The Colony then."

"See, I told you," Veronica said to the woman next to her: Midge, aka Connie Sheets.

"So, the question is—"

A detective named Bob Shepley rushed into Crawford's office. "Got a homicide down at the Town Docks," he blurted.

"Which one?" Crawford asked.

"Australian," Shepley said. "All the way at the end."

The Town Docks was the only public marina in Palm Beach. It provided berthing for boats up to 260 feet in length. There were three fixed dock structures: Brazilian, Peruvian, and Australian, named for the adjacent streets. Australian accommodated the largest yachts.

"You know the name of the vic?" Ott asked, getting to his feet.

"Sure do," Shepley said. "Asher Bard."

Crawford's head jerked back reflexively. "Ah ... sorry, ladies. We're gonna have to reschedule."

Veronica nodded. "Understand. Poor Mr. Bard. Seemed like a nice guy."

"We'll be getting back to you soon," Crawford said to the women, quickly ushering them out of his office.

He and Ott hustled out the back of the building, piled into a white Crown Vic, and were at the Town Docks in five minutes. There were four black and whites in the parking lot, lights flashing but no sirens. Crawford saw a cluster of uniforms at the end of the dock. He and Ott ran down to the end and walked up a gangplank. Crawford nodded at two uniforms who pointed to the stern of the large yacht. "Back there, the gym," one of them said.

Bard's 250-foot ship, the *Mandalay,* was built by the renowned German yard of Abeking & Rasmussen and boasted a number of special features, including a twenty-four-seat movie theater, a full owner's deck, and multiple outdoor lounge areas with spa pools. A bright red helicopter perched on a deck near the *Mandalay*'s stern.

They ran down the starboard side and turned into a room that had expansive windows on three walls and a ten-person mahogany dining table in the middle. They were ushered through that room into another one, which was a compact gym. At the center of it, next to a stack of weights and high-tech machines, was the body of Asher Bard. He was not dressed for the gym but was wearing blue jeans, a blue and white sport shirt, and fancy shoes with double buckles on the sides.

Crouched beside the body were two crime scene techs. One was Sheila Stallings, the other Dominica McCarthy. Dominica looked up at Crawford, shot him a quick smile, and looked back down at Bard's body. Crawford refrained from saying *Long time no see*.

"Hey," Ott said to Dominica and Stallings, "glad we got the A-team."

Crawford studied Asher Bard's bloody head. It looked like his skull had been caved in. He saw a forty-pound kettlebell with a smear of blood on the floor near the victim. Sheila was snapping pictures of it.

"What do you think?" he asked Dominica, pointing at the kettlebell. "Got hit over the head with that?"

"Yeah, but I'm trying to figure out why he was here," she said. "I mean, based on what he's wearing, he wasn't working out."

Sheila chimed in. "More like he was showing someone around. Whoever it was, musta got behind him and smashed him over the head with that."

"Except it weighs a lot," Dominica said. "How would a perp raise it over his head, then bring it down on him?"

"Got hit on the back of the head, not the top, maybe?" Crawford said. "So if the perp was behind him, he could swing that thing like a baseball bat. Grip it with two hands even."

"I buy that," Dominica said. "He—assuming it's a he—still has to be pretty strong."

Crawford nodded. "Let's also assume that if Bard and his

killer were walking around on the boat, the killer wasn't wearing gloves."

"Meaning there're either prints on the kettlebell or he wiped it clean," Dominica said.

"Yeah, we're not seeing anything—" Sheila started.

"So they probably got wiped," Crawford said, turning to Shepley. "You got here first, right?"

"Yeah."

"Who called it in?"

"Pretty sure it was the boat's captain."

"Where's he now?"

Shepley shrugged. "I don't know. He met us when we first got here."

"Hey, Charlie?" Ott said, getting up from a crouch beside Bard's body. "Maybe the killer snuck on board, then ambushed Bard."

Crawford thought for a moment, then shook his head. "A yacht like this, I can tell without even looking, has sensors all over the place. Deck-vibration detectors, motion detectors, you name it. Guarantee you they got high-tech stuff everywhere."

"Yeah, probably right," Ott said.

A man in a white uniform and a captain's hat came to the door and hesitated. "Can I come in?"

"Sure. Come on in, Captain," Crawford said. "Watch where you step."

"I'm Jeb Peroni," he said, staring down grimly at Asher Bard. "I was just making a call to his boys and one of his business partners."

"Sorry about what happened," Crawford said, standing up and introducing everyone. "We'd like to ask you a few questions."

"Sure. I'll do whatever I can to help."

"Thanks. First of all, how did you come across Mr. Bard? I mean, did you hear something or what?"

Peroni shook his head. "No, see, I live on the boat. I'm the only one who does. I had gone to Publix to get some groceries, and when I came back, I went to the gym for a workout. That's when I found him. Called you guys right away."

"How long were you at Publix?" Crawford asked.

"Not long, fifteen minutes maybe, but since I was close, I had a quick lunch at Green's ... You know, on North County."

"Oh, yeah, we know Green's," Crawford said with a nod. "So, it happened in that timeframe. What was it, an hour, roughly?"

"Um. Call it an hour fifteen."

"What time did you go to Publix?" Crawford asked.

"Twelve thirty."

"So you got back from Green's at around one forty-five?"

Peroni nodded.

"Is it possible someone either was waiting for him on board or snuck on while he was here?" Ott asked.

"Possible but highly unlikely," Peroni said. "This ship's got every security device known to man. Asher and I used to talk about the ship's security, and I told him the only way anybody could ever get on board undetected was if they dropped down from a helicopter."

"So, the obvious question is, have you checked any of the cameras to see what they caught?" Crawford asked.

Peroni sighed. "I was just going to tell you," he said with a shrug. "Asher called me earlier and told me to shut off the whole security system."

"He did?" Crawford said. "Did he say why?"

Peroni looked down at the two techs and lowered his voice. "No. I just assumed he was going to have a ... visitor."

"A woman, you mean?"

Peroni nodded. "Which ... was, obviously, not the case."

"So, it would seem as though Bard let the killer on board?"

Peroni nodded slowly. "That's what it seems like. Yes."

"Why do you think they'd go into this room?" Ott asked.

"All I can think is Asher was giving whoever killed him a

tour of the boat. That is, someone who'd never been on it before."

"So probably not a friend?" Ott asked.

"I wouldn't think so, but probably someone he knew," Peroni said. "I know he had some enemies, but this is just terrible."

Crawford nodded and took out his pocket recorder. "Tell me about those enemies you know about."

"Well, I heard he had issues with a rival in the media business, but I guess that would be kind of normal."

"Remember a name?"

"Sorry, I don't," Peroni said, shaking his head. "Then I heard the state attorney here was out to get him."

"Harlan Brody?"

"Yes, and I heard a father of one of those girls from ten years ago."

Crawford nodded. "You mean the girls he had ... relations with?"

Peroni seemed to shrink a little at that. Then he said: "And I'm guessing maybe some other men in business. I heard it could be pretty cutthroat, the business he was in."

"Anyone else?" Crawford asked.

"Not that I'm aware of."

"So, he never mentioned anyone, or you never overheard him talk about other ... enemies?"

Peroni thought for a moment. "No, but if I think of anyone else, I'll give you a call."

Crawford reached into his wallet, took out a card, and handed it to Peroni. "Thanks for all your help."

"Yes, we appreciate it," Ott added.

"Happy to help," Peroni said, then took one long look at Bard, slowly shook his head, and walked out.

Crawford walked over to Dominica and bent over. "So, no viable prints on the kettlebell?"

"Actually, I got a partial, but I don't know. I'm not too optimistic about it," Dominica said. "What are you thinking?"

"That the only explanation for Bard to tell the captain to turn off the security system was that he had someone coming on board after the killer."

"Like who?"

"Like maybe the wife of a Broadway producer Balfour told me about."

Dominica nodded. "That would make sense."

Crawford heard footsteps and looked up. Two big black men blotted out most of the sun that had been brightening the room. It was Tyrell and Darnell.

One of them, Darnell, looked like he'd been crying. Both of the men's eyes shot to Asher Bard prone on the floor.

"Oh, Jesus, no," Darnell said, choked up.

Tyrell knelt down beside Bard's body, unintentionally shoving Sheila Stallings aside.

"Oh, my God, my God," Darnell said, joining Tyrell and gently touching Bard's face.

Tyrell turned to Crawford and fixed him with a hostile look. "How did it happen? What the hell happened?"

Crawford stepped closer to the brothers. "We don't know. We're trying to figure it out."

Darnell put his hand on Bard's arm and lowered his voice. "Oh, Daddy, Daddy. Who coulda done this?" And, unashamedly, he started to weep.

Crawford glanced over at Dominica, not sure what to make of Darnell's inconsolable reaction. He turned to Tyrell. "I'm sorry about your loss. I didn't realize how close you were to Mr. Bard."

Tyrell shot him a look, the hostility undiminished. "Close? Didn't you hear my brother?"

"Yes, but I—"

"Asher Bard was our father. You never bothered to find out our last names, did you?"

Darnell looked up and said through tears, "We're Darnell and Tyrell Bard."

In a rapid-fire monologue, Darnell explained that their mother had been Bard's cook and the three had lived in the maid's quarter of Bard's house. One day, when the boys were two and four years old, respectively, their mother was broadsided in her car by a drunken driver on her way home from church. Bard, unmarried and childless, stepped up and adopted the boys.

Tyrell held up a hand to his brother. "Enough, man, they don't want to hear our life story."

Crawford turned to Tyrell, then Darnell. "I know it's painful, but do either of you have any thoughts at all about who might have killed your father?"

Tyrell nodded. "Right before he came over here, I heard him say on his cell, 'I got you cold, motherfucker. Those #metoo broads are gonna hang you by the balls'"—he glanced over at Dominica and Sheila—"excuse the language."

Ott looked up from taking notes in his old leather notebook. "Is that pretty much verbatim?"

"Yeah, I got a good memory," Tyrell said.

Crawford glanced over at Dominica, who was paying close attention.

"That call will show up on his cell," Dominica said, reaching into Bard's pants pocket for his cell phone.

Crawford looked back at Tyrell. "But I'm assuming you don't know who he was talking to?"

"If I did, guy'd be dead by now."

Crawford believed him.

"So, after that call, your father left?"

"Yeah, about five minutes later."

Dominica held up a cell phone to catch Crawford's attention. "Looks like a burner," she said.

Darnell seemed perplexed. "What's a burner?"

Tyrell turned to his brother. "Like a throwaway phone."

"What does what your father said on the phone mean to you?" Crawford asked Tyrell.

"Pretty obvious, I'd say," Tyrell said. "'I got you cold' sounds like he's threatening someone. Same with that #metoo thing, like he had something that would harm the guy he was talking to. Problem is, I got no clue who that was."

Crawford turned to Darnell. "And neither do you, right?"

Darnell shook his head. "Sorry, man." He reached down and held the cold hand of Asher Bard.

"Well, I'd just like to say again, we're sorry for your loss," Crawford said, and Ott, Dominica, and Sheila all nodded. "With your permission, we'd like to come to your house and investigate. See if we can find some evidence that'll help track down the person who did this."

Darnell looked at his older brother.

"Yeah, sure," Tyrell said. "When?"

"How's tomorrow morning?"

"That's good."

Crawford nodded. "In the meantime, do me a favor: don't go into his bedroom. I don't want any evidence contaminated."

"Understand."

"And what about ... Did Mr. Bard have a home office there?"

Tyrell shook his head. "No, he just went to the office on Royal Palm Way."

"Okay," Crawford said, "my partner will go there and investigate."

Ott nodded and smiled.

Crawford knew the reason for the smile.

TYRELL AND DARNELL LEFT A FEW MINUTES LATER, AND Crawford turned to Ott. "Pretty incredible, huh?"

Ott nodded. "Never saw that coming. Bard being their father."

"Yeah. So, the big question is, is it the same killer for both?"

Dominica looked up. "You couldn't have two more different MOs."

"Yeah, I know," Crawford said. "A stabbing and a bludgeoning."

"A stabbing, then throwing a woman off a roof after cutting out her tongue," Sheila added.

"All I can say is this perp is pretty strong," Dominica said. "To swing that forty-pound kettlebell like a baseball bat?"

Crawford nodded. "My hunch is it's the same guy, but I got nothing to back it up with."

Ott shrugged. "I don't know," he said. "Could be two."

Crawford nodded. "Yeah, definitely could be."

Ott got up from the crouch he was in. "Well, I'm gonna go around the rest of the ship, see if I find anything else."

"I'll go with you," Sheila said, glancing over at Dominica, who nodded.

"All right," Crawford said. "I'm heading back to the station. See if any of Bard's friends know who the guy he had that conversation with might be."

"See you back there," Ott said.

"Can I hitch a ride with you, Charlie?" Dominica asked.

"Sure. You done here?"

She nodded and got to her feet.

A few minutes later they walked down the gangplank of the *Mandalay*. A TV news crew and a reporter waited at the end of the gangplank. A beefy uniform stood between them and boarding the *Mandalay*. The reporter recognized Crawford. "Hey, Charlie, is it true Asher Bard got killed on his boat here?"

"I don't have any comment," Crawford said as he and Dominica brushed past them.

The reporter was, as reporters are, insistent. "I hear he was killed with a barbell or something. Can you confirm that, give us a few details?"

Crawford just kept beelining toward the Crown Vic. As he approached it, he went around the passenger side and opened the door for Dominica.

"Thank you, Charlie," she said, getting in.

The reporter was right behind him. "The gentleman detective," he said. "C'mon, Charlie, gimme something here."

Crawford turned to him. "It's a big boat."

The reporter shook his head and chuckled. "Thanks. How newsworthy."

Crawford got in, turned the key, and left the reporter and his crew behind.

"Still can't get over it," Dominica said. "Those two being Bard's adopted sons."

"Yeah, guess it just shows nobody is all bad. I mean, I had that guy pegged as just a complete scumbag, but those boys loved him."

"Seemed like he did a good thing. Adopting them."

Crawford nodded. "And I guess he treated 'em well," he said, glancing at the parking lot. "Hey, do me a favor: when you get a chance, will you check out the surveillance cameras here?"

Dominica nodded. "Sure. I should be able to get to that later this afternoon or first thing tomorrow at the latest."

"Appreciate it."

Dominica gazed out the window. "I wonder what exactly Bard had on the guy. #metoo could be just about anything."

"Yeah, sure could," Crawford said, tapping the steering wheel a few times. "Speaking of which, did I ever tell you about my #metoo incident?"

Dominica's head swung around hard. "No, but I'm all ears."

"So, it happened just last year ... I'm not quite sure where to start."

"How 'bout the beginning," Dominica said.

"Okay, so I got a call from my ex-wife"—he stopped at a light—"who married a doctor after me. I told you that, right?"

"Yeah, the rich surgeon."

Crawford nodded. "Well, early part of last year they got separated; then one night he—the doctor—showed up at the apartment where she was staying and, apparently, was really drunk. She lets him in and he starts trying to kiss her and she fends him off. But he's not taking no for an answer. Backs her up in a corner and tries to take her top off. So she starts screaming at him. He puts his hand over her mouth and keeps going. Puts his other hand up her skirt, and she breaks free and runs into a bathroom and locks it. Finally, after pleading with her to open up or he's gonna break the door down, he goes away."

"Jesus, that's pretty scary."

"Yeah, no kidding. Then, like a week later, he comes back. She won't let him in and he's talking through the door saying he came to apologize. How he was under a lot of stress and he's feeling really bad about it now and wants to apologize face-to-face. So, after a while, she lets him in."

"Uh-oh."

"Uh-oh is right. Long story short, he's drunk again, tries to kiss her and actually rips off her top until she knees him you-know-where and escapes to the bathroom again." Crawford took a deep breath. "But this time she's got her cell on her and calls me."

"Oh, Jesus, just what you want to get dragged into."

"Yeah, actually, I did," Crawford said, pulling into the parking lot at the station and turning off the engine. "I mean, this guy was dangerous. So what happens is she tells me the situation—completely freaked out—then puts me on speaker, wanting me to say something to the guy."

Crawford shook his head at the memory.

"And?" Dominica was riveted.

"So, I didn't know what to say. I mean, here I am, a thousand miles away. What am I gonna say, 'You're a bad boy, knock it off?'"

"So, what *did* you say?"

"Well, fortunately, I had just read this article somewhere about the woman who started #metoo. And I go, 'Listen, Dan'—that's his name—'I know Tamara Burke, and I'm gonna call her right now unless you get the hell out of Jill's apartment and never come back.' And, of course, he goes, 'Who the hell's Tamara Burke?' And I go, 'The woman who started the #metoo movement.'"

"Except it's Tarana, not Tamara," Dominica said.

"Yeah, I know, Jill told me that later. But what the hell does Dan know?"

"So, did it work?"

"As drunk as he was, he beat it out of there. I could almost hear his footsteps over the phone."

"Good for you, Charlie. I'm impressed."

He shrugged. "I didn't tell you the story to impress you."

"Yeah, I know. So, what finally happened to Jill and Dan?"

"The next day she filed divorce papers and is now a rich woman going out with a guy in advertising ten years younger than her."

"Good for her. I'm glad it had a happy ending."

Another shrug. "Well, sort of."

25

CRAWFORD WAS FULLY PREPARED FOR A TEDIOUS REST OF the afternoon. He'd need to make a lot of calls and ask the same question over and over again: *As a friend of Asher Bard, did you ever hear him mention a man he knew who had skeletons in his closet relating to the mistreatment of women?*

That sounded a little lame, not to mention the first part of the conversation would be him breaking the news about Bard's death. He figured some of them might have gotten the word before he called, because bad news traveled faster than a speeding locomotive in Palm Beach. But most probably wouldn't have heard yet.

It occurred to him that he needed to listen very carefully to people's reactions when he broke the news about Bard's murder. Because it just might be that one of them was the killer. But then, it didn't seem to matter much, because all he was getting was answering machines.

Finally, on his fifth call—to Roddy Sproul—he got a live human being.

"Hello."

"Mr. Sproul, it's Detective Crawford. Have you heard about Asher Bard?"

"No, what happened?"

"Sorry to have to tell you, but he was murdered."

"Oh, my God, that's terrible. How?"

That would be the first thing anyone would want to know, but Crawford had no intention of going into great detail. He wanted to keep it vague.

"It took place on his boat. My question to you is, did he ever mention anyone who may have threatened him, or maybe someone he had a grudge against. Or someone he was scared of?"

Sproul didn't answer for a few moments. Then: "Well, that's not usually something guys talk about except maybe with their best friend, and I wasn't his best friend. But I do remember something. About a week ago on the golf course, I overheard him say something to Joe Mitchell about someone out to get him, and he was going to turn the tables on him."

"Get him for what?"

"I don't know. I just kind of heard the tail end of the conversation."

"And who was he talking about?"

"I don't know that either. You gotta talk to Joe."

This was a good lead. "Thank you, that's helpful. And I also need to ask you where you were between the hours of twelve thirty and one forty-five this afternoon."

Sproul laughed. "You gotta ask what you gotta ask, I guess. I just finished up a long, slow eighteen at Poinciana. Want to know who I played with?"

"No. You're pretty low on my suspect list."

"Thank God for that."

A few minutes later Lord Sunderland called back, breathless.

"I know why you called. I just heard about Asher."

"What did you hear?"

"Just that he was killed on the *Mandalay*."

"Do you have any idea who might have done it?"

"Absolutely none. I mean, I guess the poor man had enemies, like a lot of men in high places, but there's no one I can possibly think of who'd do something like that to him."

"So, you heard how it happened?"

"He was beaten to death on his boat is what I heard."

"Okay. I'm asking everyone I talk to this: Where were you between twelve thirty and one forty-five this afternoon?"

"I was, well, I was visiting a friend."

"And who was your friend?"

Long hesitation. "I'd rather not say."

"I'd rather you did."

"She's married."

"She's also your alibi."

"Stephanie Saint Germaine."

The name meant nothing to Crawford. "I'll need her number."

Deep sigh. "Oh, God." Reluctantly, he recited a New York-area phone number.

"Thank you."

"I wish I could say *you're welcome.*"

He heard the familiar steps of Ott, who walked in and plopped himself down in "his" chair.

"Anything?" Crawford asked.

"Nah. I scoured the boat. Nothing. But what occurred to me is that it didn't make sense, Bard giving a tour of the boat to a guy he just said 'I got you cold' to."

"You left out 'motherfucker.'"

"I'm trying to clean up my act for my date with Jennifer Atwood," Ott said. "But seriously, did you think about that, why they were wandering around the boat?"

Crawford nodded. "Yeah, I did."

"I mean, what were Bard and the killer doing in the gym?"

Crawford shrugged. "Good question." Ott shrugged back. "You know who I came up with as a suspect?"

"Who?" Ott asked.

"Harlan Brody."

Ott lurched forward in his chair. "Holy shit, never thought about him."

"Motive, right? Bard set back his career five years."

Ott was nodding vigorously. "Yeah, embarrassed the shit out of him, too. Made him a laughingstock."

Crawford nodded. "Guys don't forget stuff like that."

"Or forgive."

"I'm putting myself in Brody's shoes. He's been waiting a long time to nail Bard, then star witness Grace Spooner gets murdered and kills his case. It's pretty extreme, but maybe he's thinking, it's time to take the law into my own hands."

"Makes sense."

Crawford stroked his cheek. "The question is, how do we approach the guy? It's not like we drop by his office and say, 'So, Mr. State Attorney, we know Asher Bard was high on your shit list. Did you kill him?'"

Ott laughed. "We could say, 'Excuse us, sir, but did you have any role in bringing about the demise of Asher Bard?' Sounds better."

Crawford smiled. "Seriously, I've been thinking about it and don't have a clue how to approach it."

"Maybe we talk to Rutledge," Ott said, referring to their chief.

"Yeah, let him question Brody."

"I don't know, man, can you see him doing that?"

"Not really," Crawford said. "Oh, before I forget, Roddy Sproul, the golfer, told me how a week ago on the golf course, Bard said something to Joe Mitchell about someone out to get him. How he was going to 'turn the tables' on the guy."

"That's interesting. I better circle back to Mitchell. Hey, what about Mitchell as the doer?"

"I don't know, you know him better than me. What do you think?"

Ott shrugged. "Guy's kinda murky, but I'm not sure I see him swingin' a forty-five-pound kettlebell."

Crawford looked at his watch. It was six fifteen. "Well, whatever we're gonna do, it can wait 'til tomorrow."

"What are you gonna do now?"

"I got a couple more hours' worth of calls to make."

"Why don't you give me half of 'em."

"Okay, but don't you have a hot date with Jennifer Atwood?"

Ott smiled broadly. "Tuesday night."

26

CRAWFORD WENT TO THE GYM EVERY OTHER MORNING. Usually Monday, Wednesday, and Friday. His gym, called Ultima Fitness Performance—formerly just plain Ultima—had moved from Clematis Street to the less convenient fourth floor at 625 North Flagler. They had cut back on their hours, too, so it was not only less convenient now but also open less often. Still, Crawford liked the trainers and was a creature of habit, so for at least the foreseeable future it would remain his gym. He usually got there right around seven and did a nonstop fifty-minute workout, which allowed him to get to the station by eight or a little after.

He was doing his ten minutes of stretching, which preceded weight training and aerobics, when he heard a voice above and behind him. "Sure beats that two-thousand-calorie breakfast at Green's."

He turned to see *The New Yorker* reporter, Quinn Casey.

"You still hanging around down here?"

"Yeah, especially now, after what happened yesterday," Casey said. "I was hoping to catch you here."

Crawford held up a hand. "Sorry, but I don't have time for a million questions."

"Okay, but do you have time for information that might help in your investigation of Asher Bard's murder?"

"You have something?"

"Yeah, I think so."

"Tell you what, I'll buy you one of those fancy waters after my workout"—he pointed to where a few metal-top tables were set up—"and we can sit over there."

Casey nodded. "Sounds good. Now let's see you sweat out those sausages from the other day."

Crawford smiled and got back to work.

A half hour later, both still sweating a little, even after showers, Crawford and Casey sat down, expensive non-alcoholic drinks in front of them.

Crawford wiped his brow with a towel. "So, whatcha got, Quinn?"

"I got nothing but speculation."

"Which, as you know, is usually pretty worthless."

"It may be, but if I was going after a suspect, the guy I'm going to tell you about would be top of my list."

Crawford nodded. "Who and why?"

"Khalid Al-Ansani and a hundred reasons why. No, actually, forty million reasons why."

"Keep going."

"Do you know anything about him?"

"We talked a while back. Fact is, I'd never even heard of him until a little while ago."

Casey took a sip of his drink. "Well, when they came up with that old cliché 'he knows where the bodies are buried,' my guess is they were talking about Khalid. Maybe because he was the one doing the actual burying."

"Seriously?"

"Word was that, early on in his nefarious career, some of his business rivals would just vanish—poof, gone. I heard they found one of 'em out in the desert outside of Riyadh getting picked at by vultures. There were a lot of other things that were rumored, not all of them substantiated. Probably plenty of bullshit thrown in, too."

"Sounds like you know a lot about the man."

"I'll give you a little taste ... you in a big hurry to get back to your office?"

"I'm okay."

"Well, I won't drag it out too long," Casey said. "So, anyway, Al-Ansani starts doing deals, like, in the first grade, practically."

"What do you mean? What kinds of deals?"

"I got 'em all catalogued in my office up north. He went to some fancy private school somewhere—Switzerland, I think—and, so the story goes, had a Libyan classmate whose father wanted to import towels. So Khalid found an Egyptian classmate whose father manufactured them. And just like that, he's off to the races. Next thing you know he hears about some big construction company who's got these trucks that have traction problems in the desert sand. So, he gets his father to lend him some money and buys a bunch of trucks with really big wheels. He's, like, twenty-one at the time."

"When I was twenty-one, all I cared about was beer and babes."

"Me, too," Casey said. "Then he steps up in class and somehow gets an in with Lockheed—you know, the aircraft company—and next thing you know, he's selling fighter jets to the Saudi Arabian government one minute, then to Iran the next. So, by 1990, age, like, thirty or thirty-two, he's a bona fide billionaire. But then, ten years later, because maybe he's not minding the store the way he should—with all the wives and mistresses and yachts and mansions all over the world—he hits a bad patch. A couple of bankruptcies, the French government puts him under house arrest in Paris for something, a scandal here, a financial bust there."

"Wow, man's got a hell of a history. But, on the surface anyway, it appears he and Bard were friends. I mean, back when that scandal about the young girls was taking place, they were both knee-deep in it. Then he has him over for his birthday bash …"

"Appearances, man. Hey, Hillary Clinton went to Donald Trump's wedding."

Crawford shrugged. "That's true."

"But here are the facts. You ready?"

Crawford nodded.

"Bard sold his duplex in Olympic Towers in New York to Al-Ansani four years ago for forty-five million dollars, of which only five million was in cash."

"You don't mean, literally, cash?"

Casey laughed. "No, no, not like he showed up with a wheelbarrow full of C-notes. What happened was, one of Al-Ansani's companies had just gone belly-up. The flagship, I think it was. So Bard agreed to take back a mortgage for forty mill."

"Meaning he basically funded the whole sale."

"Basically, and the way I heard it, Al-Ansani never even made the first payment."

"And I'm guessing it's a pretty hefty monthly number."

"No kidding. Try over two hundred thousand a month. Two hundred thousand times four years is—I've done the math —over nine and a half million."

Crawford shook his head. "That's a world I can't even begin to comprehend."

"You and me both. So, after a bunch of letters from his lawyers trying to get the money, Bard gets pissed off. And, according to a very good source, he tells Al-Ansani he's going to foreclose on him. Can you imagine the public humiliation of that? Front page of the *Post* and the *Daily News*: 'Former Billionaire Heading to Poor House.' Something like that. Even highfalutin' rags like mine would be all over the story."

"So, he kills Bard to prevent that from happening?"

"Maybe."

"That's all you got. A maybe."

"Seems like a pretty good motive to me. You got something better?"

Crawford pondered for a few seconds. "I'm thinking that sounds like a decent theory. But it doesn't jibe with something else I heard."

"What's that?"

"Well, according to someone who I'd also call a reliable source, Bard was overheard on his phone saying something like, 'I got you cold, and when it gets out, the #metoo women are gonna be all over you.'"

"He said that?"

"Yup, in so many words. According to this source, who'd have no reason to lie."

Casey nodded. "So, who does that lead you to?"

"That's the problem, no one. Not yet anyway," Crawford said. He was not about to broach his state attorney theory to Casey. That was something he wasn't ready to go public with. Especially to a reporter.

Casey shrugged. "Well, just thought you'd want to know about that Al-Ansani thing. Consider it my scoop to you."

"Hey, I appreciate it," Crawford said. "I'd say it's time I have another conversation with Khalid."

CHIEF NORM RUTLEDGE DIDN'T WANT TO TOUCH THE Harlan Brody thing with a ten-foot pole. "That's like ... I don't know, J. Edgar Hoover killing someone," Rutledge said after Crawford put forward his theory in Rutledge's office.

Not the most timely comparison, but Rutledge's points of reference were frequently dated and often far-fetched.

"Or a famous football player and movie star," Crawford responded, "who ran through airports in commercials and ended up killing his ex-wife."

Ott nodded in agreement.

"He got off, right?" Rutledge said.

"Yeah, but come on," Crawford said, catching a whiff of something.

Ott had once commented about how Rutledge's office smelled of Chinese food and Labrador retriever farts. He had voiced his observation about the latter once immediately after he and Crawford had exited Rutledge's office.

"How is a Labrador retriever different from any other dog?" Crawford had asked.

Ott was ready with the answer. "All we had growing up were Labrador retrievers," he said with a shrug, "so they're the only ones I know."

At the time Crawford had just rolled his eyes, shaken his head, and let it die.

"So, Norm," Ott was revving up. "You don't think it's worth having a conversation with Harlan Brody? 'Cause, let me tell you, when he was in Charlie's office the other day, the man was out for Bard's blood." He turned to Crawford. "True, right?"

Crawford nodded his agreement.

"How do you propose this little Q&A of yours take place?" Rutledge said, already foisting the job off on Crawford and Ott.

"I don't know," Crawford said. "I've been thinking more about it, and maybe we get someone in his office, one of his assistants, to tell us where he was between twelve thirty and one forty-five yesterday. That way, if he's got an alibi, we don't need to talk to him."

"Or piss him off," Rutledge said. "What else is goin' on?"

"I'm getting the runaround from this guy Khalid Al-Ansani. Called him four times, no call back."

Crawford watched Rutledge conjure up a response. "Maybe he hopped on his magic carpet and beat it out of town?"

Crawford glanced at Ott, who looked like he was upwind of another Labrador retriever gas emission. "Time to dust off that résumé and get it over to *Saturday Night Live*, Norm."

"Come on, Ott, where's your sense of humor?"

Ott shook his head slowly. "Hey, we got two stiffs down at the morgue. And you're yukkin' it up here."

"All right, all right, who else do we need to talk about?"

"Joe Mitchell," Ott said. "I got my suspicions about him."

"You talk to him since Bard's murder?"

"Haven't tracked him down yet. Charlie said that golfer, Roddy Sproul, overheard Bard tell Mitchell something about a guy who was out to get him, then Bard said he was gonna turn the tables on him."

Rutledge perked up. "Well, doesn't that jibe with what what's-his-name ... Darnell said?"

Crawford nodded. "Tyrell. Yeah, it does, but I also got that *New Yorker* reporter telling me about a credible motive Al-Ansani might have."

"Sounds like you're kind of all over the place," said Rutledge.

"Yeah, at the moment we kind of are," Crawford said.

"Well, then, you need to do something about that," Rutledge said.

Crawford shot a quick glance at Ott. He could see that Ott was getting squirmy, the way he did when he had gotten his quota of Rutledge.

"All right, I'm going over to Bard's house now, and Mort's going to the man's office. Maybe we can dig something up."

"Let's hope so," Rutledge said, "'cause these two cases are starting to fester. And festering cases are not what we need in this town. Because when a case begins to fester—"

"Okay, Norm, we got the idea," Crawford said, heading him off at the pass before he could launch into a long riff that went nowhere.

Crawford and Ott quickly walked out of his office. The wit

and wisdom of Norman K. Rutledge, Crawford was thinking. Rutledge could no doubt write a book about his lifelong career in law enforcement. His title: *The Man, The Myth, The Legend.* Crawford's title: *The Life of a Perfectly Average Police Chief.*

27

CRAWFORD HAD CALLED EARLIER IN THE MORNING AND had spoken to Tyrell, who said it would be okay if Crawford came over to his father's—soon to be his and his brother's—house at ten o'clock. Crawford had asked crime scene tech and newly reinstated *friend with benefits* Dominica McCarthy to come along with him. The fact that he had missed the tiny scratch on the Cadillac CTS in The Colony Hotel surveillance tape, and she had spotted it, reminded him of just how good she was.

They got to Bard's house a few minutes late. Darnell opened the door.

"Hello, Detective, and—"

"My associate, Dominica McCarthy," Crawford said. "She was at your father's boat yesterday. She's a crime scene technician."

"I remember," Darnell said with a smile. "How could I forget?"

"Hello, again," Dominica said.

"So, you want to see his bedroom?"

"Yes, please," Crawford said.

"Just follow me."

"We would also like to take a look at his cell phone, if you know where it is. As you remember, yesterday he just had that burner on him."

"Yeah, I remember. I don't know where his iPhone is."

"Maybe we call the phone number when we get in his bedroom," Dominica suggested.

"Good idea."

They followed Darnell into a huge foyer with black and white tiles in a checkerboard pattern, through a large, expensively decorated living room Crawford guessed wasn't used much, then down a long, dark hallway and into a bedroom that had a massive bed.

There was a chaise lounge next to the bed which, surprisingly, had clothes stacked on it in a messy heap. "Surprisingly" because the rest of the house was so immaculate.

Darnell saw Crawford looking at it and chuckled. "Dad wasn't the neatest guy around. He'd just toss his clothes on that"—pointing at the chaise lounge—"before he went to bed."

"I can relate," Crawford said. "I do the same thing on a chair."

Dominica smiled, familiar with Crawford's clothes pile. She pulled out her Samsung Galaxy. "Why don't I call his cell number now."

"Good idea," Crawford said. "What's his number, Darnell?"

Dominica dialed it. A phone rang across the room. Crawford took out a pair of milk-white vinyl gloves, pulled them on, crossed the room, and opened a door. It was a walk-in closet that could have accommodated a Sherman tank. The ring seemed to be coming from a blue silk bathrobe hanging from a brass hook. Crawford reached into a pocket of the bathrobe and pulled out an iPhone, then went back out into the bedroom.

"You mind if we take this with us?" Crawford asked Darnell.

"No. Just bring it back, please."

"Don't worry," Crawford said, putting the iPhone in his pocket.

Dominica pointed at the heap of clothes. "That's probably a good place to start," she told Crawford. "Go through Mr. Bard's clothes. Check his pockets."

Crawford nodded.

"You don't need me to stick around, do you?" Darnell asked.

"No," Crawford said. "We probably won't be long. I'll come get you when we're done. Where will you be?"

"In the family room," Darnell said. "It's on the other side of the living room. Off the kitchen."

Crawford nodded. "I saw it. Thanks."

As Darnell walked out, Crawford and Dominica went over to the chaise lounge. Dominica picked up a pair of pants and went through the pockets. She found some change—two quarters, a dime, a nickel, and two pennies. She held them up to Crawford.

"You can't keep that, you know."

"Aw, darn."

Crawford picked up a pair of dark green shorts and reached in one of the pockets. He pulled out a handful of golf tees. "So, the guy really did play," he mumbled to himself.

"What?" asked Dominica.

"Nothing. Just found these."

Dominica smiled. "You *can* keep them."

"Gee, thanks."

Crawford's cell phone rang. He looked down at it. It was Ott, who was at Asher Bard's office on Royal Palm Way.

"Hey, Mort, what's up?"

"Got something good for you."

"I'm all ears."

"I just found Bard's checkbook and guess what? One of the last checks he wrote was for three hundred grand. Made out to Amazing Grace, LLC, the night Grace Spooner got killed."

28

CRAWFORD AND DOMINICA SPENT TEN MORE MINUTES AT Asher Bard's house and found nothing of interest except his cell phone. They were in a hurry to join Ott at 350 Royal Palm Way.

They parked in the underground parking area below Bard's office building and took the elevator up to the second floor. Ott introduced Dominica to Jennifer Atwood, and then Crawford, Ott, and Dominica went into Asher Bard's office.

"I pretty much turned the place upside down. Nothing much until I found this." Ott picked up a big black checkbook, the kind that had three checks to a page, opened it, and pointed at a stub. The date said "3/14/19" and, sure enough, it was made out to "Amazing Grace, LLC" for three hundred thousand dollars. The date was one day before Spooner was killed.

"Wow," Crawford said, looking at Ott. "This makes things a little more complicated."

Ott nodded. "No kidding. Not to mention, it leaves a lot of unanswered questions. Like, did he give it to her that night at the The Colony?"

Crawford nodded. "Did she change her mind once she got

the check—if she got the check—and decide she wasn't going to give Quinn Casey the interview?"

"Or what about this?" said Dominica. "Maybe Bard offered her the check, but she turned him down. Said she didn't care about the money, just wanted to get her story out there and testify. He got pissed off, realized the only way to stop her was to kill her."

"Yup," Crawford said to Dominica. "That definitely could've happened."

"We got a real problem here, boys," Dominica said, running a hand through her hair.

"What's that?" Crawford said.

"In all those scenarios, the principals are dead."

"Yeah," Ott said. "That is a problem."

"Did you find anything else?" Dominica asked Ott.

Ott pointed to a large file cabinet. "I haven't been through it yet."

"Looks like it might be a big project," Dominica said.

Ott nodded as Crawford saw movement and looked toward the door. He saw a flash of red fabric and remembered Jennifer Atwood was wearing a red silk top. He thought he saw Dominica glance over, too.

Crawford pointed to a laptop on the corner of Asher Bard's desk. "Taken a look at that yet?"

Ott shook his head. "Haven't had a chance. Mainly just went through his desk. His checkbook was in the top drawer."

"But you didn't see anything else that caught your interest?"

"Nah, the check was the big news."

"Quinn Casey told me that Grace Spooner never cancelled her breakfast with him," Crawford said.

Dominica nodded. "Which either means she never got the check from Bard, or she did and told him to keep it."

"Pretty tough to turn down that kind of money, though," Ott said.

"I got another scenario: she could have planned to cash Bard's check and screw him at the same time," Crawford said.

"You mean, take Bard's money *and* spill the beans to Casey?" Dominica said.

Crawford nodded. "Lots of ways she could have played it," he said. "I'm going to see if I can get a court order to check Bard's account and Grace's to see if the check was cashed."

"Good idea," Ott said. "Want a hand with that?"

"Nah, shouldn't be too difficult," Crawford said, opening the MacBook Air laptop.

The computer was on, which was fortunate. He'd assumed he'd have to ask Jennifer Atwood for the password.

He sat down in Bard's desk chair and started reading Bard's emails while Ott and Dominica attacked the large file cabinet.

Ten minutes later, Crawford had skimmed all of Bard's incoming and sent emails for the last ten days and had seen nothing that jumped out at him. They seemed mostly to go to and come from business contacts, or women. Clearly, Bard mixed business with pleasure. Crawford intended to get Jennifer Atwood's permission to take the laptop back to his office, where he could study it more closely.

He scanned the task bar and clicked *Reminders*. It looked pretty much like a to-do list. Things like, 'Golf shoes,' 'Tina re. St. Bart's trip,' 'Get Theranos book.' Then one caught his eye: 'Sub. beneficiaries to T and D.' He glanced out the big picture window, then back at the line in *Reminders*. A good guess was T and D were Tyrell and Darnell.

He turned to Ott and Dominica. "Got a quiz for you."

"Fire away," Ott said.

"Says here on his *Reminders*, 'Sub.'—S-u-b-dot—'beneficiaries to T and D.' What's that mean to you?"

"Simple," Dominica said without hesitation. "Substitute, in a will, somebody or somebodies for Tyrell and Darnell."

"Meaning, put Tyrell and Darnell in and take somebody else out?" Crawford asked.

Dominica nodded. "Yeah, exactly."

"Wow, you're quick," Ott said. "I was still trying to figure out who or what T and D were."

"So, are you thinking"—she turned to Crawford—"if Bard was taking somebody out of his will and replacing them with Tyrell and Darnell, that could possibly be a motive for murder?"

Crawford nodded. "Could be. What I've dug up about Bard is, one, he's never been married, and two, he was an only child. Which means he didn't have any natural heirs to leave his money to. Seems like Tyrell and Darnell were about to get the bid. But apparently Bard never got around to it."

"Or else it wouldn't still be in *Reminders*, you mean?" Dominica said.

"Exactly."

"You think we could get our hands on his will?" Ott asked.

"I don't know; I was thinking of that. We could try. Might be some worthwhile information in it." Crawford glanced toward the door separating Bard's office from Jennifer Atwood's office and saw what he thought was a shadow. "All right, Mort, why don't you stick around and go through the rest of that file cabinet."

"What are you gonna do?" Ott asked.

"Just drop in at Khalid Al-Ansani's house. Guy hasn't called me back, and I've got a lot more questions for him." Crawford turned to Dominica. "You want to help Mort or head back?"

"I've got to get back. I'm getting results on that burglary at the south end," Dominica said.

Crawford nodded. "All right, let's hit it then."

"See you, Mort," Dominica said.

"Later, beautiful."

Crawford and Dominica walked through the door into

Jennifer's office. She was on her computer. She turned to them and smiled. "Find anything useful?"

"A few things maybe," Crawford answered. "Would you mind if I took this computer with me?" He held it up. "I'd like to have a closer look at it back in my office."

She looked alarmed for a split second, but quickly erased it with a smile. "Sure, but how about … Can you maybe pick it up a little later? There are a few things on it I need for bookkeeping purposes. Also, a few bills on it I need to pay."

"Of course. But if I can get it as soon as possible, I'd appreciate it."

"No problem," Jennifer said. "Anything else?"

"Yes, do you have a copy of Mr. Bard's will, by any chance?"

Again, a flash of alarm; again, it evaporated quickly. "That's something you'll have to get from Mr. Bard's attorney, Berkman Ross."

"He didn't keep a copy here in the office?"

"No, I think maybe he did in the New York office."

"Could you give me Mr. Ross's phone number, please?"

"Sure." She wrote a number on a pad, tore it off, and handed it to him.

"Thanks," Crawford said. "And we appreciate your cooperation. My partner's gonna stick around a little longer."

"Sounds good," Jennifer said with another smile.

Crawford and Dominica went down to the underground parking lot and got into the Crown Vic.

Just as they did, Dominica's cell phone rang. She looked down at the caller ID. "The call I've been waiting for."

She clicked on the speakerphone. "Hey, Paul."

"Hey, doll," the male voice said.

"You're on speaker," Dominica said. "I'm with Charlie."

"Oh hey, Charlie … So I got a hit for you from that surveillance footage at the Town Docks parking lot. Turns out that a midnight blue Caddy CTS that was there when that guy got killed is registered to a certain John E. Begay."

"You're the best," Dominica said. "Took you a while, but it was worth the wait."

"Yeah, thanks, man," Crawford said.

"No prob. Catch you guys later." Paul clicked off.

Dominica turned to Crawford. "Well, well, isn't that interesting."

"Sure is. Mort and I need to pay the brothers a visit. Want to come?"

"When?"

"About an hour. I've got a re-interview with this guy Al-Ansani. Right after that."

Dominica shook her head. "'Fraid I can't. Got to dust for prints at the break-in."

"Well, we'll miss you."

"Thanks. Give those yahoo brothers my best," Dominica said. "On another subject, was it me, or did you notice Jennifer was kind of *hovering*?"

"I was just going to ask you that," Crawford said. "Like she was trying to eavesdrop, right?"

"Yeah, that was my impression."

Crawford shrugged. "Maybe just curious."

"Maybe."

CRAWFORD WAS BACK ON KHALID AL-ANSANI'S BACK porch, two houses down from Rose Clarke's, questioning the Saudi Arabian mystery man. Al-Ansani had answered the door himself and was apologetic about not having returned Crawford's many calls to him. He said a business "emergency" had come up that required his full attention which had now, he volunteered, been resolved. Crawford mused to himself that Khalid Al-Ansani, at least according to Quinn Casey, had

had more than his share of business emergencies over the years.

Crawford, nursing a glass of ice water, decided to plunge right in. "Mr. Al-Ansani, it's come to my attention from a reliable source that you have a substantial mortgage on a condo in New York City that you bought from Asher Bard."

"Yes, I do. What does that have to do with anything?"

"Was Bard about to foreclose on it?"

Al-Ansani shook his head. "His lawyer sent a few notices to me and my lawyer, but we would have worked it out—Asher and me."

That wasn't exactly a no.

"I was told the principal was forty million dollars and there was close to another ten million in deferred interest."

"Like I said, we would have worked it out." Al-Ansani said it like it was no big deal and the whole subject was starting to irk him.

"But haven't you had four years to *work it out?*"

Al-Ansani shook his head and took a long pull of his Perrier. "I get it. What you're implying is this may be a motive for me to have killed Asher. Is that it?"

"You tell me. Is it?"

"I don't make a habit of going around killing my friends."

But what about your enemies?

Crawford nodded. "That's good to know. And while I'm tossing out hypotheticals and possible motives, what about this one? The woman who was murdered at The Colony, Grace Spooner, and who, I believe, was going to testify that you had sex with her when she was a minor, was there at the exact same time that you were there. At The Colony. You were on the second floor, she was in the penthouse."

Al-Ansani rolled his eyes theatrically. "And I never went anywhere near the penthouse. Not only that, I had no idea she was there. How was I supposed to know that?"

At least he wasn't denying knowing Grace Spooner this time.

"I don't know. One hypothetical would be that Asher Bard told you she was there. Maybe—and this just came to me this moment—maybe Bard told you she was there and suggested you, let's say, eliminate Grace Spooner as a witness in exchange for discharging part of, or maybe all of, your debt to him."

"Do you really believe any of these preposterous allegations?"

"I wouldn't call them allegations. They're just ... what-ifs, conjectures, theories. You'd be surprised how many what-ifs, conjectures, and theories turn out to be what actually happened."

Al-Ansani tapped on the table impatiently. "Look, I've been very cooperative with you, and I've listened to all of your nonsense, but I really don't want to do it anymore. So, in the future, if you want to talk to me again, call my lawyer. His name is Anthony Barton. But, please, if you're just going to float nonsensical scenarios, don't waste either of our time."

Crawford got to his feet. "Thank you very much, Mr. Al-Ansani, for suffering through my nonsensical scenarios. If you do see me again, I will be reading you your rights and pushing your head down right before you get in the back of my police car."

29

CRAWFORD PICKED UP OTT AT THE STATION AT ELEVEN thirty a.m., and they drove over to the Puss in Boots in West Palm.

They got no answer when Crawford leaned on the buzzer at eleven forty-five.

"I got a feeling people in this line of work don't see a whole lot of the morning," Ott said.

"I got a feeling you're right," Crawford said with a nod. "Tell you what, let's go around back. I think there's a back entrance to the Puss executive suite."

They walked around back and saw the same black Ford F-150 pick-up and Cadillac CTS parked in the same spots as when Crawford and Dominica had visited the strip club.

Ott flicked his head at the truck and car. "The executive vehicles?"

"Yup." Crawford pointed. "That's the Caddy Dominica spotted."

They walked up to a door and Ott hit the buzzer. After a few moments, they heard the thudding sounds of slow-moving footsteps.

The door opened a crack. Frank Begay squinted out, naked except for frayed Jockey underwear.

He groaned. "Not open. Come back at five."

Crawford pushed the door open. Begay didn't resist.

"We need to have a few words with your brother," Crawford said.

"So, 'zat mean I can go back to bed?"

"No. Since you're up, you're included, too."

Another groan.

"Go get him, will ya?" Ott said as he and Crawford walked in.

"All right, all right," Frank said, shuffling off.

"This place smells a lot like Rutledge's office," Crawford said.

Ott nodded knowingly. "Labrador retrievers."

Johnnie Begay appeared. Same Jockey underwear, but his had a hole in one side.

"How 'bout you put some clothes on," Ott said.

"What the fuck is this?" Johnnie snarled.

"Put a shirt on, at least," Ott said. "It's too early in the morning to look at your flaccid bodies."

"Whatever the fuck that means," Johnnie said.

"You just roll out of bed sayin' *fuck*, Johnnie?" Ott said.

"Fuckin' right. What do you want?"

Frank came out of the back and threw a blue plaid shirt at his brother.

"We want to ask you some questions," Crawford said.

"Jesus Christ," Johnnie said. "Not again."

"A few days back, your car was caught on camera at the lot on Australian in Palm Beach. What were you doing there?"

Johnnie glanced at Frank and smiled broadly.

Crawford had a sudden premonition that he wasn't going to like the answer.

Johnnie scanned the room with his hand. "You think this

place is all I got to show for years of hard work and keepin' my nose clean?"

"Answer the question," Ott said.

"Hold on," Johnnie said. "I'm tryin' to answer it. I got a Regulator 41 down there at the docks."

"What's that?" Crawford asked.

"A fishing boat," Ott told his partner.

"A hell of a nice fishing boat," Johnnie said.

"So, exactly where were you the day before yesterday between twelve thirty and one forty-five?" Crawford asked.

"On my boat," Johnnie said. "About three miles out."

"You know Asher Bard?" Crawford asked. "And don't bullshit me like last time."

Johnnie sighed and rubbed his unshaven face. "Once upon a time a long time ago I knew him. Haven't seen him or said a word to him since ... shit, ten years ago."

Crawford looked over at Frank.

"Yeah, same with me," Frank said.

"So, that's what you woke us up for?" Johnnie asked.

"Yeah. And to see if you found out who put the wood to my partner the other night," Ott said.

Johnnie shook his head.

Ott glanced at Frank. "How about you?"

"No idea."

"Okay, boys, we're done. You can go back to bed," Crawford said, heading to the door.

Ott's eyes were stuck on Johnnie's holey underwear. "Ever thought about getting one of your girlfriends to darn up those skivvies of yours?"

30

"Score one for the Begays," Crawford said.

"Yeah," Ott said, getting into the Vic. "You never heard of a Regulator?"

Crawford turned the car key. "Nah, not much of a fisherman."

"So, how you feel about having Norm in on the Archie-girls interview?" Ott asked.

"Knowing him, he'll probably try to score their phone numbers."

Khalid Al-Ansani had jumped to the top of Crawford's list as a leading candidate for the murders of Grace Spooner and Asher Bard. Also-rans for either, or both, murders were—in no particular order—Lord Ainslie Sunderland, Joe Mitchell, and Harlan Brody. Scratched from contention were Johnnie and Frank Begay. Long shots included... well, there really weren't any to speak of at the moment.

Crawford was back at his office, making calls and wrapping up loose ends. He had just called the office of State

Attorney Harlan Brody. He had asked for 'Mr. Brody's appointments assistant,' which in the old days would have meant his secretary. He had been bounced around—reminding him of his experiences with the Motor Vehicle Department—for the last fifteen minutes. If there was one thing Crawford wasn't, it was patient, and he was getting frustrated.

"State attorney's office," said a chirpy voice.

"My name is Detective Crawford, Palm Beach Police. I'm working on an investigation and would appreciate you telling me where the state attorney was yesterday between the hours of approximately twelve thirty and one forty-five."

"Why do you want to know?" the woman asked, going from chirpy to all business.

"I'm just trying to establish a time line," he said, not even sure what he meant by that.

"The state attorney was down in Miami for a morning conference, Detective. Then a twelve-thirty lunch with donors."

"So when did he get back to his office, do you know?"

"Around four. I'm still not sure why you want this information."

"Well, thank you very much," Crawford said, eager to end the conversation. He clicked off.

So much for Harlan Brody as a suspect ... No self-respecting politician aspiring for higher office would ever miss a donor's lunch: the opportunity to put the bite on rich people eager to buy some influence always had to be a top priority.

Crawford just wished he hadn't had to identify himself but knew that without saying who he was, he wouldn't have gotten the information.

OTT HAD MADE AN APPOINTMENT WITH JOE MITCHELL.

This time, instead of a stroll on the beach, they were meeting at Mitchell's house on Indian Road.

Ott was met at the door by the same housekeeper he encountered last time he was there.

He followed her back to Mitchell's home office that had floor-to-ceiling bookshelves on three sides. He noticed half a shelf, above Mitchell's head, seemed to be the entire oeuvre of the news anchor Bill O'Reilly. *Killing Kennedy, Killing Nixon, Killing Reagan, Killing Patton* ... Ott had a silent chuckle to himself. Everything except *Killing Bard*.

Mitchell gave Ott a dead-fish handshake. "So, what can I do for you this time, Detective?"

"Quite an impressive collection of books, Mr. Mitchell."

"Thanks. Are you a reader?"

Ott leaned back in his chair. "I read about twelve books a year. You know, one a month."

"Oh, really."

"Yes, but there are only three authors I read."

"And who would they be?"

"Stephen King, Harlan Coben, and Lee Child. Between the three of them, they knock out about twelve books a year."

Mitchell's eyes narrowed. "I see. So, you just read popular fiction then?" It was clearly a put-down.

Ott nodded. "Yeah, whatever you want to call it."

Mitchell glowered. "Well, what can I do for you?"

"You can remember a conversation you had on the golf course a while back. You were playing with Asher Bard, Robbie Sproul, and I'm not sure who the fourth was."

"Yes, I remember. The fourth was Eric Hobson."

Ott wrote the name down in his dog-eared notebook. "We've heard that during that round of golf, Mr. Bard directed a comment to you. He told you someone had threatened him, but he'd learned or come across something that was going to 'turn the tables' on that person. Sound familiar? Do you remember him saying that, Mr. Mitchell?"

"No, but it sounds like Asher. He was always trying to get leverage on everyone."

Ott leaned toward Mitchell and turned up the volume. "Are you saying you don't remember him saying that to you, or who he was talking about?"

"That's what I'm saying. I think the person who told you this—who I deduce was Roddy Sproul—had me confused with someone else."

"The only 'someone else' it could have been is the man you just told me about, Eric Hobson."

"Yes, so I suggest you talk to Eric."

"Mr. Mitchell, my source was sure it was you who Bard said that to."

Mitchell shrugged. "I don't know what to tell you, but it wasn't. Maybe you should ask *your source* how many of those South African beers he'd had before he heard this."

AFTER CRAWFORD GOT OFF THE PHONE WITH HARLAN Brody's assistant, he called Berkman Ross, Asher Bard's attorney. The law firm's receptionist asked him for his name, and he said, "Detective Crawford, Palm Beach Police." A few moments later Berkman Ross picked up.

He skipped the *hello*. "I'm assuming this has to do with Asher Bard, Detective?"

"Yes, it does. I'm one of the investigators on his murder. My first question is, did Asher Bard ever tell you about someone who had threatened him or whom he may have feared?"

"Not that I'm aware of. Wasn't my job to keep track of Asher's enemies, but I'm sure he had a few."

"Next question is, do you have in your possession, or know where I can get my hands on, Mr. Bard's will?"

"What do you need that for?"

"I'm hoping it may shed light on who his killer might be. It's kind of a long shot but worth checking into."

"Yes, I do have a copy. It's funny, because he called me last week and said he wanted to come in and change something on it."

"Did he say what?"

There was a long pause.

"No, but I could take a guess."

"Tell me."

Ross sighed. "Couple weeks ago, he talked about cutting his assistant out of it."

"You're talking about Jennifer Atwood?"

"That's who I'm talking about."

"Why was he going to do that?"

"It's kind of a long story, but she's in his will for ten million dollars."

"Wow, he was a generous boss."

"Well, there's more than meets the eye about their relationship—" He paused like he wasn't sure he should go on.

Crawford realized he needed to give Ross a little prod. "Keep going, Mr. Ross, this may be critical to my investigation."

"Well, Asher's dead, so I suppose the usual discretion isn't necessary anymore. See, back about twenty years ago, Jen was Asher's girlfriend. Not totally exclusive because ... well, I'm sure by now you know all about his appetite for women. At one point, she kind of manipulated him into asking her to marry him. Then, he reneged. But along the way, she got him to put her in his will."

"To the tune of ten million dollars."

"Exactly. But then a couple months ago he was in here on another subject, and he started talking about Jen. How he pays her five hundred thousand a year, not to mention a big bonus and, you know ... how that was plenty. Why did he also need to leave her ten million? Particularly since those two boys, Tyrell and Darnell, had become so important in his life."

Crawford was digesting the numbers. "He was paying her five hundred thousand a year? Plus a bonus?"

"Yeah, the bonus worked out to another two to three hundred thousand."

"That's incredible. And, as of right now, Jennifer Atwood's still in Bard's will as a ten-million-dollar beneficiary?"

"Sure is. As of now and forever. That's the will that's gonna stand unless—"

Crawford could imagine the light bulb snapping on over Berkman Ross' head.

"Okay, I get it now. You're asking me these questions because you suspect Jen may have had something to do with Asher's murder?"

"I'm looking at everyone in his life," Crawford said. "What about Tyrell and Darnell, what were they getting?"

"Well, they both had trust funds ... and now I'm thinking what you probably suspect, that maybe Asher was going to will Jen's ten mill to the boys."

The problem was there was no way in hell Crawford could see Jennifer wielding a forty-pound kettlebell as a murder weapon. Not that she couldn't hire someone to do it.

"So," said Crawford, "since yesterday you've had plenty of time to think about who might have killed your client. Who have you come up with?"

"The state attorney, Harlan Brody, hated Asher with a passion," Ross said. "I know what you're thinking ... a guy that high up would never do it."

"Anyone else?"

"Why are you dismissing Brody?"

"I just am."

"Why?"

"Trust me, I looked at him, but he's got a solid alibi."

Ross sighed. "Damn," he said. "Nobody I'd love to see in the slammer more than that arrogant prick."

"Sorry," Crawford said as his cell phone rang. "Thank you very much for the help. Gotta take this other call." He clicked off.

"Hello."

"Crawford, what the hell are you up to?" Speak of the devil, it was a clearly apoplectic Harlan Brody.

"'Scuse me?" Crawford said innocently.

"You know damn well. Calling my office and asking 'em where I was when Asher Bard was killed."

"Oh, that? Mr. Brody, my partner and I make about a hundred calls like that in the course of a typical investigation," said Crawford, exaggerating it about threefold. "It's called a routine question, and I'm sorry if you were offended."

"Offended. Are you fucking kidding me, I was totally pissed off. You pull a stunt like that again and, I promise you, you're in deep, deep shit."

Crawford's first instinct was to push back, but he let it go. "I said I'm sorry. I'm in the middle of an important interview and need to go now."

IT WAS WHAT CRAWFORD CALLED A "CATCH-UP" SESSION and Ott referred to as a "shoot the shit" session. Both of them were reviewing what they had done, or found out about the two cases, in the twenty-four hours since they last sat down together.

Ott told Crawford he'd spent another two hours going through the big file cabinet in Asher Bard's office but hadn't come up with anything like the three-hundred-thousand-dollar bombshell: the check to Grace Spooner. It was mostly files relating to Bard's business. Crawford asked him if he happened to notice that Jennifer Atwood seemed to be spending an inordinate amount of time keeping an eye on what the three of them were saying and doing in Asher Bard's office when they were all there. Ott said he'd been aware but had chalked it up to natural curiosity to learn what they'd found out about her longtime boss. Crawford flashed back to what he had seen on Asher Bard's computer and made a mental note to go and get the MacBook Air from Jennifer Atwood once he and Ott were done.

Next, Crawford summed up his conversation with Bard's lawyer, Berkman Ross. He grabbed Ott's full attention by starting out saying, "You're about to go on a date with a multi-millionaire."

Crawford left out the part about Bard's eleventh-hour desire to change his will. His gut still told him Jennifer Atwood was a long shot for the murders, and he didn't want to dampen his partner's spirits unnecessarily.

When he'd finished replaying his conversation with Berkman Ross, Ott said, "Wow, five hundred K a year and another two hundy in bonus. I should marry that woman and retire from my long, distinguished career in law enforcement."

"Yeah, but before you marry her, you gotta at least have one date with her."

"Coming right up."

"Might want to get a ring beforehand."

Ott chuckled. "I should."

Crawford stood up.

"Where you going?" Ott asked.

"To see Jennifer."

"You bastard, you gonna try to steal her away from me, aren't you?"

Crawford laughed. "I'm gonna get Asher Bard's computer."

Ott chuckled. "Yeah, a likely story."

CRAWFORD WENT OVER TO JENNIFER'S OFFICE AT 350 Royal Palm Way, got the MacBook Air without incident, then brought it back to his office.

He spent the next hour going over Bard's emails again. This time he went back two months on both Asher's sent and received emails. There were some steamy back-and-forths with a number of women, some vituperative rebukes of executives in his media company over a takeover that had apparently blown up, some kindhearted messages to adopted sons Tyrell and Darnell, and many notes to Jennifer Atwood requesting her to attend to certain tasks. But what there wasn't was a smoking gun. Nothing even close. Crawford had hoped for more.

He closed the computer and looked at his watch. It was 7:10 and his stomach was growling. It was time to call it a night. Then he had one last thought. He picked up the computer again and punched *Reminders* on the task bar. He scrolled down, not finding what he was looking for, then scrolled up and down one more time.

But the reminder that had said "Sub. beneficiaries to T and D" was nowhere to be found.

31

THERE WAS NO MYSTERY WHO HAD ERASED 'SUB. beneficiaries to T and D.'

Crawford called Ott right away. "You getting ready for your big date?"

"I'm actually on my way to pick her up. What's up?"

"That thing about Tyrell and Darnell under *Reminders* in Bard's computer? It miraculously disappeared."

Ott didn't hesitate. "So, Jennifer disappeared it, huh?"

"Only person who could have."

"Okay, after a couple glasses of wine and once I've got her under my spell, I'll slip into a little business Q&A."

"That'll be romantic."

Ott laughed. "I don't hear you telling me not to."

"Maybe we're both guilty of what Dominica and Rose always accuse me of."

"The case first, everyone else second?"

"Something like that."

Crawford heard Ott flick on his blinker.

"Think we got a problem, Charlie?"

"I don't know. Maybe."

"Gotta go, I'm at her house."

"Dazzle her, big man."

"That's your department, but I'll do my best."

CRAWFORD GOT ANOTHER CALL FROM DAVID BALFOUR. "How'd it go?"

"Good and bad," Balfour said. "I was a very convincing bluffer. Missy bought it that you broke in to Jenkins's studio."

"And the bad?"

He exhaled. "Jenkins beat the hell out of Missy."

"What for?"

"She said he was pissed off about all the work he did for nothing."

"You mean, painting the fakes."

"Yeah."

"How's she doing ... Missy?"

"Not so good. She's at Good Sam"—Good Samaritan Medical Center in West Palm Beach—"with a concussion, a broken arm, and bruises all over her face."

"Jesus, I'm sorry."

"Will you go after the guy, Charlie?"

"Jesus, David, I can't now. I'm going twenty-four seven on my two homicides," Crawford said. "Tell you what I'll do, though. I got a guy here I'll put on it. Name's Bob Shepley, he's a real bulldog."

OTT HAD HER LAUGHING FROM THE GET-GO. TELLING HER stories about his past life in Cleveland had a way of doing that.

Jennifer was looking at a menu now.

"If we were in Cleveland, one of the entrees would be *The Polish Boy*, which you'd find hard to resist," Ott said.

"Do tell: What's *The Polish Boy*?"

"Grilled kielbasa, French fries, and coleslaw all crammed into a monster bun and doused with barbecue sauce. See, in Cleveland, fries are a condiment."

"Sounds yummy. What other local favorites would I find irresistible?"

"Glad you asked. If *The Polish Boy* didn't whet your appetite, I would heartily recommend a pierogi."

Jennifer cocked her head. "I'm not familiar with a pierogi."

"A pierogi is an Eastern European dumpling that you fill with potato, cheese, and sauerkraut, then top it off with sautéed onions, heavy on the butter, with a generous dollop of sour cream."

"Wow, that sounds delicious. I'm ready to move."

Ott laughed. "Do I detect a note of sarcasm?"

"Maybe a tad," she said, holding up her thumb and forefinger, half an inch apart. "I've always wanted to live in a place that has a burning river."

"Yeah, the good ol' Cuyahoga. We're best known for that and the Rock & Roll Hall of Fame."

"Well, the Rock & Roll Hall of Fame truly is something to be proud of."

"Yeah, no kidding, all those guitars from my rock gods," Ott said. "Not to mention John Lennon's elementary school report card, James Brown's jumpsuit with SEX spelled out in rhinestones, and my favorite, Jim Morrison's Cub Scout uniform."

Jennifer laughed. "That's hard to picture. Jim Morrison in a Cub Scout uniform."

"No kidding. But he came from a military background. His father was an admiral in the Navy."

"Yeah, I guess I knew that."

Ott had been looking for a segue to the Asher Bard case as they ordered dinner and another glass of wine.

The Rock & Roll Hall of Fame wasn't much of a segue, but it was time.

"Jennifer, can I ask you about something?"

"Sure. Anything." She laughed. "Well, maybe not *anything*. This *is* our first date."

He put his hand on her hand. "I'm a cop, right?"

"Is a detective the same thing as a cop?"

"Pretty much. I'm actually a homicide cop. Meaning I just do homicides."

"Okay," she said with a smile, "where are you going with this, Mort?"

"So, I'll cut to the chase. As you know, my partner and I are the lead detectives on your boss's murder, and I have a bunch of questions for you."

Jennifer's smile slid into a frown, and she pulled her hand out from under his. "Is that why you asked me out to dinner, to spring twenty questions on me?"

Ott shook his head robustly. "No, I asked you out for dinner because I found you attractive. And, by the way, I don't have twenty questions."

"What, only fifteen?"

"Fact is, when I asked you out, I didn't plan to talk about Asher Bard's murder at all, but since then certain things have ... come up."

"Like what?"

"Well, like the fact that something disappeared from *Reminders* on Asher Bard's computer."

Her eyes darted away from Ott's. "Okay," she said slowly. "Guilty."

"Why did you do that?"

"Because I thought if you two saw that, it would open up a whole can of worms."

"Well, we did see it, and now that can of worms is open. You might as well tell me about whatever it is you were trying to hide."

"How long do you have?"

"All night."

Jennifer sighed. "Okay, you asked for it."

Ott nodded.

"Twenty years ago, I was hired by Asher Bard as his personal secretary. I always suspected it was, well, because of my looks. I'd never really had a bona fide job before—" She paused, like she wasn't sure she wanted to go on. "Anyway, about a year into it, it developed into more than a job."

Ott knew when to hold his tongue.

Jennifer sighed again. "So ... we, ah, started sleeping together. I guess I kind of looked at it as a boyfriend-girlfriend thing, but under wraps. He didn't want anybody to know about it. I didn't really know why. At one point, he talked about getting married, and, I have to admit, I was game. I thought I loved him, but then I started to notice things about him. The most obvious was that he was a serial cheater. But, also, a few ... um, other things."

"Like what?"

"Well, he lied to people, but it was almost like he didn't know he was doing it," Jennifer said. "So anyway, one day I discovered I was pregnant." She took a long sip of her chardonnay. "I told Asher I wanted to have the child. He tried to talk me out of it, but I was adamant ..."

Ott noticed tears forming in her eyes.

"So, I had the baby. Named her Laura." Jennifer's breathing became more labored, and her voice dropped lower. "Laura was born with autism, which turned out to be what's now called low-functioning autism or level three autism. Meaning as severe as it can possibly get. Poor girl needs around-the-clock care. Yes, she's still alive—oh, God, aren't you glad you asked me out, Mort. What a fun date, huh?" Jennifer tried to laugh through the tears that she was mightily trying to hide.

Ott put his hand on hers again. This time she didn't pull it away.

"While I'm spilling all these secrets, I've got something that might actually be helpful to you."

"I'm all ears."

"Okay, so a few days before Asher was killed, I heard him say something like, 'you expose me and I'll expose you.' Then he said, and I remember this loud and clear, 'you get your girls to rat me out, and I'll get mine to do the same to you.' And now you're going to ask me who was he talking to and, I'm sorry, but I have absolutely no idea."

"No idea at all?"

She shook her head. "Sorry, Asher spent half the day on the phone."

"I appreciate everything you've told me"—he patted her hand—"and I'm glad you're sharing all this with me."

"Yes, but I mean, on a first date? It must be a little overwhelming."

"Maybe this is a special first date."

Jennifer went on to tell Ott about all the caregivers she had coming and going throughout the day when she worked for Asher Bard and how he rarely visited his child. To his credit, or maybe because of his guilt, from that point on, he compensated Jennifer very generously.

The waiter brought their entrees, which they ignored. Ott told Jennifer that he had a niece with autism, but clearly it was not as severe as Laura's.

He glanced at his watch. It was already ten fifteen.

"You want to hear the other half now?" Jennifer said.

"The other half?"

"Yes. See, I figure if I keep blathering away, you'll never get around to asking me your next question."

"I've already forgotten my questions," Ott said, waving the waiter off as he approached with the wine bottle. "So, what's the other half?"

"About Asher. Something I was sworn to secrecy about,

but since he's ... no longer with us, guess I don't have to keep it a secret anymore."

"And that would be?"

"That Tyrell and Darnell are his natural sons."

Ott's head snapped back.

"Weren't expecting that, were you? Asher went out with this model up in New York. A pretty well-known black model whose name I'm not going to disclose. One thing I'll say about Asher is he was fertile. So anyway, he made up a story about adopting them when their mother was killed in a car accident. His cook or something."

"I heard she was his cleaning lady."

"Whatever. It wasn't true."

"So, what about taking you out of his will?"

She looked surprised. "You knew it was me?"

"My partner talked to Berkman Ross. Why was he going to do that?"

Jennifer smiled and nodded. "Because I went to Asher and said in so many words, 'give the money to the boys.' Even with all Laura's caregiving and medications, I was putting away a ton of money every year. I'd finally gotten to the point where I had enough to last me three lifetimes, and Laura's set for life, too. Plus, she was in his will anyway. Might as well let the boys have it. Go buy themselves a Lamborghini or something. Asher never really spent that much on them."

Ott patted her hand. "Wow, that's quite a story."

"Every word is true. I'm sorry about erasing that thing on Asher's *Reminders*. I just didn't want to explain the whole thing. But, turns out, you're a pretty good listener."

"Here's the only problem," Ott said with a smile. "Now that there's nothing left to talk about, I'm worried about our second date."

"I'm sure we can come up with something," Jennifer said with a smile. "We can always just go to the movies."

32

After a good-night kiss at Jennifer's house in the Northwood historic district of West Palm Beach, Ott called Crawford and filled him in on his long conversation with her. Then he told Crawford, who had never thought of Jennifer as anything but a long-shot suspect in Asher Bard's death, that in no way was she involved. There were women who had men killed for money—there were even some women who could kill a man with a forty-pound kettlebell, or at least hire someone to do it—but Jennifer Atwood was not one of them.

Ott was in bed by eleven forty-five and in Crawford's office at seven thirty the next morning. Crawford had a Dunkin' Donuts extra-large coffee, and Ott had his big mitt wrapped around a container of office rotgut.

They had barely had time to sit down when they heard the unmistakable thudding steps of Chief Norm Rutledge.

"Oh, shit," Ott said two seconds before Rutledge poked in his head with the black-shoe-polish hair.

"I got a call last night," Rutledge said, glaring at Crawford, "from the state attorney."

"Oh, shit," Ott said again. "What did he want?"

Rutledge sat down on a windowsill. "Seems your partner was inquiring as to Brody's whereabouts when Asher Bard was killed."

"Yeah, Norm, we talked about this day before yesterday. Do you have no recollection of that conversation?"

"Yeah, we talked about it but didn't decide on anything."

"We all agreed even state attorneys can have deadly motives."

"Yeah. Yeah. Yeah. Anyway, Brody suggested maybe I needed to step in here and get these cases wrapped up. He said, and I quote, 'When the lead detective's crawlin' up my ass, looking at *me* as the possible killer, then it's clear he ain't got jack-shit.'"

Crawford wondered how it was that all these people had crystal-clear memories of past conversations.

"Christ, we're only a week into the first case," Ott said. "Did you point out to the state attorney that we got a pretty good clearance record?"

"He knew that. But we're talking about now. The present tense. Not last year or the year before."

"Okay," Crawford said. "So what's this all mean? What are we supposed to do that we're not already doing?"

Rutledge looked totally blank. Then, after a moment, "Well, that's what I wanted to talk to you about."

"Okay, so let's talk," said Crawford.

"Hey, don't get that way," Rutledge said. "A lot of guys would welcome me in."

Crawford did a quick search of his brain and couldn't think who 'a lot of guys' might possibly be. "Tell you what, Norm, since you're dying to get involved, here's something you'll want to be in on."

"What's that?"

"Our interview with the three women who provided entertainment at Asher Bard's birthday party last week."

A smile appeared on Rutledge's face. "And just what kind of entertainment did they provide?"

"The kind where a lot of skin is displayed," Ott chimed in.

Rutledge smiled his lecherous smile. "I actually think I'd be very helpful. I'm particularly good at eliciting confessions."

"Oh, are you, now?" Crawford said. "Because these women are not suspects."

"Well, I'm good with women in general."

Crawford shot Ott a quick eye roll.

"I saw that," Rutledge said.

"Dude would have enjoyed Puss in Boots," Ott said to Crawford.

"What's that?" Rutledge asked.

"You playin' dumb, Norm?" Ott asked.

"Never heard of it," Rutledge said.

"It's a strip club in West Palm," Crawford said.

Rutledge's smile widened. "You guys seem to have a lot of *interesting* interviews."

"These three women," Crawford said, "their names are Veronica, Betty, and Midge. That ring a bell at all?"

Rutledge brightened. "Sure. The girls in *Archie*."

Just as Crawford figured, Rutledge read a lot of comics. Probably still did.

33

Crawford, Ott, and Rutledge had just gathered in Crawford's office when his desk phone rang.

It was Janine at the reception desk. "I got a Veronica, Betty, and Midge here."

"Thanks, Nance. Show the ladies back, please."

"You got it."

Two minutes later, they walked in. "Welcome back," Crawford said. "Norm"—he extended a hand toward Rutledge—"this is Veronica, Betty, and Midge."

Rutledge bowed slightly. "Enchanté, ladies."

No. He didn't actually say that?

Betty glanced at Crawford and almost cracked up.

The women all sat down in the extra chairs Ott had brought in. Once again, except for Midge, they were dressed for Sunday services: Veronica in a dark dress that fell below her knees, Betty in the same pantsuit she wore last time, and Midge in a dark dress that sported relatively modest cleavage.

"So, ladies, as I told my chief here"—Crawford glanced at Rutledge—"we were just beginning to talk last time when my partner, Detective Ott, and I got pulled away on other business."

"The murder of Asher Bard," Ott added.

Veronica, Betty, and Midge nodded.

"So, here's what we need to know. When you were at CPB, the restaurant, and The Colony Hotel, did any of you see anything that was in any way suspicious, or out of the ordinary, or that just didn't seem right to you?"

"What the detective is trying to say is," Rutledge put in, "was there anything that made you think a crime either was about to be committed or had been committed?" He leaned forward as if he wanted to sneak a closer look at Midge's chest.

Betty was the first to respond. "I'm sorry but I didn't see a thing. I mean, everything just seemed pretty normal. Guys drinking a lot, a lot of laughs, everyone just, well, just having fun."

Veronica and Midge nodded.

"Yeah, I mean, me, too. I agree with that," Veronica said.

"What about in the hotel?" Crawford asked, taking out a photo of Grace Spooner. "Did you ever see this woman at all?"

The three passed the photo between them, and all shook their heads.

"Which one of you was with Asher Bard?" Ott asked.

None of them moved to answer.

"Look, you're not going to get in trouble," Crawford said. "We just need to know."

Midge's eyes flicked to Betty.

"Promise me I won't get in trouble?" Betty said.

"You have my word as Chief of the Palm Beach Police Department," Rutledge said pompously.

"You sure?" Betty said.

Rutledge gave her a smarmy smile and nodded.

"Can I smoke here?" Betty asked nervously.

"Sorry," Crawford said.

"Okay, I was with him," Betty said, clutching her purse with white knuckles.

"And did he ever leave the room?" Crawford asked.

Betty shook her head. "Nope."

"And after ... when you left, did you leave together?"

"Yup. Went back to the restaurant."

"And did you see him leave the restaurant after that?" Ott asked.

Betty shook her head.

Crawford eyed Veronica and Midge, then came back to Veronica. "You were with the man with the turban, right?"

She nodded.

"Same question. Did he ever leave the room?"

"No."

"And you went back to the restaurant together ... after?"

She nodded. "Well, what happened was, I left first, and he came a little after me. I figured he didn't want to be seen with me. You know, in case he knew someone staying at the hotel."

"I understand," Crawford said. "And you didn't see him leave?"

Veronica shook her head.

"So, that leaves you, Midge," Rutledge said with a fawning smile. "I had an aunt named Midge."

"That's not my real name."

"Your *nom de plume,* huh?"

"What?"

"So, who were you with?" Rutledge asked.

"Lord Sunderland."

"So, as my men asked the other girls, did he ever leave the room while you were there?"

"Yes, he did."

Rutledge's eyes went wide. "He did?"

"Yes, for ten, maybe fifteen minutes."

"And about what time would you say this was?" Rutledge asked.

"Eleven or so."

Rutledge smiled at Crawford, then Ott.

"Did he say where he went?" Rutledge asked.

"No, he didn't," Midge said to Rutledge, "but I have to tell you, Detective, he was very drunk."

"I'm the chief. My men are detectives."

"Sorry ... Chief," Midge said.

"That's okay," Rutledge said. "So, he just came back and didn't say anything about where he'd been?"

"I didn't ask. Tell you the truth, I kind of nodded off for a little while."

"So, it could have actually been more than ten or fifteen minutes?" Crawford cut in.

"Coulda been, I guess."

"Did you notice anything different about him? When he came back," Ott asked. "Maybe he was breathing faster or something. Or maybe you saw ... some blood on him."

"It was dark. I didn't notice anything like that. He was still really drunk."

"So, then what happened?" Rutledge asked.

"We got dressed and went back to the restaurant."

"And you didn't see him leave CPB after that?"

"No."

"Thank you, Midge," Rutledge said, smiling triumphantly. "Thank you very much."

"You're welcome."

Betty, still holding tightly onto her purse, spoke up. "I did see someone famous, though."

"Oh, yeah? Who was that?" Crawford asked.

"Well, not famous, but I'm kind of a news junkie. A guy I've seen on the news a few times."

Ott caught Crawford's attention and mouthed, *Joe Mitchell*.

"Is the man's name Joe Mitchell?"

"I'm not really sure, but that doesn't sound familiar."

Ott had his iPad out and Googled Mitchell. A block of photos came up. "Is this the man?" Ott asked, handing Betty his iPad.

She took it from him. "No, the man I saw wasn't as old as him. He was wearing a blue baseball cap. I've seen him on CNN or maybe it was MSNBC."

"When you saw him in the hotel," Crawford asked, "what was he doing? Where was he?"

"Waiting for an elevator."

"Was he alone?" Ott asked.

"Yes, I think so."

"Not with that woman, Grace Spooner?" Crawford asked.

"Definitely not."

"Was it Joe Scarborough?" Rutledge asked.

"No, I know who he is. Definitely not him."

"Chris Matthews?" Rutledge asked.

Betty shook her head.

"Wolf Blitzer?"

"Okay, Norm," Crawford said, "we can't go through the entire CNN and MSNBC rosters."

Rutledge looked chastened.

"He's not an anchor," Betty said. "Just on every once in a while."

Crawford nodded. "Tell you what," he said, reaching for his wallet and a card, "if you remember who it is, or if you see him on TV, call me, please."

"I sure will," Betty said.

Crawford looked at Rutledge. "Got anything more?"

Rutledge shook his head. "No, I don't think so. You got the ladies' phone numbers, I presume?"

Crawford nodded.

"I want to thank you for your cooperation," Rutledge said.

"Mort, anything else?" Crawford glanced at Ott.

Ott shook his head. "Nope. I think that does it."

"Okay, well, thanks," Crawford said, and they all got to their feet.

The women nodded and walked toward the door.

When they were out of earshot, Rutledge said, "Now that's what I call a productive interview."

"You mean with Betty?"

"That's exactly what I mean. I think we got our guy, don't you?"

"I got my doubts," Crawford said. "I've met Sunderland, and I sure as hell didn't peg him as a killer."

"Plus, he was clearly shitfaced," Ott added.

"You don't think drunks have ever killed people before?" Rutledge said.

"The guy who did this was methodical and professional," Crawford said. "Not only that, he had a murder weapon with him. A knife and probably duct tape. Somehow I don't see Sunderland having those things stashed in his bathrobe pockets."

"Not only that," Ott said. "I'm not really seeing much of a motive."

"What do you mean?" Rutledge said. "How 'bout being worried about getting convicted at his upcoming trial?"

Ott nodded. "Yeah, maybe."

Rutledge shrugged. "Okay, so when he left the room, where the hell would the guy have gone, then?"

"I don't know," Crawford said. "It's a reasonable question."

"We need to talk to him," Rutledge said. "If he doesn't have a good answer, we bring him in."

Crawford wasn't sold, but he was certainly curious. He nodded and glanced over at Ott, who nodded back.

"Where's he live?" Rutledge asked.

"On Middle Road," Crawford said.

"Well, isn't that convenient."

"Said he walked to the party and back."

"I'm liking this guy more and more," Rutledge said. "What about you, Ott?"

Ott shrugged. "Like I said, maybe, but I got my doubts."

"You always have your doubts."

"I just don't think we should go charging in with the cuffs out," Ott said.

"Don't worry, we'll give the guy his say," Rutledge said.

Ott smiled. "By the way, Norm, I didn't know you could speak French. Pretty impressive."

Rutledge beamed with pride.

"Thank you, Ott ... Or should I say *merci buckets?*"

He would say that.

34

CRAWFORD, OTT, AND RUTLEDGE WALKED IN ON A farewell between Lord Sunderland and his daughter. Crawford guessed she was about twenty-five and in no way looked like his preconceived image of a duchess, which was how Sunderland introduced her. "The Duchess of Norwich," to be exact. She was wearing stylishly ripped blue jeans and a tight-fitting red silk top. Apparently, she'd flown down from New York, where she had gone to visit friends, hoping to catch Dad and a few "toffs" in Palm Beach before flying back to London. Crawford had absolutely no clue what a "toff" was. Maybe Rutledge did, being a linguist and all.

Sunderland saw his daughter off, then came back into the house and sat down with the three of them.

"Beautiful room," Rutledge said. Crawford had noticed before Sunderland seemed to have a thing for chintz, particularly pink and green hues.

"Thank you," Sunderland said. Then to Crawford, "This is getting to be a regular thing, Detective."

Crawford nodded. "The reason we're here—"

"—is because we have reason to suspect you may have firsthand knowledge about the death of Grace Spooner,"

Rutledge took over. "The woman killed at The Colony last Tuesday."

Sunderland's face suddenly twisted into a half frown, half snarl. "What in heaven's name are you talking about?"

"I'm going to go through the facts one by one," Rutledge said.

Sunderland raised his hands. "Okay."

"Fact number one, you went to a room on the second floor of The Colony with a woman you met earlier in the evening at Asher Bard's birthday party. Correct?"

Sunderland nodded. "Yes"—he glanced at Crawford —"that's exactly what I told the detective."

"Then at some point, and we believe it was around eleven o'clock that evening, you left the room for between ten and fifteen minutes, though it may have been longer."

"Okay, Chief ... is that what I'm meant to call you?"

"Yes, that is my title. Like Lord is yours."

"Okay, Chief, let me tell you exactly what happened." He glanced at Crawford once more. "Again, as I freely admitted to Detective Crawford, I had a lot to drink at the party. As we say in my country, I was trolleyed, pissed, or as you would say, shit-faced, hammered, wasted."

"So I heard," Rutledge said.

"I got out of bed, put on a bathrobe, and went to the loo. But it turned out it wasn't the loo at all; it was actually the door out of the room."

Takes some serious champagne imbibing to confuse those two doors, thought Crawford. But for someone really drunk, he could see it.

"So, now I'm out in the hallway, and it took me a few moments to realize it was not the loo. I turned and pressed the buzzer of the room I'd come from, then knocked on the door. I got no answer. I think my friend, Betty, may have winked off."

Crawford glanced over at Rutledge, whose jaw had dropped into freefall. Ott seemed to be fighting a smirk.

"So, I remembered thinking, even in my sozzled state, that I didn't have many options. Either go down to the main desk and get a key or—" He noticed Rutledge's incredulous expression and asked, "Do you want me to go on ... Chief?"

"So, what happened next?" Rutledge asked.

"I knocked on the door next to my room, and a woman opened the door. I was going to ask her if I could use her phone to call the desk and get a key, but she slammed the door in my face. You sure you want me to go on?"

Rutledge hesitated, then nodded.

"Then I went and knocked on another door. This time there was no answer. So I tried another one, and a man came to the door. He didn't look too friendly, but when I told him I had locked myself out and needed to call the front desk and get someone to bring me a key, he let me in. I was about to piss my pants, so I dashed into his loo and let loose. Good thing, or I would've pissed my knickers in the hallway somewhere."

"Okay, Lord Sunderland," Rutledge said. "I think we got the idea. One of us will call the front desk and confirm that someone brought up a key to you that night."

"Yes, nice young chap, he was," Sunderland said.

Crawford got to his feet. "So, Norm, that about does it, right?"

Frowning, Rutledge stood up, nodded, and sighed. "That about does it."

35

Crawford went back to his office afterward, then headed home around seven that night. On the way, he called Dominica to see if she could do a spur-of-the-moment dinner. She said, unfortunately, she had her aunt and uncle in town, and they had dinner plans.

Then, automatically almost, he thought about giving Rose a buzz. But then he remembered: *Oh yeah, John the shrink.* So, instead he stopped by Publix and got one of his old favorites—the fried chicken eight-piece special: two breasts, two wings, two thighs, and two drumsticks along with a side of shredded coleslaw. Wash it all down with a couple Sierra Nevada Torpedo IPA beers. It didn't get much better than that.

Something was bothering him, though, and he couldn't quite put his finger on it. The woman, Betty, telling them about recognizing a man she had seen on the news walking toward the elevator. Wearing a blue baseball cap. Then, ME Bob Hawes saying the driver of the Cadillac that picked Grace Spooner up the night she died was also wearing a dark baseball cap.

He put down one of the chicken drumsticks, took a sip of his beer, and gazed out his window for a few minutes.

Then he got up, grabbed his keys, and quickly walked down to his car. Fifteen minutes later he was at The Colony Hotel. It was eight twenty when he walked up to the desk. The man who had been there the night of Grace Spooner's murder was on duty again. He looked up at Crawford and smiled. "Welcome back, Detective."

He remembered his name was Rick Hodding. "Thanks, Rick. I have a favor to ask. That surveillance camera aimed at the bank of elevators ... Can I take a look at the server, please?"

"Sure, it's in the room behind me," Rick said, pointing. "You need any help?"

"No, thanks, I should be able to manage."

First, he walked back over to the CCTV camera slanted down at the elevators. He remembered from last time that The Colony had something called a Super High Definition 4MP Infrared Dome 4 system. He had Googled it and found it was top-of-the-line. He went back into the room behind Rick Hodding and went through two hours' worth of digital tape from the night Grace Spooner was killed.

At 10:24 that night, he found exactly what he was looking for.

CRAWFORD WAS WAITING FOR DOMINICA MCCARTHY when she walked into her cubicle of the Crime Scene Evidence Unit at eight the next morning. He was sitting in a chair opposite her desk, a Dunkin' Donuts extra-large coffee in one hand, a half-eaten blueberry donut, his version of "health food," in the other. And a tea for Dominica, just the way she liked it.

"Top of the morning to you, Charlie," she said.

"Back at ya," Crawford said, handing her the tea.

"Oh, thank you. Now I don't have to drink the office bilge water."

Crawford smiled. "So, I need your help. You okay driving up to Tampa and looking into something up there?"

"That's a little vague, but, sure, I guess. This afternoon okay?"

"Yeah, that's fine. I need you to go to Grace Spooner's apartment and turn it upside down. She's got a mysterious boyfriend whose identity I need to confirm."

"What's his name?"

"That's what I need you to find out."

"But you think you know?"

"I think so. But I want to see if you agree," Crawford said. "I went through her computer pretty thoroughly, but I might have missed something. We never found her cell phone at the scene because I think the guy who killed her took it with him. But maybe there's something else in her apartment. Oh, also"—he pulled out his wallet and took out a scrap of paper—"will you try to reach this woman? Her name's Natalie Weir, a friend of Grace Spooner's. I tried her a bunch of times, but she never got back to me."

"Sure. Will do. Tampa's, what, about three hours?"

Crawford stood up and patted her on the shoulder. "The way you drive, two-fifteen, two-thirty, max."

CRAWFORD FILLED HER IN A LITTLE MORE, GAVE HER Spooner's address and the name and number of her boss. Then he drove to 350 Royal Palm Way, Asher Bard's office. Ott, who was with him, told Crawford that Jennifer Atwood had said she planned to keep working there until the end of the month. She said there were a lot of loose ends and unfinished business she felt were her obligation to wrap up and finalize.

On the ride over, Ott told Crawford he had another date scheduled with Jennifer for later that week. She was going to serve what she referred to as her "signature dish": lasagna with sausage, it turned out. He'd assured her he'd be wanting seconds.

Ott and Crawford had just walked into the office and had said their *hellos* to her.

"Jennifer," Crawford said. "That big file cabinet in Bard's office seemed to be a hundred percent business files and records; where are his files that relate to personal matters?"

"Over there." She pointed at her desk. "The files on either side are all personal."

"You mind if we appropriate your desk for a while?" Crawford asked.

"No, whatever you need to do," Jennifer said. "Just bear in mind that a lot of Asher's stuff is up in New York."

"Yes, I understand." Crawford knew that and had actually contemplated taking a quick trip up to New York, getting a search warrant, and going through Bard's office there. He couldn't really spare the time but thought he might find something there that might help crack the case. But now, he might just have enough here to accomplish that.

"Why don't you go ahead and sit in Jennifer's chair," Crawford said to Ott. "Go through the files on the right, and I'll take the ones on the left."

Ott nodded as Crawford went and got another chair on wheels. He rolled it over to the left side of the desk.

"What exactly are we looking for?" Ott asked, sitting in Jennifer's chair. "It's like you know, but you're not telling me."

"Here's the thing," Crawford said, lowering his voice. "I have a suspicion, a strong suspicion, who our perp is, but I don't want to lead the witness, meaning you. In other words, I want to see if you come to the same conclusion as me. Same with Dominica."

"Okay," Ott said with a shrug. "You're not even going to give me a little hint?"

"No, it'll be better if you come to the same conclusion on your own that I came to."

Ott shrugged and pulled out the first file.

AN HOUR LATER, THEY WERE STILL LOOKING. FOR WHAT, Ott had no clue. Crawford, on the other hand, was in search of confirmation, though he had no idea what form it might take.

Ott had just removed a file simply labeled "NY." He opened it.

There was just one sheet of yellow-lined paper in it. Both sides of the sheet had dates and short notes next to the dates. The notes were, for the most part, only a few lines long. He was ninety percent sure that Asher Bard had written them because they matched the handwriting in his checkbook.

To make it a hundred percent, Ott got up and walked into Bard's former office, where Jennifer was now sitting. He held up the front side of the yellow-lined sheet. "Is this Bard's handwriting?"

"Yes."

"Thanks." He walked out of the larger office and back to Jennifer's desk.

Crawford looked up. "Got something?"

"I hope so."

The first note was dated "2/3/19" and read: "Contacted by NY. Said story was going to land me in a jail cell. Told him to f- himself. Hung up."

The next entry read: "2/4/19: Called again, said 3 of the girls—named names—were prepared to testify in new trial. Hung up again."

"2/6/19 Called again. Said story, along with names and quotes, will run in March 2019 and did I want to comment. Comment on what, I said? 'Want me to send you the text.' Don't bother, I said."

"2/12/19 No calls for a week. Thought he'd gone away. Then he called, said, 'maybe there's a better way.' 'What's that?' I said. 'A million dollars,' he said. 'Think about it.' He hung up."

"2/20/19: NY said 'my birthday's coming up and just wanted to know if you got me a present?' Told him not going to happen. Thought about paying but figured that was his way of trapping me. If give him $, it's proof I'm paying him off."

Ott stopped reading and looked out the window. He could see the red tile roof of the O'Keeffe Gallery at the Society of the Four Arts and beyond, the Intracoastal. A yacht like Asher Bard's was chugging north on the Intracoastal.

It suddenly dawned on Ott who NY was.

36

Upon arriving in Tampa, Dominica had first met with Kevin Malchoff and Kathleen Esposito at Advance Team, where Grace Spooner had worked. She had gotten the key to Spooner's condominium from Esposito and spent an hour searching it for information that would move the case forward. She found nothing she deemed useful except a photo of a man, which was torn in half, in the bottom of a wastepaper basket in Spooner's bedroom. She slid it into an evidence bag, which she put into her breast pocket, then called Natalie Weir, the friend of Grace Spooner whose name and number Crawford had given her.

Weir answered after the first ring. "This is Natalie."

"Oh, hi, Ms. Weir, my name is Dominica McCarthy with the Palm Beach Police Department—"

"Oh, I am *so* sorry I never called you back. I was out of town and—"

"That was actually my colleague, Detective Crawford, who called, but don't worry about it. I'm in Tampa and wondered if I could drop by and talk to you about your friend, Grace Spooner?"

A pause. Then, "How about now?"

"That would be great. Where's your office?"

Natalie told her and Dominica arrived fifteen minutes later. Natalie's company, Anderson Insurance, was on the top floor of a three-story brownstone-type building in an older section of Tampa. She had an office and a window, but it wasn't much larger than Dominica's cubicle. Natalie had a marble-topped desk with a laptop and cell phone on it. Dominica sat across from her in a chrome and black leather chair.

Natalie said that Grace and she first met at a Rotary Club meeting. She'd gone there at the suggestion of her boss to try to drum up new business. Grace had been a member there for only a few months.

"We were both single, around the same age, and ended up doing a lot of things together," Natalie said.

Dominica nodded. "Detective Crawford told me Grace was going out with a man, a married man who apparently didn't live here in Tampa. Do you know anything about him? His name, hopefully?"

Natalie shook her head. "Sorry. She never told me his name. It was all very hush-hush."

Dominica twisted a strand of hair behind her ear. "Why was that, do you think?"

"I really don't know. It was the total opposite of her boyfriend before him. Jack. Grace told me everything about him. I mean, it was almost like"—she held up her hands—"TMI. About Jack, I mean."

"I gotcha," Dominica said, reaching into her breast pocket for the photo she had found. She took it out of the evidence bag. "Is this the man, do you know?"

"See, that's the problem. I never met him. If I had, presumably I'd know his name. At least his first name anyway," Natalie said. "You know who might know, though, is a friend who Grace grew up with."

"What's her name?"

"Cheryl. Cheryl Banderas." Natalie smiled. "I remember because I asked her if she was related to Antonio. She laughed and said, 'Gee, there's a question I've never heard before.'"

Dominica typed the name on her iPad. "Do you know where she lives?"

"Yeah, a place down near you. South of West Palm."

"Ah, Lake Worth maybe?"

"No ... a little place. Lake Clarke something."

Dominica typed "Lake Clarke, Florida" and "Lake Clarke Shores" popped up. It was just south of West Palm.

"Lake Clarke Shores?" Dominica asked.

"Yeah, that's it."

"So, when you say they were friends growing up, you mean—"

Natalie nodded. "Back when things were really bad for Grace. They were together at that halfway house or whatever you call it. I got the feeling Cheryl is still going through hard times."

"What do you mean?"

Natalie sighed. "Just some things Grace told me. She's had major depression, doesn't have a job, doesn't really have much of a life s'posedly."

"Well, thank you, Natalie, I can't think of anything else I need to ask you. I really appreciate your help."

"You're welcome," Natalie said with a smile, "and please apologize to the other detective for me not calling him back."

"I will. I'll be speaking to him shortly."

TEN MINUTES LATER, SHE WAS ON THE PHONE WITH Crawford.

"I already looked up Cheryl Banderas's address," Dominica said. "She lives in Lake Clarke Shores. Know where that is?"

"Know? It was the first place I lived when I first moved down here. Beta Court, to be exact. Where's she live?"

"1920 Barbados Drive."

There was a long pause. "Holy Christ."

"What?"

"When I went through Asher Bard's checkbook, there was a stub that said 1920 Barbados, LLC for three hundred thousand dollars. Right after Amazing Grace, LLC for the same amount."

"You're kidding."

"No," Crawford said. "So, obviously, Bard was buying her off, too."

"And hiding her identity."

"A little more subtly than Amazing Grace. Where are you now?"

"About halfway between Tampa and West Palm."

"Well, put the hammer down and meet me at 1920 Barbados Drive as soon as you can."

"I'm already doin' ninety-five."

"Well, then Christ, slow down. I can wait."

"Aw, I'm touched, Charlie. You're concerned about my well-being."

37

CRAWFORD WAS WAITING ACROSS THE STREET IN HIS unmarked Crown Vic when Dominica cruised down Barbados Drive an hour and fifteen minutes later. He hit his flasher so she'd spot him and rolled down his window.

"You made good time," he said as she pulled up parallel to him.

She tapped the steering wheel. "Got the fastest car in the fleet here. Is she home?"

Crawford nodded. "Yeah, TV's on. Let's go pay her a visit."

Dominica nodded and drove past Crawford and parked.

They both got out of their cars and walked toward 1920 Barbados.

"How'd it go at Bard's office?" Dominica asked as they stepped up to the front porch.

"Good," Crawford said, hitting the buzzer. "Tell ya later. You want to play good cop or bad?"

Dominica's response was quick. "Bad."

A few moments later, the door opened and a woman with tousled brown hair appeared. Behind her was a thick cloud of cigarette smoke.

"Who are you?" the woman asked, then took a long drag on her cigarette.

"Palm Beach Police. Ms. Banderas?"

"Yeah," she said. "What do you want?"

"I'm Detective Crawford and this is my associate, Dominica McCarthy. Can we ask you some questions about Grace Spooner and Asher Bard?"

"Oh Christ," she groaned. "And I s'pose you want to come in?"

Based on the wall of smoke, he didn't really, but … "We won't take too much of your time."

She turned and went in as Crawford and Dominica followed. The place smelled awful. Like a hundred people sat around in a circle and chain-smoked all day long. But the only one there was Cheryl Banderas, along with her seemingly antisocial, one-eyed cat, and a minimal amount of thrift-shop furniture.

Crawford and Dominica sat on a rickety, burnt-orange sofa that was missing an arm. Cheryl took a seat opposite them in a pea-green beanbag chair that looked like it had lost a fair amount of its stuffing over the years.

"Our understanding is that you grew up with Grace Spooner and remained good friends?" Crawford started out.

"Yes, that's true. Not that we saw each other much, but we stayed in touch."

"Ms. Banderas," Dominica said, summoning up her hard-ass tone. "We are well aware of the payoff you received from Asher Bard. I assume you know he was killed?"

Cheryl nodded. "Yeah, can't say I was heartbroken."

"That three hundred thousand dollars was to prevent you from talking about what happened ten years ago. Hush money, basically."

Cheryl hesitated, then, "Yeah, I guess that pretty much sums it up."

"And, we're assuming, you cashed that check?" Dominica

asked.

"Yeah, I did. Didn't you see the new Ferrari out front?" Cheryl said with a goofy smile. "I was kidding. I'm actually thinking about going to look at new houses."

"Now that Bard's dead, you know, you're under no obligation to honor that agreement anymore," Crawford said.

"I still don't want to talk about it," Cheryl said.

"Why not?" Dominica said. "A good friend of yours was brutally murdered."

"'Cause I just want to forget about it. What happened back then ruined my life. I kinda doubt I'd be sitting here in this dump doing nothing all day if what happened then never happened."

"Yeah, but at least you're alive," Dominica said.

"Cheryl, we really need your help," Crawford said. "We don't want the murderer of your friend to get away with it, and I'm sure you don't either."

Cheryl shrugged. "What's it matter now?"

"What if it was the other way around and you were killed?" Dominica said. "Wouldn't you want Grace to cooperate and do everything she could to find your murderer?"

"Yeah, but what happened to her was because of her boyfriend and didn't have that much to do with Asher Bard."

Dominica glanced at Crawford then back at Cheryl. "Spell that out, will you?"

Cheryl leaned forward. "How much you gonna pay me?"

"We're cops, Cheryl," Dominica said. "We don't pay people, we arrest them."

"I heard of cops paying informants money," Cheryl said.

Crawford thought about hitting her with the old "it's your civic duty" speech but stifled it. "We really need your help," he said instead.

Cheryl lit a cigarette off of one that was down to its filter. "I'll think about it," she said with a long sigh. "What do you want to know?"

"Thank you," Crawford said.

"I just said I'll think about it."

"Can you tell us what you know about Grace's last boyfriend?"

"She told me he's famous, but I never heard of him."

Crawford tapped his fingers on the side of the chair. "You're talking about Quinn Casey, right?"

"This man, right?" Dominica held up the two pieces of the photo she had found.

Cheryl nodded. "That's him. She told me she met him when he was doing a story about Bard. Seemed really blown away he was interested in her, even though she was a beautiful woman. She told me he went to Princeton and that one in England, what's the name? Starts with an O, I think."

"Oxford." Crawford had read that Casey had gone there when he first Googled him.

"That's it," Cheryl said. "But after a while, Grace told me, he got really possessive and jealous. When he was up in New York he wanted to know what she was up to every night he wasn't around. Accused her of going back to her old boyfriend."

"Jack Marin, you mean?"

"Yeah, exactly," Cheryl said. "She finally just couldn't deal with it anymore. He wanted to know where she was every goddamn minute"—she shook her head— "and he was a married man."

"So, what happened?" Crawford asked.

Cheryl shook her head and took a drag down to her toes. "A couple things. One, he beat her up a couple months ago. He was drunk, she said. Like that makes any difference. Then he did it again. She emailed me some photos of her face and neck. Not pretty."

"Could we see the photos?" Crawford asked.

"Sure," Cheryl said, standing up. "I'll get them."

She went over and got her laptop from a small desk,

brought it over, and opened it up. There were nine photos in a grid pattern. Grace Spooner looked as though she'd done a couple of rounds with Muhammad Ali.

"Son of a bitch," Crawford said.

Dominica shook her head. "How could someone—"

"She finally said *screw this I'm outta here* and told him she was done. He flew down the next day and apparently really lost it. Said how could a woman who grew up in a trailer park and went to some bush-league junior college break up with a great man like himself."

Crawford shook his head. "He said that?"

Cheryl nodded.

"So, what happened?" he asked.

"She was intimidated because he got so out of control, but then he apologized, and they kind of got back together. I think he went back down to Palm Beach to work on that story of his. Then a few days later, she told him she wanted to have dinner with him. This time she was really going to end it for good but wanted to do it face-to-face. So, she drove down to Palm Beach, and that was the last I ever heard."

"But you have a theory about what happened, right?" Dominica asked.

"A theory? Hell, no, I know exactly what happened," Cheryl said. "The bastard killed her."

Crawford eyed Dominica and nodded. "I'm assuming part of that money Bard paid you was to get dirt on Quinn Casey, right?"

"Yeah, Bard knew I knew stuff about Casey."

"So, you told him stuff, like about Casey beating up Grace."

"Yup," Cheryl said, "among other things."

Crawford nodded. "And what did Bard say?"

"He didn't say anything. Just had this big shit-eating grin —" Cheryl put her hand over her mouth. "Oops, sorry."

Crawford laughed. "That's okay. I've heard the expression."

It was time for sweet-talking Charlie to step up.

Cheryl was on at least her eighth Marlboro since they'd arrived. Their clothes were, no doubt, saturated with the stench of cigarette smoke and would have to be torched, and all they had was Cheryl's absolute conviction that Quinn Casey had killed Grace Spooner. That wouldn't get them very far in a court of law.

"Cheryl," he said gently, "how would you feel about helping to bring this guy down? The guy who beat up your friend and, we suspect, eventually killed her?"

"I thought that's what I'd just been doing," Cheryl said with a shrug. "Giving you all that info."

"Yes, and we're very appreciative," he said, then amping up what Rose called "the charmin' Charlie smile," "but I'm thinking of you in a more prominent role."

"Role? What do you mean?"

"You ever do any acting?" Crawford asked. He didn't glance at Dominica for fear she'd be giving him her *Where the hell you going with this?* look. He'd seen it on several occasions in the past.

"Yeah, like, back in junior high."

"Perfect. You don't need to have an Oscar on your mantel for this role. In fact, all you have to do is talk on the phone. Think you can handle that?"

Cheryl smiled. "You seem like a very persuasive man. Not that I really know what you're asking."

"What I'm asking is for you to play a role. Want to hear about it?"

"Sure." She shrugged again. "Why not?"

"Okay," he said, glancing over at Dominica, "I'm thinking this will work best as a two-woman play."

Dominica cocked her head to one side. "Oh, do you now? Do tell."

38

After rehearsing with Cheryl Banderas for the next half hour, Crawford felt she was ready to get into character. He gave her Quinn Casey's cell phone number. She dialed it and put it on speaker. After a few rings, Quinn Casey picked up.

"Hello?"

"Mr. Casey, you don't know me, but I was a friend of your friend, Grace Spooner."

"Who are you?" Casey asked gruffly.

"Someone who's got a few deep, dark secrets about you."

"I'm gonna hang up unless you get to the point."

"Okay, point is I have a bunch of photos of Grace after you beat her up. I bet there are people in the media who would love to see them."

"No clue what you're talking about."

"They come with emails about where and when they happened. Tampa, Florida, to be exact. A surveillance camera recorded the action in one." That was a Crawford invention.

"What do you want?"

"What most people want, money."

"And who the hell are you?"

"Ms. Anonymous."

Crawford shot her a thumbs-up. She was better than he expected.

"I just figured out who you are," Casey said. "You're Cheryl. Grace's friend from way back."

Cheryl flashed a frightened look at being ID'd. "I don't know what you're talking about."

"Look, I'm getting bored with this, Cheryl. Send me the photos you got, and maybe I'll give you a couple bucks." He reeled off his email.

"Couple bucks ain't gonna do it."

Crawford nodded and smiled. The girl was brazen.

"Goodbye, sweetheart." And Casey clicked off.

Cheryl looked surprised as she looked over at Crawford. "Sorry, I thought I was doing so well."

"You were," Crawford said. "He's just playing hardball. He'll be back."

Dominica patted her on the shoulder. "Yeah, good job. We haven't heard the last of him."

AFTER GETTING CHERYL'S PERMISSION TO OPEN SOME windows, Charlie went around and opened every one of them. But the place still reeked, so he suggested they go out on the wood deck behind her home. Crawford brought out a bottle of water, Dominica a Coke, and Cheryl her umpteenth cigarette of the day.

"How many of those do you knock back in a day?" Crawford asked.

"Four packs," Cheryl said. "It's my only vice."

Dominica laughed. "Otherwise, you're pure as the driven snow, right?"

Cheryl smiled. "Pretty much."

Crawford turned to Dominica. "Okay, have you figured out what your role is yet?"

"I think so."

"I figured. So, what is it?"

Dominica leaned back in the plastic chaise. "When Casey calls back, if Casey calls back, Cheryl's gonna set up a meet where Casey can pay her to lose the photos. And instead of Cheryl being there, it's gonna be me. And you're gonna be hiding nearby."

"Pretty close. And I'm thinking we might as well do it right here."

"Okay. Question?"

"Shoot."

"How we gonna explain Cheryl morphing into me?"

"Ah …"

"You haven't quite figured that out yet, have you?"

"Still working on it."

Cheryl blew a well-constructed series of smoke rings. "Wait a minute, why can't I do it?"

"Sorry, Cheryl," Crawford said, "it's way too dangerous. Casey could show up with a gun."

"Yeah, but you'll be behind the sofa or whatever, right?"

"Probably in your hall closet."

"All right, so I'll be safe then?"

"Theoretically," Crawford said. "It's still a risk, and we don't put citizens in risky situations."

He thought for a moment about calling Ott for backup but decided he didn't really need him.

"But what about poor Dominica?" Cheryl said. "You don't mind putting her in a risky situation?"

Dominica looked amused. "Yeah, Charlie, what about poor me?"

Crawford chuckled and said to her, "You know what you're doing."

"Fact remains," Cheryl said, "Dominica's gonna have to explain why she's there and I'm not."

"I want to talk to you in private for a second," Crawford said, searching his mind whether Casey had ever met or seen Dominica.

"Come on," Cheryl said. "Whatever you have to say, you can say in front of me."

Crawford thought for a few moments. "Okay, I've already said it, Cheryl. My superiors take a dim view of putting a private citizen in a dangerous situation."

"But you'll be watching," Cheryl said. "Quinn Casey does something, you shoot him."

"It's not quite that simple."

He turned to Dominica. "Has Quinn Casey ever seen you?"

Dominica shook her head. "No, but I think you should let Cheryl do it."

"Please, Dominica—"

"No, she's right," Dominica said. "Both of us will be a few feet away, ready to neutralize Casey." Dominica turned to Cheryl and smiled. "Plus, she's good and feisty."

Cheryl beamed. "Thank you, Dominica."

AS THEY EXPECTED, QUINN CASEY CALLED BACK WITHIN the hour.

"Okay," he said. "Where do you live? I'm going to come over and pay you for those photos."

"You got a nice, big, fat check for me?"

"Yeah, ten thousand dollars."

Cheryl scoffed. "Forget it. I want ten times that."

"*You* forget it. The most I'll give you is fifty."

Cheryl responded with a long dramatic pause. "All right. The last name is Banderas. B-a-n-d-e-r-a-s."

"Where do you live?"

"1920 Barbados Drive in Lake Clarke Shores."

"I'll be there in an hour."

"Why so long?"

"I'll be there in an hour," he repeated.

DOMINICA WAS LOOKING OUT THE WINDOW, PLAYING sentry. Crawford was next to her, talking on his cell phone to Ott. They had driven their cars several blocks away so they wouldn't be spotted. Crawford clicked off.

"So, you figure Casey giving Cheryl a check will hang him?" Dominica asked.

"Put it this way: it's a start," Crawford said. "I mean, he could say he was just trying to save his job. Figuring the bad press from the photos could get him fired."

"Or, he doesn't want his wife to get wind of his affair with Grace."

Crawford nodded. "Yeah, so we're gonna need more than him giving Cheryl a check. But, like I said, it's the first step."

Dominica pointed at a white Ford Taurus that had pulled up in front of Cheryl's house.

"He's here," she said, and Crawford walked quickly to the front closet. Dominica went into the kitchen and positioned herself just inside the door.

"Okay, Cheryl," Crawford said. "We got you covered."

"You better," Cheryl said gamely. "Break a leg, right?"

A few moments later, the doorbell rang.

A tense look spread over Cheryl's face.

She walked to the door and opened it.

There were two men there. One was wearing a policeman's uniform.

"Ms. Banderas?" the man in uniform asked.

"Yes, who are you?"

"Officer Lembeck, and this is the man I understand you talked to a little while ago, Mr. Casey."

Casey was smiling, but it was more like a smirk.

Crawford groaned silently. He had heard the name Lembeck before and thought he was with the West Palm Police Department. He took out his phone and scrolled to West Palm PD.

Lembeck took a step closer to Cheryl. "I have reason to believe you were trying to extort money from Mr. Casey. Is that true, Ms. Banderas?"

"What do you mean, 'extort money?'"

"I mean, threaten to expose him for actions supposedly recorded by a surveillance camera. And photos of a woman with bruises and wounds supposedly inflicted by Mr. Casey."

"Yeah, I have the photos right here," Cheryl said. "Would you like to see them?"

Crawford found Lembeck's name in the West Palm PD personnel roster.

"Let me ask you a question," Lembeck said. "Do any of the photos show Mr. Casey inflicting harm on Ms. Spooner?"

Cheryl thought for a second. "Well, no."

"And do you have a surveillance tape showing Mr. Casey inflicting harm on Ms. Spooner?"

In the closet, Crawford was regretting coming up with that invention.

"No."

"But in a phone call a short while ago, you tried to extort a hundred thousand dollars from Mr. Casey in return for those photos and footage. Is that correct?"

"Well, I—"

"Is that correct or not?"

"Well, I guess—"

Lembeck turned to Casey. "Mr. Casey, would you like me to arrest this woman for attempting to extort you?"

Casey's smug expression turned into a look of contemplation. He didn't say anything for a few moments.

"No, Officer, I don't believe that the lady's ill-advised actions should result in her being arrested. A simple apology will be acceptable to me."

"But you beat her up," Cheryl said with a flash of anger. "Twice. She told me."

"I'm sorry to have to tell you this," Casey said. "But, clearly, you have me confused with someone."

Cheryl's face flushed red with rage.

"Ms. Banderas," Lembeck said, "I strongly suggest you apologize to Mr. Casey or I *will* be forced to arrest you for extortion."

Cheryl shook her head. "This isn't right. He's the one you should be arresting."

"Ms. Banderas, last chance."

Casey's smirk was back with a vengeance.

"Ms. Banderas, I mean it, one last time."

Cheryl sighed deeply and dropped her voice. "I apologize," she said, her voice muffled.

"Sorry, I didn't hear you," Casey said.

"I apologize." Not much louder.

"You're going to have to speak up," Lembeck said.

"*OKAY, OKAY, I APOLOGIZE ... I FUCKING APOLOGIZE,*" Cheryl said so loud the neighbors across the street could hear.

39

Crawford, Dominica, and Cheryl Banderas were back out on the wood deck behind her house.

"What if he'd actually arrested me?" Cheryl said. "I mean, it was pretty close."

"I think it was what is known as 'sending a strong message,'" Crawford said. "I doubt he would have ever arrested you."

Dominica nodded. "Or else we would have come out and saved you."

Cheryl smiled. "That was fun, actually."

"You were good," Crawford said.

"Never too late for Hollywood," Dominica said.

Cheryl smiled. "Sure beats hangin' around watching soap operas all day long," she said. "What's our next move?"

Crawford laughed. "Afraid we're going to have to retire you as an honorary cop."

"Aw, come on."

"Sorry, but we'll let you know how this turns out. Don't worry, we'll get him."

"You sure?"

Crawford nodded.

"You gotta," Cheryl said.

"We will," Crawford said, though he wasn't sure what the next move was.

CRAWFORD AND DOMINICA WERE HEADED BACK TO THE station. It was five forty-five.

"Want to get a bite a little later?" Dominica asked.

"I do, but I can't," Crawford said. "Gotta work. I feel like I'm making progress, then I take three steps backward. In this case, I know who did it, but I can't nail him."

"What exactly are you going to do?"

"Go to that little park on the other side of South County and ponder."

"Seriously?"

"Yeah, that's what I do when I'm at a dead end. That's my spot," Crawford said. "It's like how Ott goes to the dog park and hangs out, even though his dog died last year."

"Yeah, what's that about?"

"That's where he thinks. Comes up with stuff."

"And the little park is your spot?"

"Yup."

"Now that I think about it, I've seen you there a couple of times. Why didn't you ever tell me this?"

"I guess I didn't think you'd find it very interesting."

"No, it actually is."

Crawford turned right into the police station driveway.

"So," said Dominica, "what if, when you're at your little spot in the park, you figure out right away how to crack the case?"

Crawford chuckled. "Well, if that happens, I'll give you a call right away. We'll go get dinner."

Dominica's head shot up. "Oh, I forgot to tell you something. Rose asked if you and I wanted to go to her house for dinner on Friday. Spend some quality time with her and her friend, John the shrink."

"Yeah, let's do it. What time?"

"She said seven."

"But if I'm a little late, that's okay, right?"

Dominica nodded. "We both know how it is when you're on a case. Case first, women second."

"You don't really believe that?"

"Ah, yeah, I really do."

They got out of the Crown Vic. Crawford walked Dominica over to her car and lowered his voice. "I'd give you a big, slobbery kiss right now, but someone might be watching."

Dominica held out her hand and, in case someone was listening, said, "So nice to spend part of the day with you, Detective."

Crawford laughed and shook her hand. "The pleasure was indeed mine, crime scene tech McCarthy."

40

Right after Crawford walked into his office, Bob Shepley stopped by to give him an update on Roy Jenkins, the art forger.

"Guy skipped town," Shepley said. "His landlord thinks he might be headed back to where he used to live."

"Where's that?"

"Charleston, South Carolina."

"You contact anybody up there?"

"Not in Charleston," Shepley said. "But I just spoke to an old buddy who lives in Mount Pleasant, near there. He mentioned a Charleston cop named Nick Janzek."

The name was vaguely familiar to Crawford, but he didn't know from where. "So call the guy," Crawford said.

"Only problem is he's a homicide cop."

"So what? It's a good place to start."

Shepley shrugged. "All right. Later, man." He walked toward Crawford's door.

"Oh, hey, keep me in the loop," Crawford said.

"Will do."

Nick Janzek? Nick Janzek? Then, he remembered. He had been an All-American lacrosse player at Boston College. They had crushed Dartmouth three years in a row, Janzek making goals just about every time he got his stick on the ball.

Before Crawford went to the little park across from the station, he stopped by his office and made a call. It was to *The New Yorker* magazine in New York. He knew, even though it was past six o'clock, he'd find plenty of people still there. Running a magazine was not a nine-to-five operation. And it would be a short call because he had only one question: whether a certain person worked at the magazine or not.

Five minutes later Crawford was sitting on the bench in the small park across the street from the station. Many of the old familiar questions were banging around in his head, still unresolved. How come the camera that recorded the comings and goings of guests on the penthouse floor of The Colony Hotel didn't show Grace Spooner's murderer coming to the door and going inside? Why did Grace move from the Chesterfield to The Colony late in the day when she had already paid for the night—by courier, in cash—at the Chesterfield? With all the surveillance cameras in the Australian dock area, why wasn't there any footage of Asher Bard's murderer coming onto Bard's yacht?

Those were the recurrent questions, but there were others, as well.

Two hours later he was still there, oblivious to everything around him—the South Country Road traffic, a few night strollers who passed by in ones and twos, even the rain. Yes, the rain, as he suddenly realized he was three-quarters soaked. Talk about getting lost in your thoughts ... He finally got up, crossed the street, and went down the driveway to the police station parking lot. He hit his car clicker, opened the door, and drove back to West Palm Beach. He planned to get started at seven o'clock the next morning, since he had a full day planned.

As he crossed the bridge from Palm Beach, he hit the speed dial he'd created for Tyrell and Darnell Bard. Tyrell answered, and they had a ten-minute conversation, ultimately planning to meet at the Ultima gym first thing in the morning, although Darnell couldn't make it because he had a doctor's appointment.

That would be the start of what Crawford predicted would be a long, long day.

TYRELL WAS DECKED OUT IN BLACK UNDER ARMOUR tights and a neon yellow muscle shirt. The Rock didn't have much on him.

"Lookin' good," Crawford said, sidling up to Tyrell. "This where you normally work out?"

"Hell, no, heard this place is for pussies," Tyrell said, and the guy at the front desk turned around and frowned. "LA Fitness, man."

Crawford nodded. "So, I don't know for sure if this guy's gonna show, but if not, I guess you'll just have to do a pussy workout."

Tyrell laughed. He walked over to the hand weight rack, hefted a pair of seventy-pound hand weights, and did three sets of fifteen reps.

To try to keep up, Crawford attempted to do the same with a pair of forties. He normally did thirties and stopped after seven reps. Fortunately, Tyrell wasn't watching him. Crawford put the hand weights back on the rack and looked around just in time to see Quinn Casey walk through the front door and head straight back to the locker room. Crawford noted what he was wearing: faded blue jeans and a collared white sport shirt. A few minutes later he walked out clad in two-tone Nike fleece training pants and a long-sleeved shirt with a swoosh high up on the left side.

Casey saw him, waved, and came over. "Hey, Charlie. How ya doin', man?"

Crawford nodded and got Tyrell's attention. "Hello, Quinn. Like you to meet a friend of mine, Tyrell." Tyrell approached them. "Think you knew his father."

Tyrell looked Casey over like he was a cockroach.

"Hello, Tyrell, Quinn Casey," Casey said, taking a step to shake Tyrell's hand, but Tyrell didn't move. "And who would your father be?"

"Asher Bard," Tyrell said.

Casey blanched but recovered. "Never had the pleasure."

"Oh, I think you did," Crawford said. Then to Tyrell, "That the name?"

Tyrell nodded and eyed Casey. "Told me he was going to meet you at his boat."

Casey was frowning now. "I don't know what you're talking about."

"It's pretty clear," Crawford said, then launched into his bluff. "His father was Asher Bard. And Asher told him he was going to meet you on his boat three days ago. Then we know what happened."

Casey slowly shook his head. "You know, Charlie, I had a lot of respect for you. Your perfect clearance record. How you went about solving cases. But now you're grasping at straws—" Then, like he had a brainstorm, "Wait a minute, I bet you were behind that thing with the woman yesterday."

Crawford played dumb. "What woman?"

"You know. Cheryl somebody. Yeah, you were, weren't you?" Casey said, shaking his head.

He took a few steps and picked up a pair of boxing gloves. "So, you and your pal Tyrell here are trying to pin Bard's murder on me, is that it?"

Crawford felt his footing was none too solid. "Are you

saying Tyrell was mistaken when he heard his father say he was going to go meet you?"

Casey took a step closer. "Yes, Charlie, that's exactly what I'm saying. Tyrell's badly mistaken and a dead man ... well, a dead man doesn't make for much of a witness."

Tyrell glared at him but didn't move. Crawford could see his swelling rage wasn't far from exploding.

"Well, I've got a workout to get to," Casey said. "Nice to meet you, Tyrell."

He walked away.

"What are we going to do?" Tyrell hissed. "Just let him go?"

"That's all we can do at the moment." Crawford lowered his voice. "I need more evidence."

"I want to kill that asshole," Tyrell said.

"Just do what I said," Crawford said. "Hang in a little longer. For now, you gotta just take it out on that speed bag over there."

Confronting Quinn Casey was only one of the reasons Crawford had come to the gym. As Tyrell went to hammer the speed bag, Crawford headed for the locker room. He went in and started opening locker doors. There were only about ten or twelve men in the gym at this hour, so it shouldn't be too difficult to find Quinn's. He'd told Tyrell the night before that one of the reasons he wanted him there was to act as a sentry. He'd told him he was going to go into the locker room at some point and if Tyrell noticed Quinn Casey heading in that direction, to cut him off. Distract him. Whatever it took to keep him out of the locker room. Tyrell assured him he would, even if it meant taking him out at the knees.

Crawford had opened several lockers with clothes in them but no blue jeans and white sport shirt. He opened two more; still nothing. Finally, he opened one and saw the blue jeans hanging on one hook and the white shirt on another.

He felt for a lump in the blue jeans and pulled out a

brown wallet. He opened it and saw a New York driver's license. Quinn Casey had a cocky smile in the photo. When Crawford called *The New Yorker* the night before, he had spoken to an office staffer named Tony. Crawford had ID'd himself and asked Tony a simple question: Does a man named Arnold Riegart work there?

Tony hadn't hesitated. "Yeah, he's a photographer. Why?"

Then Crawford had asked a second question: Does Arnold work with Quinn Casey?

"Yeah," said Tony. "In fact, they're working on something together now."

And there it was.

The night Crawford had gone to The Colony Hotel and met with Rick Hodding, he had discovered it was Arnold Riegart's credit card that had been used to make a reservation for Grace Spooner and another penthouse room on the sixth floor. Crawford suspected Quinn Casey had either borrowed the card or stolen it from his coworker so he couldn't be traced to the transaction. On both sides of Casey's wallet were rows of cards. He pulled out an Amex card in the name of Quinn T. Casey. Next, a Visa card, also Quinn T. Casey. He realized they were the only credit cards Casey had in the wallet and figured he must have returned the "borrowed" credit card to Riegart.

There was a bunch of what appeared to be receipts in the fold next to Casey's cash. He pulled them out. One from a Citgo for forty-one dollars' worth of gas, another from CVS for toothpaste and contact-lens cleaner. A third one, from Home Depot, caught his eye.

It was from ten days before, and there were three items on it: duct tape, nylon rope, and a knife. Crawford had not been looking for the receipts, but it was an even better find than what he *had* been looking for. The knife said "Gerber knife" and cost $54.91. The duct tape ... well, it spoke for itself. Used to cover the mouth of Grace Spooner and keep her from screaming. And the rope answered the question he'd been mulling ever since Spooner's body was discovered: why the hallway camera didn't show the perp entering Spooner's penthouse.

There was one more receipt, partially torn. It was from Buccan, a Palm Beach restaurant, for $109.14. It was dated the night before Grace Spooner's death. Crawford wasn't sure whether it had any significance or not.

Feeling exhilarated, Crawford took out his iPhone and snapped a few shots of the Home Depot and Buccan receipts. Then he took two more close-ups of Casey's Amex and Visa cards.

He put the receipts back where he found them, then the wallet back in the blue jeans and the jeans back on the hooks in the locker. He walked out of the locker room back into the gym.

Quinn Casey was lying on a bench, bench-pressing what looked to be around two hundred pounds. Crawford walked over to him and waited for him to finish.

"Pretty good, Quinn. Bet you had no problems swinging a forty-pound kettlebell?"

Casey eyed him coldly. "What are you talking about?"

"You know damn well ... what killed Asher Bard."

Casey shook his head and played disgusted. "Give it up, Charlie. You got nothing, absolutely nothing on me."

"Oh, you'd be surprised," Crawford said. "I'm curious about something, why you changed Grace Spooner's reservation at the last minute from the Chesterfield to The Colony."

"I have no clue what you're talking about," Casey said, wiping his brow with a gym towel.

"Sure you do," Crawford said. "You used your photographer's credit card so your name wouldn't show up. You did that, my guess is, because you found out about Asher Bard's birthday at The Colony and moved Grace Spooner there at the last minute. Why? Because since Bard was there, at the hotel, the cops would assume he did it. Or one of his friends, maybe. Gotta hand it to you, pretty slick move."

"You got one hell of a fertile imagination, Charlie." But Crawford could see he'd gotten to him. "Now, if you don't mind, I'd like to get back to my workout."

"I don't mind," Crawford said with a smile. "Just a few more things and I should have this thing wrapped up."

41

He went straight to The Colony Hotel next. He felt confident the theory he had hatched was going to prove correct. He'd called Ott and asked him to meet at the front desk at nine o'clock. He got there a little early and waited for Ott. In the meantime, he introduced himself to the woman who was at the desk.

He saw Ott shamble through the front door and come up to the desk. "What are we doin' here, Charlie?"

"I'll explain as we go along," Crawford said. Then to the woman working the front desk, "This is my partner, Detective Ott."

"Detective," she said with a smile.

"Denise," he said, reading her gold name bar.

"So, what we'd like to do is look back at your list of guests staying on the penthouse floor last Tuesday," Crawford said to Denise.

"Okay," she said, punching a few keys on her computer. "That's pretty easy."

"Thanks."

Denise looked up at Crawford. "You want me to just read

off the names? Turns out eight of the ten rooms up on six were occupied."

"Yes, please," Crawford said. "Just go right down the list. Better yet, can you just show me the names?"

"Sure." She turned the computer screen so he could get a better look. "Can you see okay?"

"Yes," he said, reading down the list.

The seventh name he saw was the name he was looking for. Arnold Riegart. Room 609.

He pointed to the name. "Bingo."

"Who's Arnold Riegart?" Ott asked.

"A photographer at *The New Yorker*."

Ott nodded slowly. "Ok-ay."

Crawford turned to Denise. "Is anyone in 609 now?"

Denise shook her head. "It was vacant last night."

"Would you mind giving me the key for it? And holding off checking a guest in, please?"

"Will do," Denise said, reaching for the key, then handing it to Crawford.

"Thanks," he said. "I'll probably get it back to you in an hour or two."

She nodded, and Crawford and Ott walked toward the elevator bank. Crawford pulled out his iPhone and dialed.

"Hi, Dominica," he said. "You doing anything?"

"Nothing that can't wait. What's up?"

"Can you bring your bag of tricks and come over to room 609 at The Colony Hotel right away?"

"Sure. That a proposition, Charlie?"

As they walked to the elevators, Crawford explained to Ott that Quinn Casey had used his photographer's credit card to pay for room 609. That way there'd be no trace of Casey being the one staying there.

Ott walked toward the bank of elevators that went to the penthouse where Grace Spooner had stayed.

"No, not those," Crawford said, pointing to two elevators on the opposite side. "These here."

Ott frowned. "Wait, those go to the penthouse, too?"

"Yeah, the ones on the other side of the building."

An elevator opened and they got in.

"Holy shit," Ott said with a wide smile.

"You put it together yet?"

"Yeah, so two separate hallways, right?"

Crawford nodded. "You got it."

"Which is why we never saw the perp go into Grace Spooner's suite on the hallway camera."

Crawford slapped him on the shoulder. "Exactly. Because he never did. Plus, he was on this side, not the other one."

The elevator door opened on the sixth floor.

Ott was shaking his head. "So ... you figure he went from his terrace to her terrace?"

Crawford nodded as he slipped the plastic card into the lock for penthouse 609. "Which was easier than you think. He probably didn't even need the rope."

"Well, I'll be damned," Ott said, following Crawford into the room. "So, I'm guessing you saw Casey on the surveillance tape on this side?"

"Good guess."

Ott slowly shook his head. "One hell of a smart perp, this guy."

"Hey, what do you expect? Princeton and Oxford."

There was a knock on the door. Crawford went over and opened it. It was Dominica.

"Hey, boys," she said, "so catch me up."

Crawford turned to Ott. "Mort, why don't you do the honors."

Dominica was a quick study and got it right away.

A few minutes later they walked out onto the penthouse terrace.

"To get to her terrace, he figured he might need a rope," Crawford said as he scrolled to a photo on his iPhone and showed Dominica the receipt from Home Depot. "He bought the rope"—he pointed to it on the receipt—"the day before Spooner's murder."

Dominica read the other items on the receipt. "Along with a knife and duct tape."

"Kind of makes it an open-and-shut case," Ott said.

Dominica looked around. "Even though it was over a week ago, I should be able to lift a print of his. Or find hair, DNA, or a rope fiber."

"See what you can come up with," Crawford said. "We probably don't need 'em to put him away, but it sure would help."

"Why wouldn't we need 'em?" Ott asked, then it dawned on him. "Oh, I get it, 'cause we got Casey's mug on the surveillance camera on this side."

SURE ENOUGH, AS CRAWFORD HAD SEEN BEFORE ON THE hallway surveillance camera, there was Quinn Casey walking down the hallway, blue Yankees cap on his head, a crimson knapsack on his back.

Crawford pointed at the knapsack. "Guess what he's got in that?"

Ott nodded knowingly. "Rope, duct tape, and a badass knife. We ready to take him in?"

"Just about," Crawford said. "There's one more camera I'd like to take a look at."

"Which one?" Ott asked.

"At the Brazilian Court." The hotel where Quinn Casey had told Crawford he was staying.

"What if we run across him there?"

"Well, then, we got a jail cell with his name on it."

Ott nodded. "Sure do."

Dominica stayed behind at The Colony while Crawford and Ott drove to the Brazilian Court at 301 Australian Avenue.

Turned out they found what they were looking for much quicker than at The Colony. The reason was because they knew the exact date when Quinn Casey made his three purchases at the Home Depot on Palm Beach Lakes Boulevard. Then, they guessed, he took a twelve- to fifteen-minute drive—if he made no stops—from the Home Depot to the Brazilian Court. Ten minutes later, they found what they were looking for. It was from a camera that covered the Brazilian Court's parking lot, and the footage was clear: Quinn Casey parking his blue Cadillac CTS. Then, getting out of the car with a distinctive orange-tinted Home Depot bag in hand, crossing the parking lot, and heading for the front entrance of the Brazilian Court.

"Bingo on two counts," Ott said, "the bag and the car."

"I don't know why we didn't think to check his car," Crawford said.

"We're slipping," Ott said.

"Well, while we're here, let's go get him."

They walked quickly to the front desk of the Brazilian Court.

The man who they had spoken to and who had given them permission to study the tapes of the parking lot was talking on the phone. He held up his hand, signaling *just a moment.*

Crawford nodded. A few moments later, the man hung up.

"Yes, detectives, how can I help?"

"We need to see Quinn Casey. What room is he in?"

The man shook his head slowly. "Oh, I'm sorry, but Mr. Casey checked out two hours ago."

Ott groaned.

If something was handy, Crawford would have flung it across the room.

"Okay, thank you," Crawford said, trying to stay cool, but what he really wanted to do was yell, *Jesus, what next?*

42

CRAWFORD STEPPED AWAY FROM THE DESK. Ott followed him as Crawford turned and pulled his cell phone out of his pocket. "I'm gonna call Rutledge," he said. "Why don't you get Casey's plate number and put a BOLO out on his car."

Ott called in the "be on the lookout" order as Crawford dialed Rutledge's cell phone.

"Yeah, Norm, our suspect, Quinn Casey, just checked out of the Brazilian Court. He was scheduled to stay through the end of the week, so he's in the wind. I need you to dispatch men to the airport, here, Lauderdale, and Miami, also the train station, bus station, and ... even ships departing Miami."

"I'm on it," Rutledge said. "What are you gonna do?"

"First, I need to call a guy, then Ott and I are going to go find the son of a bitch."

Crawford dialed the number he had called the night before. "*The New Yorker*," said a woman.

"I'm trying to reach Arnold Riegart, please."

"Arnold's not in, but I can give you his cell number?"

"Please."

She read the number to him.

"Thank you," he said, clicking off, then he dialed the number.

Arnold Riegart picked up on the first ring. "Riegart."

"Mr. Riegart, my name is Detective Crawford, Palm Beach Police. I'm one of the lead detectives on the Asher Bard and Grace Spooner murders and have a question for you."

"Okay, whaddaya wanna know?" Riegart asked in a pronounced Brooklyn accent.

"Quinn Casey used your Visa credit card to pay for two rooms at The Colony Hotel last week. Question is, does he still have your card?"

"No, he just used it that one time. Gave it right back to me. He said he was having problems with his Mastercard, paid me back with a check right away."

"That's all I need to know," Crawford said, making a mental note to get a copy of Riegart's Visa statement. "Thank you."

"No problem."

"Oh, also, do not contact Casey or tell him we spoke. Okay?"

"Uh, sure, you got it."

Crawford clicked off.

"What now?" Ott asked.

"I'm thinking he may make a run to New York. Thinking that might be the hardest way for us to find him. It's about eighteen, nineteen hours by car. See if you can find a statie in the Jacksonville area to set up a checkpoint for his Caddy. If he's making a run, he'll be in the Jax area in about two hours. Assuming he went straight up 95 from here."

Ott nodded.

"I'll do the same for the Florida Turnpike and I-75. Try to find someone in Gainesville to keep an eye out."

They walked out of the Brazilian Court, then to their Crown Vic, and started making calls. Ten minutes later, they had state troopers set up on I-75 near Gainesville and I-95 near Jacksonville on the lookout for a blue Cadillac CTS.

"What if he went down to the Keys to just hide out and be invisible?" Ott said.

"Good call," Crawford said. "See if you can get someone down there. He'd already be past Miami by now if that's where he's headed."

Ott had his phone out and had clicked on a map of the Florida Keys. "Maybe Islamorada or just past there, Duck Key. That's about a three-hour drive."

"Sounds good," Crawford said, who had gone down to Key West five years before after burning out up in New York. His sense of the geography down there, however, was somewhat tequila-challenged.

As Ott put a call in to the state police jurisdiction for that area, Crawford's cell phone rang.

It was Rutledge. "Jackpot," Rutledge said. "The guy's pounding the hound."

Fortunately, Crawford could understand Rutledge-ese. He was saying that Quinn Casey was on a Greyhound bus.

"Shit, man, that was fast," Crawford said.

"I don't dick around," Rutledge said.

"Where's he going?" Crawford asked.

"Bought a ticket to Atlanta. My guess would be to go somewhere from the Atlanta airport."

Crawford Googled *Greyhound West Palm to Atlanta* on his iPad. "So, that means it's on the Florida Turnpike now, then I-75, makes stops at ... Fort Pierce, Melbourne, Rockledge, Titusville, then Orlando where there's an hour-and-twenty-minute layover."

Ott had clicked off his call and was listening intently.

"See what the driving time is to Rockledge and Titusville from here, will ya?" Crawford said to Ott.

Ott nodded and started working his iPhone.

Crawford looked down at his watch. It was almost three

o'clock. "So, the Greyhound left West Palm at 2:05. I'm thinking we catch up and get on board in either Rockledge or Titusville," Crawford said on his cell to Rutledge.

"Okay," Rutledge said. "You need backup?"

Crawford thought for a second. "Nah, I think the idea is to take him by surprise. We show up with the cavalry, and no telling what could happen. He could take a hostage. The fewer the better is the way to go."

"I hear you," Rutledge said. "Keep me in the loop."

"Yeah, will do," Crawford said, turning to Ott. "All right, me and Leadfoot here gotta get our asses in gear."

43

They only had a quarter of a tank, so they had to gas up at the Chevron on Okeechobee Boulevard. While Ott filled up, Crawford ran inside and bought two hats and two pairs of sunglasses.

"Any-chance-to-go-fast" Ott fishtailed out of the Chevron station and was on the Florida Turnpike ten minutes later, doing ninety.

"This is nothing," Crawford said, looking down at the speedometer. "Dominica was doing ninety-five on her way back from Tampa."

Ott pushed down on the accelerator.

Crawford chuckled. "Never gonna let a woman go faster than you, huh?"

"That's a sexist comment."

"Yeah, accurate, though."

"Hey, I'm a big fan of Danica Patrick," Ott said, referring to the female race car driver.

"Quit yappin' and eyes on the road."

Crawford made several calls on the way to alert the state police not to arrest a speeding white Crown Vic. Ott kept his speed to just over ninety-five.

"Can't really enjoy the countryside going this fast," Crawford said, hitting the button of the calculator on his iPhone.

"What are the times again for the Hound?" Ott asked.

Crawford looked down to where he had written the schedule. "Forget Fort Pierce and Melbourne. It gets in to Rockledge at five." Crawford checked his watch. "I think we can make that easy. You could even slow down to ninety."

Ott chuckled. "Yeah, then you'd tell Dominica."

At exactly 4:26, Crawford saw a Greyhound bus up ahead. They were gaining on it rapidly.

"Slow down," Crawford said as he reached in the back for one of the hats he'd bought. The one he planned to wear himself was a twill bucket hat that had a Harley-Davidson logo on it. He put it on along with a cheap pair of wraparound sunglasses. Ott glanced over. "Very chic."

"Now you speak French, too?" He handed Ott another hat as Ott slowed down to seventy and stayed back behind the Greyhound.

It was a black felt cowboy hat. "I like it," Ott said, putting it on. "Like something Richard Petty'd wear."

Crawford glanced back down at what he had written. "Greyhound gets in to Rockledge in half an hour."

And at that, Ott tromped on the peddle and went roaring past the Greyhound. Just to be safe, Crawford put his hand up over his face even though the Harley-Davidson bucket hat and big wraparounds made him unrecognizable.

THEY AGREED THAT TWO MEN WITH FUNNY HATS boarding the Greyhound at Rockledge, Florida, might attract attention and decided only Crawford would get on the bus. Ott would follow in the Crown Vic.

They were in the men's room of the bus station in Rockledge. Crawford figured that with the bucket hat pulled low and cheap sunglasses on, he could only be recognized by his mother and maybe Dominica. He looked at his watch again. The Greyhound wouldn't get there for another ten to twelve minutes.

"I'd hunch over a little, too, so you don't look so tall," Ott said.

Crawford nodded. "All right, you better get back in the Vic."

Ott punched Crawford's shoulder. "Go get him, man."

THERE WERE FOUR PEOPLE IN LINE TO BOARD THE Greyhound. A woman with a small child, a short man dressed in cargo shorts and a faded Rolling Stones T-shirt, and a tall woman in tight black jeans and a loose-fitting blouse.

Crawford cut in line behind the woman who was in front of the man. The man made a noise somewhere between a snarl and a groan but didn't say anything.

Crawford handed his ticket to the bus driver as he got on board. He wished he had a suitcase or even a knapsack to look more like a traveler, but he didn't. He was hunched over, to make him look older and shorter, and immediately saw Quinn Casey in the third to last row, in an aisle seat. He was glad Casey had left a couple of rows behind him.

The bus was only about half full, which Crawford figured owed to the fact it arrived in Atlanta at three a.m. He shuffled back slowly, close behind the tall woman, and as he got to Casey, looked away. Then he sat down in the seat directly behind him.

He was sitting next to a woman who gave him a look like, *with all the empty seats on this bus, why do you have to sit next to me?* He gave her a nod anyway. She didn't acknowledge him and glanced out the window. The bus driver started up the bus. They backed up, then the driver drove slowly out of the station bay. Sun streamed through the windows of the bus as Crawford felt for his SIG Sauer in his shoulder holster. There was no point in delaying his move. The woman next to him evil-eyed him, like, *why is this guy in the dopey hat and bad shades reaching inside his jacket?* And, *why is he wearing a jacket on such a hot day?* Or maybe that was Crawford's imagination running on overdrive.

The last thing he wanted was for his fellow passenger to tip off Casey with a gasp at the sight of his pistol. He glanced over again, and she was looking out the window.

Now or never.

He slipped the SIG Sauer out of its holster and pressed the barrel to the back of Casey's head. "Hands in the air, Casey."

Casey didn't react right away.

"*Now.*"

A few heads jerked around and Casey's hands went up. Crawford stepped around, pulled out his handcuffs, and slipped them onto Casey's wrists.

"I'm placing you under arrest for the murders of Grace Spooner and Asher Bard."

44

OTT WAS BEHIND THE WHEEL DOING A MERE EIGHTY miles per hour back to Palm Beach. Crawford was riding shotgun, and Quinn Casey was in the back seat, handcuffed.

"What did you do with the knife?" Crawford asked Casey.

"What knife?" Casey spat back.

"A Gerber StrongArm 420 tactical knife, to be exact," Crawford said, turning in his seat so he could watch Casey.

"The one you used at The Colony Hotel," Ott added.

"I don't know what you're talking about," Casey said.

"Probably tossed it in Intracoastal or somewhere," Ott said.

"It doesn't matter," Crawford said, "the ME's matching up the stab wounds from one just like it right now. Got a pretty distinctive blade, he told me."

Casey tried not to react, but Crawford noticed his head jerk back a fraction.

"Why'd you do Spooner?" Ott asked. "We understand Bard was about to expose you as a serial woman-abuser. Probably get you fired from your *New Yorker* and *CNN* gigs. But why Spooner?"

Casey was dead silent.

"Well, since the cat's got Quinn's tongue," Crawford said, "I got a theory."

Ott tapped the steering wheel and smiled. "You always do, Charlie. Let's hear it."

"Spare me," groaned Casey.

"Well, I don't need to tell you this, Quinn, but you got a pretty nasty temper. So, the way I figure it, you were out to dinner with Grace the night before she was killed—"

"You mean the night of, don't you?" Ott asked.

"No, the night before. I found a receipt from Buccan. Looks like Quinn had a steak and Grace had veal chops. Or maybe the other way around. Anyway, I went there, to Buccan, showed Grace's photo and yours to the maître d' who was on duty that night. He remembered you both because he said you got loud and belligerent. Directed your wrath at poor Grace. So, as I know from Grace's friend Natalie Weir, part of the reason Grace came down from Tampa was to end her relationship with you."

"No more abuse, no more beatings, no more Quinn," said Ott.

"That was the idea. The other reason she came was because she had agreed to let you interview her for *The New Yorker*, and you were paying her." Crawford's eyes drilled into Casey's. "Okay, that part was fact, this part is conjecture, but conjecture based on facts: I'm sure you figured, given your superior intellect and persuasiveness, that you could talk Grace into continuing the relationship. But she said absolutely no way in hell and threw you a curve: she threatened to tell your wife about the affair if you didn't stop badgering her. But you kept on and didn't let up. So, after a while, you left Buccan. She went to the Chesterfield, you went to the Brazilian Court. What you didn't know—until, I'm guessing, you got an irate call from your wife—was that Grace called her. She had had enough of your bullying and beatings."

"No shit," Ott said with a look of disbelief on his face.

Casey was struggling mightily to keep a straight face, but his eyes were blinking a lot more than usual.

Crawford was eyeing Casey like he wanted to see past his eyes and into his brain. "I know this because I had a conversation with your wife a little while ago. Not to mention, the waiter at the Buccan said he overheard the word 'wife' half a dozen times."

Casey finally looked away, his eyes refocusing into a thousand-yard stare.

"Tell you what, Quinn. I think I'd be authorized to let you plead down from double-homicide-one to a lesser charge. That is, if you give us a full confession."

Casey turned to Crawford, his eyes squinty and hateful. "Not in a million years."

Crawford raised his hands and shrugged. Then he turned to Ott. "You want to hear the rest, Mort?"

"Absolutely. This is good," Ott said enthusiastically. "Beats the hell out of listening to shit on the radio."

Crawford smiled and nodded. "So, later that night, Quinn, who I can only imagine is seething with rage, decides he's going to get his interview, then kill Grace. His marriage just blew up, Grace just cut him loose. So—gotta hand it to you, Quinn—he does a masterful job of setting it all up: He moves Grace from the Chesterfield to The Colony so Bard and his friends seem like the likely perps, goes to Home Depot and gets the murder weapons, gets a room on the same floor as Grace in someone else's name—"

"—that would be Arnold Riegart."

"Exactly. Oh, wait, I forgot something."

"What's that?"

"Flash back to a couple weeks ago ... Quinn goes to Avis or Budget or wherever, right after he sees Johnnie Begay, who he ran across researching Bard, driving a blue Caddy CTS, and rents the exact same car. Tries to set up the poor, unsuspecting Johnnie redneck as the killer."

Ott shook his head, almost in admiration, then glanced at Casey in the rearview mirror. "Man, gotta give you credit, Quinn, you're the damn Einstein of killers."

"Yeah, so all that's left to be done before he kills Grace is to get his interview ... but, surprise, surprise, Asher Bard beats him to the punch. With that three-hundred-thousand-dollar check, he owns Grace. So now—sorry, Quinn—interview's off."

Ott was nodding. "So ol' Quinn's totally screwed."

Crawford nodded back at him, then drilled in to Quinn Casey's dark eyes. "You have anything you'd like to say, Quinn?"

Casey didn't move or say a word.

"One last thing I don't have a theory about is why you killed Asher Bard in his gym." Crawford shrugged. "I mean, why there?"

Nothing from Casey.

"Maybe he just asked Bard to give him a tour of the boat, and when he saw a good murder weapon and perfect opportunity, he jumped at it?" Ott said.

Crawford nodded his head. "Maybe. And maybe we'll never know. Or why Asher Bard turned off the boat's security system. I talked to a woman who Bard was supposedly having an affair with, asked her if she was meeting him that afternoon, but she just played dumb. Anyway, here's the reality: It doesn't much matter if we don't have every single detail exactly right because, fact is"—he eyed Casey—"we can place you on the same floor as Grace Spooner at The Colony Hotel. And we have forensic evidence—fibers from that rope we can prove you bought. Plus, fingerprints and DNA." He stretched it a little. "All you had to do was climb around, over to her terrace." He paused. "You think that might be enough for a jury, Quinn?"

"Not to mention," Ott piped in, "we're still waiting for a

positive ID of DNA found under Grace Spooner's fingernails."

"Oh, yeah, I forgot about that," Crawford said, taking a pocket recorder out of his jacket and holding it up. "What do you say, Quinn? Time to talk?"

45

NOT ANOTHER WORD WAS SAID ON THE RIDE BACK, EXCEPT for Ott cursing out a driver for trying to cut him off on Okeechobee Boulevard.

Crawford glanced back in the rearview mirror a number of times and never saw Quinn Casey change his expression. He was just staring out his window, looking like he'd rather be any place in the world other than in the back seat of a car that could use a new set of shocks.

When they got to the station, Casey asked if he could make a call. Crawford had relieved him of his cell phone when they were on the Greyhound and decided he didn't want Casey to use it to make the call. There were too many things that could happen. Casey could drop it in the toilet or disable it in a lot of different ways, and Crawford was betting on it revealing evidence that could be useful to Casey's prosecution.

Crawford handed him his own phone.

"Thank you, Charlie, that's very kind of you," Casey said.

"You're welcome." He pointed at a room nicknamed "the guilty room." "That room at the end on the left. It's all yours."

"I suppose you got a couple bugs in there."

Crawford chuckled. "We don't need to bug your conversation. We already got you dead to rights."

"You think so, huh?"

"I know so."

"I got a New York lawyer who'll run circles around any Florida prosecutor."

"I guess we'll just have to see about that."

"I guess we will."

IN THE END, QUINN CASEY COPPED A PLEA.

He chose to follow the suggestion of his attorney and the lead of many other criminals before him: Ariel Castro, the Cleveland man accused of holding three women captives in his home for a decade, who pled guilty and got a lesser sentence than the death penalty. Subway restaurant pitchman Jared Fogle, who pled guilty to possessing and distributing child porn and got only five years. The Texas man who killed his pregnant wife and her father in 2009, who pled it down to second-degree murder.

Casey's plea bargain got him twenty-eight years but with no possibility of parole. Crawford did some quick math and figured that meant he'd be behind bars until he was sixty-two.

He deserved longer, but it was far from the worst possible outcome.

46

CRAWFORD AND DOMINICA, ROSE, AND JOHN THE SHRINK were out in back of Rose's house on the ocean. It was a night in the low eighties, so clear you could see forever. A smoke-belching tanker appeared to be only a mile offshore, but it was probably more like ten miles out. Crawford was grilling two thick rib eye Kobe steaks Rose had provided because John the shrink had stated he was not "a griller ... Well, except at my job maybe." He followed his little accidental joke with one of those heh-heh-heh laughs. Maybe he wasn't a griller, but he was pretty good at knocking back Rose's Macallan single malt scotch. Crawford had brought two bottles of Santa Margarita pinot grigio because he knew both Dominica and Rose liked it.

Rose was telling them about a difficult real estate deal she had recently closed on. "I don't know who was worse, the buyer or the seller," she said. "The seller claimed there was ten more feet of frontage on the ocean than he actually had, and the buyer wanted the seller to throw in all the furniture because, as he said, 'it's mostly junk anyway.'" Rose shook her head and groaned. "Half of it was stuff the seller had just bought at Restoration Hardware and Walker Zabriskie two years before."

"But you got it done, right?" Dominica asked, taking a sip of her pinot grigio.

Crawford stood at the grill, giant fork in one hand, beer in the other. Dominica had picked him up a six-pack of an IPA called Audrey Hopburn. Rose, Dominica, and John sat at the distressed-wood dining table.

"Yeah, I got it done," Rose said, "but, man, was it bloody. The buyer called the seller a liar at the closing table. The seller wanted me to give up a chunk of the commission, but I told him, 'Forget it. I earned every penny.'"

Dominica raised her wine glass. "Well, here's to you and another million-dollar payday."

"Not quite, but thanks," Rose said as Crawford raised his beer bottle and John his near-empty glass of scotch.

Then Rose raised her glass and looked up at Crawford. "And to you, Charlie, for taking yet another miscreant off the streets of Palm Beach."

"Couldn't've done it without Dominica," Crawford said.

"That's an exaggeration," Dominica said, "but I'll take it."

Rose turned her head to John. "And to you ..."

"Yes?" said John.

"To you ... for sorting out the various neuroses of the head cases of Palm Beach and making their twisted lives a little more tolerable."

A bemused look appeared on John's face. "I guess that's a good thing."

AN HOUR AND A HALF AND SEVERAL DRINKS LATER, THE four of them were finishing off an ice cream cake that Dominica had picked up at the Carvel store on South Dixie in West Palm Beach. It was called "Fudgie the Whale" and was a Crawford favorite from having grown up in the heart of Carvel-land in the New York metro region.

"This is really good," John said. "I've never had it before."

A slur had snuck into John's speech, which was to be expected after having downed four Macallans. Everyone else had slowed down, but John remained full speed ahead, pedal to the metal, having just poured his fifth. Crawford was already making plans to drive him home or call an Uber. But then he thought maybe John was going to spend the night with Rose.

The thought bothered him.

John turned to him. "So, Charlie"—which came out *Shaw-lee*—"do you have any regrets about taking down—that's the lingo you use, right—that guy, Quinn Casey?"

"'Regrets?' What do you mean?"

"I mean, Casey's reporting has resulted in a lot of good things over the years."

"Like what?" Crawford asked, finishing off the last of Fudgie the Whale.

"Oh, you must know?" His tone was almost, *You must know, you moron*. "His reporting about the Russian mafia in Little Odessa put away about twenty of the ringleaders, then that series of reports about the corrupt president of Nicaragua, or maybe it was Panama, which caused that coup that got him voted out of office. That's just for starters."

"Quinn Casey killed two people ... just for starters," Crawford said matter-of-factly.

"I'm well aware of that," John said. "But what if I were to prove Quinn Casey's actions and reporting saved—oh, I don't know—a hundred lives over the years, and if he kept on doing what he was doing, maybe the world would be a better place because of it? Would you maybe consider not arresting him for those two murders?"

Crawford was dumbstruck. He glanced at Dominica and Rose to see if it was just him. He could tell from their looks, it wasn't.

Rose leaned close to John. "Are you out of your mind?"

"Whaddaya mean?" John slurred.

"I mean, are you out of your mind? A guy murders two people in cold blood, and you think, 'Hey, that's okay, because he saved a bunch of people from a ruthless dictator in … Panama or Nicaragua.' You don't even know which."

Crawford glanced at Dominica. She gave him a quick eye roll.

"Pretty sure it was Nicaragua," John said. He had more. "So, let me posit this: if a man kills two people but saves the lives of hundreds—"

"Oh, for Chrissake, John." Rose raised the decibel level. "Enough. You're not going to wear us down into saying Charlie should have let Quinn Casey go. No matter how eloquent you are … and at the moment, you're not at all eloquent."

"Well, that's kind of hurtful."

"You know what they say. 'The truth hurts.'"

John lifted his glass toward his lips. Rose reached out and caught it halfway up. "You are hereby cut off."

John looked like a little boy whose favorite toy was snatched away from him. "C'mon, Rose."

Rose looked at her watch. "Jesus, it's eleven fifteen. Time we wrapped up this little shindig." Then, dropping her voice, she turned to Crawford. "You mind taking him home?"

Crawford shook his head. "No problem. Where's he live?"

Rose chuckled. "He probably has no clue. 300 Valencia Road in El Cid." Which was just over the bridge in West Palm Beach.

Crawford turned to John, who had begun babbling to Dominica. "Okay, John, I'm giving you a lift home."

"No way. I'm staying here with the hostess with the mostest," he said, beaming at Rose.

"Ain't happening, my friend," Rose said. "Cuff him, Charlie."

John had passed out on the short drive to El Cid, so Crawford and Dominica had to lift him out of the back seat, stand him up between them, put their arms around his waist, and walk him into his one-story, Spanish-style stucco house. They got him into the master bedroom as he sort of came to.

He turned to Dominica. "Hey, honey," he said. "Do *you* wanna spend the night with me?"

Dominica laughed. "Sorry. Case you didn't notice, I'm not Rose."

"I don't care," John said, leaning toward her for a kiss.

"Okay, lover boy," Crawford said, guiding John down into his king-size bed. "Time for beddy-bye."

Dominica and Crawford were back in his car after turning off the lights in John's house.

"So, what did you think?" Dominica asked.

"Of John?"

"Yes."

"I don't know. He got a little weird at the end."

"At the beginning, middle, *and* end, I thought."

"So, is that a thumbs-down?"

Dominica nodded. "Rose can do better."

"Yeah, I guess."

"You're always so nonjudgmental."

"That's not true."

"Pretty much, though."

"You ever hear me talk about Rutledge?"

"Yeah, well, you and everybody else."

They both fell silent for a while, just sitting there in the car. Crawford didn't start the engine.

Finally, Dominica turned to him. "My guess is Rose is going to come back onto the market."

"Meaning dump John the shrink?"

"Yup. That would be my guess."

"And you're telling me this because ... ?"

"You know why. Because you've got a choice to make ... again."

Crawford leaned into Dominica and gave her a long kiss. "Too late. Choice's already been made."

THE END

To find out when the next Charlie Crawford Mystery is available, sign up for Tom's free newsletter at **tomturnerbooks.com/news**.

And don't miss the new Charleston mystery series, starring Nick Janzek, a Boston cop with a dark, tragic past who moves south to start over. But Nick's not even in Charleston for 24 hours before he catches a murder case that could change the entire face of the city.

KILLING TIME IN CHARLESTON (EXCERPT)

I am pleased to bring you two chapters from the first book in a new series set in one of my favorite cities: Charleston, South Carolina. It's entitled *Killing Time in Charleston*.

Killing Time introduces Nick Janzek, a hero/anti-hero—you be the judge. He's a man with a tragic past and an uncertain future in a town that doesn't always throw out the welcome mat for Yankees. Nick, a homicide cop, hooks up with new partner, Delvin Rhett, who's fresh out of the ghetto and a recent graduate of hard knocks university. Right off the bat they have a murder, and while that body is still warm, another stiff turns up. Never a dull moment for Nick and Delvin...and you as well!

Killing Time in Charleston is now available on Amazon.

1

A YEAR AFTER WHAT HAPPENED IN BOSTON, JANZEK FLEW down to Charleston, South Carolina, for his college roommate's wedding. It took him about five minutes to fall in love with the place. Beautiful old houses, five-star restaurants on every block, streets crawling with killer women and, best of all, no snow in the forecast. What was not to love?

He had wandered off from his friend's wedding reception with Cameron, the twenty-eight-year-old sister of the bride. Together they discovered the culinary gusto of an out-of-the-way spot called Trattoria Lucca then followed it up with some jamming music at a quasi-dive he figured he'd never be able to find again. Last thing he remembered was teetering down a cobblestone street, arm around Cameron's shoulder, looking for a place that had either Lion or Tiger in its name. That Cameron, what a handful she turned out to be.

The day after the wedding he canceled his return flight to Logan Airport, then on Monday morning walked into the Charleston Police Department on Lockwood Street. The résumé he had knocked out in his hotel room that morning had a typo or two in it, but that didn't seem to bother the chief of detectives, who hired him on the spot.

Now, three months later, he was coming down the home stretch: Interstate 26, just north of Charleston. The first half of the trip down had been a little dicey, since the day he had picked for the move had turned out to be especially cold and windy. He was driving a U-Haul, his car on a hitch behind it, and had been wrestling the steering wheel of the orange-and-white cube the whole way down. A few miles before Wilmington, Delaware a gusty blast blew him into the path of a rampaging sixteen-wheeler, which roared up on his bumper like an Amtrak car that had jumped the tracks. It was a close call, but things quieted down after he hit the Maryland border.

He had the window down now and was taking in the warm salt air, which reminded him of the Cape when he was a kid and life was easy. He was looking forward to the slow Southern pace of Charleston. Kicking back with a plate full of shrimp and grits, barbeque and collards or whatever it was they were so famous for, then washing it all down with a couple of Blood Hounds, a bare-knuckled rum drink bad girl Cameron had introduced him to.

He was thinking about how he might get his lame golf game out of mothballs, psyched about being able to play year-round. One thing he'd miss would be opening day at Fenway, but he'd heard about Charleston's minor league baseball team and figured it would be good for a few grins. One thing he'd never miss would be staring down at stiffs on the mean streets of Beantown.

The ring of his cell phone broke the reverie. He picked it up, looked at the number, and didn't recognize it.

"Hello."

"Nick, it's Ernie Brindle. Where y'at?" Brindle was the Charleston chief of detectives, the man who had hired him.

"Matter of fact, Ernie, I'm just pulling into Charleston. A few miles north. Why, what's up?"

Brindle sighed. "Looks like it's gonna be trial by fire for you, bro. I'm looking down at a dead body on Broad Street...

it's the mayor. The ex-mayor, guess that would be. How fast can you get here?"

Janzek had figured he'd at least get a chance to unload his stuff from the U-Haul before his first-day punch-in.

"Thing is, Ernie, I'm driving this big old U-Haul with all my junk in it. Can't I just drop it—"

"No, I need you right now. Corner of Broad and Church."

Janzek stifled a groan. "Is Church before or after King Street?"

"Two blocks east. Just look for a guy under a sheet and every squad car in the city. Not every day the mayor gets smoked."

"Okay, I'm getting off I-26. I see a sign for King Street."

"You're just five minutes away," Brindle said. "Welcome to the Holy City."

"Thanks," Janzek said. "Kinda wish it were under different circumstances."

Janzek rumbled down Meeting Street, breathing in the fragrant scent of tea olive trees. He got stuck behind a garbage truck and his first instinct was to lay on the horn, but something told him you didn't do that in Charleston. Up ahead he saw a horse-drawn carriage jammed with gawkers. The garbage truck and the carriage were side by side—like blockers—creeping along at ten miles an hour. The smell of horse manure wafted through his open windows and replaced the sweet tea olive smell.

Janzek finally saw an opening, hit the accelerator, and slipped between the truck and the carriage. Broad Street was just ahead. He had never seen that many squad cars except at an Irish captain's funeral up in Southie. Ernie Brindle was keeping an eye out for him, and when he saw the U-Haul pull up he directed Janzek past the long line of black-and-whites to a spot in front of a fire hydrant. Janzek got out and walked over.

Brindle, a short, intense guy with hair he didn't spend

much time on, eyeballed Janzek's transportation. "Jesus, Nick, not just a U-Haul, but dragging a sorry-ass Honda behind it?" Brindle shook his head. "Thought you were s'posed to be a big-time homicide cop."

Janzek glanced back at the car that had served him long and loyally. "I'm not much of a car guy, Ernie."

Janzek looked down at the body sprawled half on and half off the sidewalk. Brindle pulled the sheet back. The late mayor was dressed in an expensive-looking blue suit, which was shredded and splattered with blood. A crushed gold watch dangled loosely from his wrist.

"So, what exactly happened?" Janzek asked, looking around at the cluster of cops, crime scene techs, and a man he assumed was the ME.

"According to a witness," Brindle said, "he was crossing the street when a black Mercedes 500, goin' like a bat out of hell, launched him twenty feet in the air."

"So... intentional then?" Janzek said.

"Yeah, for sure. Guy said he saw the driver aiming a gun."

"In case he couldn't take him out with the car?"

Brindle nodded. "I guess."

"Pointing it out the window?"

"Uh-huh," Brindle said.

"So he was a lefty," Janzek said. "Guy say whether he fired it or not?"

"He didn't think so. Didn't hear anything, anyway."

"How'd he know it was a 500?"

"He's a car salesman," Brindle said. "On his way to the bank."

Janzek knelt down next to the body to get a closer look. It was clear the mayor had landed on his face. His nose was shoved off to one side, and his forehead and cheeks looked like a sheet of salmon.

The guy he figured for the ME, who'd been talking to two

men nearby, came up and eyeballed him with a who-the-hell-are-you? look.

"Jack," Brindle said to the man, "this is Nick Janzek, new homicide guy." Then to Janzek, "Jack Martin is our esteemed, pain-in-the-ass ME."

"Good one," Martin said, crouching down next to the body then looking up at Janzek. "So how come you caught this one, Nick?"

Janzek didn't know the answer.

"'Cause I liked his sheet," Brindle said.

"Who you got him with?" Martin asked Brindle.

"Delvin."

Martin shook his head and glanced over at Janzek. "Urkel? Good fuckin' luck." Then he noticed the blue parka Janzek was wearing. "You plannin' on goin' skiing or something, Nick?"

Janzek glanced down at his coat. "Just drove down from Boston. Weather was a little different up there."

Martin nodded and kept looking Janzek over.

"Hey, Jack," Brindle said, "how 'bout examining the mayor 'stead of Janzek?"

Martin ignored him. "Boston, huh?"

"Yeah," Janzek said. "Massachusetts."

"Yeah, I've heard of it," Martin said, looking over Janzek's shoulder at the U-Haul. He shook his head, shot Brindle a look, and muttered, "Just what we need down here."

"What's that?" asked Brindle.

"Another fuckin' wiseass Yankee."

2

Picture Twelve Oaks in *Gone with the Wind*, a two-story Greek Revival-style house with enough piazza and balcony space for a small platoon of soldiers to do marching drills. Leading up to it was a long, perfect allée of live oak trees and, in between, a smooth tabby driveway. A black butler in a dark suit, white shirt, and a tie with the logo and coat of arms of Pinckney Hall on it watched from the porch as Ned Carlino pulled up in his Tesla Roadster.

Carlino got out, stretched, and looked around as Jeter, the butler, walked down the last few steps to greet him.

"Hey, Mr. Carlino," Jeter said, his bushy white eyebrows arching, "welcome back to Pinckney."

"Thanks, Jeter. Good to be back."

Ned Carlino, fifty-four years old and a stocky five eight, was not a man you'd ever mistake for Rhett Butler. Born in a socially unacceptable suburb of Philadelphia, he had gotten a scholarship to Villanova then another one to Harvard Law, and quickly became one of the best ambulance chasers around. Back then, his card read *Personal Impairment Attorney*, but everyone knew.

His first big case came at age twenty-six when Hector

Nunez, the hotheaded, power-hitting Philadelphia Phillies right fielder, lost it after a called third strike in the fifth game of the playoffs and flung his bat in disgust. It clanged off the metal railing in the boxes to the left of the Phillies dugout then bounced off the head of an out-of-work cleaning lady from across the river in Camden.

Turned out to be the best thing that ever happened to her.

Carlino, who was watching the game in a bar because he hadn't paid his cable bill, beat it over to Thomas Jefferson Hospital—where he figured they'd take her—in just twenty minutes. Practically beat the ambulance. He crept up to a woman at the nurses station in the ER and told her he was a cousin of the woman who had been hit by the bat, even though she was sixty and Hispanic. The nurse looked at him funny, but Ned was not about to be deterred.

Long story short, the former cleaning lady, Ned's new client, got four million dollars when his expert witness convinced the jury that she would have constant migraines, and possibly life-altering seizures, for the rest of her life. The expert witness was convincing, and Ned, even more so. Half of the four million went to the woman and the other half to Carlino's firm, Suozzi and Scarpetta—or Sleazy and Sleazier as one TV news reporter dubbed it. Carlino managed to wangle nearly a million for himself. He immediately paid off his cable bill, bought a BMW, and moved to the Main Line. After five years of following his sensitive nose to massive settlements—including one where he represented the widow of a three-pack-a-day smoker and wangled twenty million dollars out of National Tobacco Company—he decided to seek legal respectability and become a trial lawyer.

That was thirty years ago and, surprisingly, a few of the big Philadelphia white-shoe, establishment firms pursued him despite his low-born Italian heritage and somewhat unsavory reputation. Because—unsavory or not—Ned Carlino was a winner. Along the way, in the great tradition of all American success stories, Carlino decided he needed to burnish his image and erase all hints of his past. He first became a prodigious collector of modern art, outbidding a Connecticut hedge fund owner on a Jim Dine and several Jasper Johns. Then, in addition to his townhouse in Rittenhouse Square and his Nantucket beach house, he bought a third house on the Intracoastal in Palm Beach and a fourth on Sullivan's Island, outside of Charleston. Three years after that, he sprang for the five-thousand-acre Pinckney Hall plantation, forty minutes south of Charleston. Lastly, he became a philanthropist and sat on the boards of a hospital and a library in Philadelphia, to which he had just donated nine million dollars for a twenty-thousand-square-foot wing. *The Edward G. Carlino Research Library* was etched elegantly into the building's limestone facade.

"Jeter, grab my bag in the trunk and take it upstairs," Carlino said. "I'm going over to the guest house."

Jeter smiled wide, and his teeth looked like a freshly painted picket fence. "William is waitin' on you there, sir."

Carlino walked across the driveway then down the antique-brick path to the guest house, where he pushed open the massive mahogany door, which he'd shipped over from a tumbled-down manor house in England. He walked into the vast living room, painstakingly decorated piece by piece by Madeline Littleworth Mortimer herself. He waved at William across the room and gestured that he needed a drink. William nodded eagerly and reached for the Myers's rum bottle.

The first girl he saw was Ashley. Twenty-three, give or take, she was wearing black-and-silver spandex tights, a gypsy top, and red jellies—teen dream, circa 1994. She was shoving quarters into an antique slot machine, which was lined up next to a collector's item Gottlieb pinball machine on the far wall. She looked up and gave him a Marilyn Monroe pop of the lips and a fluttery smile.

Justine was sitting in a pudgy leather couch facing a huge

fireplace with a mantelpiece from a Normandy castle. She was wearing a miniskirt with pin-striped tights, a white silk top, and Tory Burch flats. Under the tights was one of the best pairs of legs in South Carolina. The look was girl-who'll-do-anything-to-get-ahead, circa 2019.

"Hey, Mr. C," she said, her hoop earrings jiggling beneath her Jennifer Aniston haircut. She came up to him and gave him a prodigious kiss on the lips. "So glad you're back, lover boy...I missed you *desperately*." She knew exactly what he wanted to hear.

He kissed her back then reached down and cupped her remarkably perfect breasts. She smiled up at him and pretended to like getting pawed.

"Missed you too, honey," he said, marveling at how tight her stomach was, "but I told you, lose the Mr. C, it makes me feel old."

"Sorry...Ned," Justine said with a wink. "I got the sheets all turned down."

"Hold on, girl, I haven't even had my first drink yet."

Martha was sitting on a barstool as Carlino approached. She turned to face him. William, behind her, was adding a lime wedge to his drink. Martha, twenty-five and runway-model striking, was dressed in a short tartan skirt. Her legs were spread, a few inches beyond discreet, revealing a black thong and light coffee-colored thighs. Bad girl cheerleader, circa... hard to tell.

"Welcome home," she purred.

Carlino walked over and kissed her on the lips.

"Oh, *baby,* can't wait for you to rip my clothes off," she whispered and winked at William, who pretended not to be listening, "and do all those naughty things you do." She was the one who talked dirty, but in such a refined way.

William was a six-eight former basketball player from Clemson who blushed easily. He set a drink down in front of

Carlino. "Good to see you again, sir," William said. "Hope you enjoy the drink."

Carlino took a long sip and wiped his lips. "I always do, William." Looking back at Martha, he said, "You know something? I'm thinking about changing your name. You're way too hot for Martha."

"What's wrong with Martha?" she asked, ratcheting up the smile.

"It's just not sexy. I mean, Martha Washington, Martha Stewart... Martha Wiggins."

"Who's Martha Wiggins?"

Carlino chuckled. "My old neighbor growing up. Two hundred pounds, three chins, five-day growth. I'm thinking of—I don't know—Willow or Miranda, or maybe Vruska."

Martha laughed. "What? I'm Russian now?"

He nodded.

"Of course," she said. "Whatever you want me to be."

Ned's cell phone rang. He punched the green button. "Hello, Rutledge," he said, smiling at Martha. "Yeah, I'm looking forward to seeing you and Henry down here tonight. Got a couple of girls just dying to meet you."

He looked away from Martha and listened. "Yeah, I know, terrible thing that was." He chuckled. "People just gotta be more careful how they drive in Charleston. But, hey, the good news is I got the perfect guy lined up to fill his shoes."

END OF EXCERPT

ACKNOWLEDGMENTS

My thanks to new members of my "street team"—Kirsten McDonough and Marie Parker—for your help in whipping Bedlam into shape. You did a thorough, imaginative and creative job, not to mention picked up a few misplaced modifiers and slapdash punctuation. And again to Gordon McCoun and Ted Manno. You guys are the best and I can't tell you how critical your input always is.

My thanks, also, to Nick Johansen and Rebecca Sterling for the spectacular jobs you both do.

My love to Serena and Georgie, the most incredible daughters a father could have.

ABOUT THE AUTHOR

A native New Englander, Tom dropped out of college and ran a bar in Vermont...into the ground. Limping back to get his sheepskin, he then landed in New York where he spent time as an award-winning copywriter at several Manhattan advertising agencies. After years of post-Mad Men life, he made a radical change and got a job in commercial real estate. A few years later he ended up in Palm Beach, buying, renovating and selling houses while getting material for his novels. On the side, he wrote *Palm Beach Nasty*, its sequel, *Palm Beach Poison*, and a screenplay, *Underwater*.

While at a wedding, he fell for the charm of Charleston, South Carolina. He spent six years there and completed a yet-to-be-published series set in Charleston. A year ago, Tom headed down the road to Savannah, where he just finished a novel about lust and murder among his neighbors.

Learn more about Tom's books at:
www.tomturnerbooks.com

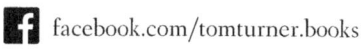 facebook.com/tomturner.books

ALSO BY TOM TURNER

CHARLIE CRAWFORD PALM BEACH MYSTERIES
Palm Beach Nasty

Palm Beach Poison

Palm Beach Deadly

Palm Beach Bones

Palm Beach Pretenders

Palm Beach Predator

Palm Beach Broke

Palm Beach Bedlam

NICK JANZEK CHARLESTON MYSTERIES
Killing Time in Charleston

Charleston Buzz Kill

STANDALONES
Broken House

For a current list of all available titles, please visit
tomturnerbooks.com/books.

Made in the USA
Monee, IL
24 April 2022